A cry rose in Elar... the steel blade pre... fling back her hea... slice her own throa... asked Kethrenan ... whimper or plead. She ...

And so the outlaw took her away. Brand ... e stonelands had the princess. A cry did sound for her, though, against the rage of battle, the war cries and the death screams of elves and goblins, long and loud and filled with terrible rage. It followed her, winding through the barren land, the sound of Kethrenan cursing.

DRAGONLANCE

DRAGONLANCE Classics

Murder in Tarsis
John Maddox Roberts

Dalamar the Dark
Nancy Varian Berberick

The Citadel
Richard A. Knaak

THE INHERITANCE

Nancy Varian Berberick

Wizards of the Coast

THE INHERITANCE

©2001 Wizards of the Coast, Inc.

All characters in this book are fictitious. Any resemblance to actual persons, living or dead, is purely coincidental.

This book is protected under the copyright laws of the United States of America. Any reproduction or unauthorized use of the material or artwork contained herein is prohibited without the express written permission of Wizards of the Coast, Inc.

Distributed in the United States by St. Martin's Press. Distributed in Canada by Fenn, Ltd.

Distributed to the hobby, toy, and comic trade in the United States and Canada by regional distributors.

Distributed worldwide by Wizards of the Coast, Inc. and regional distributors.

DRAGONLANCE and the Wizards of the Coast logo are registered trademarks owned by Wizards of the Coast, Inc.

All Wizards of the Coast characters, character names, and the distinctive likenesses thereof are trademarks owned by Wizards of the Coast, Inc.

Made in the U.S.A.

Cover art by Bradley Williams
Map by Sam Wood
First Printing: May 2001
Library of Congress Catalog Card Number: 00-103749

9 8 7 6 5 4 3 2 1

US ISBN: 0-7869-1861-6
UK ISBN: 0-7869-2615-5
620-WTC21861

U.S., CANADA,   EUROPEAN HEADQUARTERS
ASIA, PACIFIC, & LATIN AMERICA   Wizards of the Coast, Belgium
Wizards of the Coast, Inc.   P.B. 2031
P.O. Box 707   2600 Berchem
Renton, WA 98057-0707   Belgium
+1-800-324-6496   +32-70-23-32-77

Visit our web site at **www.wizards.com/dragonlance**

To Amy Bridgeman
for the Phoenix

Qualinesti

Qualinost

Bianost

"The Stonelands"

N

Kharolis Mountains

Pax Tharkas

0 1 2 3 4 5 Miles

Chapter 1

In the coffers of the elf king, in Solostaran's deep chests, lay many treasures—gold plate, rings of sliding silver, necklaces from which fantasies of jewel-work hung. His walls wore tapestries whose weavers lived in the years before the Cataclysm. He trod upon floors of white marble inlaid with black, of black marble inlaid with rose, of rose marble with gray, and all the work of dwarven craftsmen who commanded the worth of a royal ransom for their fee.

In Solostaran's treasure houses lay weapons of finest steel, swords hilted with gold, the grips made from the whole of a precious stone, of emerald and ruby and sapphire and diamond. For his most glittering ceremonies, he had helms of silver, plated in gold and wondrously bejeweled. He was no poor king, Solostaran of the Qualinesti. Yet, in the estimation of Elansa Sungold, his sister-in-law, the wife of Prince Kethrenan, his brother, the most extraordinary and valuable of all the things housed in the Tower of the Sun did not belong to Solostaran himself. This treasure belonged to Elansa, and she counted nothing owned by Solostaran or his royal kin as fair or valuable.

The Risen Phoenix, wings spread, triumphant, a wonder of sapphire and silver, cherished and jealously guarded, was Elansa's, handed to her by her mother, who'd received it from her own mother, and that mother from hers. Down the misty roads of time it had come, from the dawn of the Age of Dreams to mother then to daughter, never fallen from the kindred, never gone from the clan, bearing its magic and hope on flashing wings across the ages. A day would come when Elansa would put the treasure into her own daughter's hands.

Today, though, Elansa had no prospect of handing off the talisman as she stood in the chill darkness of the hour between night and dawn. Not even the first bird had risen to sing in the garden outside her window. Few lights shone in the city, and those that did were in the barracks beyond the orchards. The lights gleamed like fireflies, seeming to wink as the breeze stirred the naked branches between.

Elansa stood a moment, looking at those lights. She wondered where her husband was, Prince Kethrenan who was lord of all those scouts and warriors that kept their people safe. Out upon the border somewhere, far away in the cool western wood by the Straits of Algoni, or on the banks of the White-rage River, in the south near the bitter mountains . . . away with his warriors, a shining, armed presence on some border.

Elansa turned from the window. She had dressed for a journey, geared herself for riding through the forest in fine boots, warm trousers, and a flowing silk shirt. She wore her honey-colored hair over her shoulder, twined through with scarlet ribbon. Her green woolen cloak lay across her bed, the hem of it half concealing a small rosewood box. At her belt she wore a little knife, but that was no weapon, only a decoration to complete her costume. A princess abroad in her kingdom attended by twenty warriors, she would need no weapon. She needed now only one thing, and then she could leave. She needed the phoenix.

Elansa moved the rosewood box from beneath her cloak. She lifted the lid and caught her breath in wonder. The Risen Phoenix gleamed upon a bed of gray velvet. It appeared to be cut from one whole sapphire, shaped with wings wide, triumphant. Elansa, who knew the history of it, knew it hadn't been cut at all. It had been discovered, uncovered like a living thing trapped in stone. A whole sapphire shaped like a phoenix, with wings spread wide, the dwarf who'd found it had never again seen anything so wonderful, and he'd lived a long, long time. He freed it from its rocky prison, chipping away the clutching stone until the sapphire itself stood free, a phoenix risen again to life. No more had he done but polish it and hang it from a chain of silver, the links so tightly woven they ran like liquid.

He'd rid himself of it, so the story said, as quickly as he could get a good price for it. Dwarves don't like magic, not at all, and this winged sapphire beat with magic the way a heart beats with life: quietly, steadily.

Here was the sigil of Elansa's god, the Blue Phoenix whom those not elves named Habbakuk, the lord of the natural world, of the unstoppable cycle of life and death and life again. These cycles Elansa knew as well as she knew the tides of her own body. She was a woodshaper, born with the ability to know and love the very soul of the forest, to tend its health and keep it well. Legend whispered that the blood of the woodshapers had long ago mixed with that of nature spirits, and some believed that was more than folklore speaking, for it had long been the custom, seldom breached, that woodshapers would marry none outside their own clans, unwilling to dilute their ancient heritage.

Now and then, though, when the negotiations went well and enough was offered to make all parties happy, that rule bent. For a royal marriage and a seat in the places of power, Elansa's father had done the bending and given her to Prince Kethrenan. The prince and his brother the king were as pleased by the prospect of having that pure woodshaper blood come into their royal clan as though it were dower goods.

Elansa lifted the phoenix from the rosewood box. It was not large. It fit in the palm of one hand, the chain flowing over her fingers. It breathed, or seemed to, and the beat of its power was the beat of her pulse, strong and sure.

There was, beyond the city and past the shining bridges, an illness in the forest. A blight, gray and scabby and quick to kill, had touched the elms in little Bianost, shriveling the heart of the trees, in only a matter of weeks rendering them bent and leafless.

"Send us a woodshaper," cried the people. "Send us the princess whose magic can heal."

Elansa had no magic. She was neither mage nor cleric. She had this talisman, and this the people cried for, praying for the princess to bring them the healing grace, for this was the truest virtue of the artifact. With the talisman in hand, what natural skill a woodshaper possessed was transmuted. The world became as a living being to her—earth and sky, fire and wind and water, she spoke to them as she would to kin.

Elansa closed her eyes, slipped the necklace over her head, and whispered a welcome to the god. In the courtyard of the tower, out beyond her garden, she heard the jingle of bridles, the stamping of hooves. Her escort had come. She slipped on her cloak, spoke a word to a startled, sleepy servant in the corridor outside her suite, and went alone into the waking day.

The phoenix hung around her neck. Let the elf-king keep his fat coffers. She knew no better treasure than this stone warm against her breast. Every beat of her heart found an echo in the living magic of the stone, an easy rhythm with the phoenix, as though one beat were hers and the other magic's. Perhaps, she thought, the echo of a god's. So comfortable was that rhythm that she'd not gone as far as the courtyard before she ceased to be aware of it. She wouldn't feel it again until she stood in the presence of the trees of Bianost. There, with the magic to aid, she would touch the souls of the wounded trees, speak to their hearts, and infuse them with her own will and strength. Upon the wings of a phoenix rising, their illness would change into health.

* * * * *

Wind spilled down the sky in waves, tossing the tops of the trees, coming just like the sea, tumbling and leaping. High on the cold cliff, in the borderland between the Qualinesti Forest and the Kharolis Mountains, a tall, broad-shouldered man stood, watching the wind run. Brand felt its fingers in his shaggy hair and beard. He heard the sky's voice hissing, just like the voice of the sea. He'd seen the sea, once long ago, when he was a boy of ten years. It was as far away from this bitter borderland as he'd ever been.

He stood between the kingdom of elves and the hidden kingdom of dwarves. He stood in stonelands owned by no one but buzzards and ravens, fought over by bands of outlaws. They fought for the roads, rocky passages over which merchants had to travel when they went out from the towns and cities of Abanasinia and down to Tarsis. Humans and hill dwarves threading the byways between the kingdoms of Qualinesti and Thorbardin, they found themselves in a vast land of cruel realms whose varied borders changed like the wind. These were the windswept reaches populated by filthy goblin towns from which those heartless creatures came ravening at the first scent of prey. The goods they kept. The women and children they sold in Tarsis for slaves. The men and boys they killed. Should the merchants have the great good luck to encounter no goblins, they might find themselves beset by bands of outlaws whose numbers were made up of humans banished from towns and cities, disgraced dwarven sons cast out of their clans, and dark elves swept out of Qualinesti like storm-broken branches.

When these goblins and outlaws didn't have luckless travelers to fall upon, they fell upon each other, for they had their own feuds, and, for the most part, they were each other's worst enemy.

The dwarves in Thorbardin didn't care what went on outside their mountain. In Qualinost the elves liked to let the goblins and the outlaws keep each other in check, only coming out of their forest to scour the stonelands when the brigands became over-bold with the borders. In that way, dark little reigns rose and fell between the mountain and the forest, their histories recorded only in blood and dust. Brand had seen no few of these risings and fallings. He had written some of that dark history.

The wind dropped lower, sailing cold along the cliffs, whirling dust and the scent of rain before it. Brand hardly lifted his head to that lie. It hadn't rained in the borderland for two turns of the two moons.

An eagle screamed in the sky, the sound like a ripping. Lower down, at the bottom of the cliff, a darkness of ravens quarreled over something. Brand kept his eye on the black-wings. It was an old habit, one he'd never broken, as old as his habit of listening behind.

He wasn't surprised when a voice deep and low said, "Someone's found dinner, eh?"

One broad-winged raven leaped up from the feast, then dropped suddenly, clawing at the eyes of a rival. Brand thought he smelled blood when the wind changed, but maybe not. He turned to the one-eyed dwarf. "What?"

"Spotted 'em," the dwarf said. He cocked his head to give his good eye the view and looked below at the raven-feast. He pitched a rock over the side at the crowd of ravens. Shrieking, they rose, and in that instant, Brand saw the white gleam of a rib cage and the blood glistening on spilled intestines. He was too far up to see whose rib cage that was and whose guts—goat or elf or dwarf, maybe even a deer wandered out of Qualinesti, or a goblin or a human like him. The ravens hung in the sky for a few moments, then settled again.

"Spotted them," said the dwarf, "and I reckon we'll be seeing them tomorrow or the next day, heading right along the edge of the forest, the whole crowd out for a ride."

Brand grunted. "Where are they now?"

The dwarf skinned his teeth in a cool grin. "A day out from the city. 'Nother day or two, we'll see 'em riding along the edge of the forest. We'll do best to wait till they're right in the shadow of the wood, just where the ground rears up and the stones all have names."

Brand squinted away north and west. He imagined he could see them, the shining line, like a thin snake winding through the forest: elves.

"All right," he said, "how much gouging are the goblins doing on the deal?"

"Right to the bone." The dwarf snorted. "Greedy bastards. They want the whole field to loot. I told 'em you have a taking to do. Told 'em it's personal. They keep out of our way, they can have the rest. And I told 'em they could have their headman's son back, all his parts still on him and mostly working, if it all goes the way you want. Good as a standing army, one squealing goblin whose da might want him back."

"You told them they'd get him back?"

The dwarf's smile was as cold to see as the high wind was to feel. "Told 'em what you said, Brand. Every word."

Brand clapped the dwarf on the shoulder. "Good enough, Char." Beyond the ravens squabbling, out past the stony stream run nearly dry, the wind rolled across the tops of the trees, and the trees began to bend their heads.

"Smell the rain?" Char said. He squinted up at the iron sky.

Brand didn't answer. He turned his back on the forest and went away across the cliff. He found a winding way down on steps not made by dwarf or human or even stinking elves. When he was full of dwarf spirits, Char liked to say gods made these strong stone steps. Brand had no patience for that prate. He knew better. Wind and rain and storm made those steps.

Down on the flats again, Brand looked west, across the puny stream that had once been a river. Stagger

Stream they called it now, those who lived in the border-land. Years before a rockfall had blocked the river at the headwater, and only a skimp of water came down after that. Not much of that, either, since the last time it rained. Across the puny water lay the Notch, a wedge that seemed to be cut out of Qualinesti. It hadn't been. Trees simply refused to grow there, probably because there was too much stone. A farm had been there, and people had called it the Notch. Not "Notch Farm" or any name like that. Just the Notch. A man had cleared the stones and made a house and fences. He'd scraped the earth and found soil enough to grow food for his family. His goats had eaten the tough grass springing up at the edge of the wood. Sometimes, when the bold mood was on them, the farmer and his sons took deer from the forest, or game birds.

That was a time ago. Now the stone house and fences were toppled. Qualinesti had swallowed the farm. Not the forest, not that. The kingdom had claimed it, and the elves had snatched the land and not made any pretense about asking. Too close to their borders, they'd said, a troop of shining warriors in mail and bright helms. The tallest of them, the leader who had eyes that narrowed to slits when he was thinking, whom his soldiers addressed as a prince, tilted his head as though the farmer and his family stood so far below him it was hard to see them. He'd spoken in Common, pronouncing the words as though they were too coarse to pass royal lips. "Go on. Get out of here." And when the farmer and his kin stood their ground, the elf had ordered his soldiers to get rid of them.

Hooting and laughing, the elves had chased them, pricking their heels with the glinting steel of their lances until they'd driven them away into the stony foothills. Most of the family had died that winter.

Looking into the Notch, Brand bared his teeth in a wolfish grin. Sometimes, over the rim of the jug of dwarf spirits, he'd say to Char, "That place, the Notch, used to be a little fastness of stone. Not big enough, though, and no one could defend it. The ground's too flat. Me, I like the high ground. You can hold high ground forever."

Char would laugh, passing the jug or taking it back. "Are you on that horse again? Talking about holding the high ground and turning yourself into King Brand, the terror of all the goblin towns around? Ain't the goblins you got to worry about. Them elves are the ones. Whatever place you hold, they'll just run you out of there." He belched and wiped his mouth on a greasy sleeve. "Ain't like it hasn't happened before."

Brand didn't care what Char thought. He had a plan. "It just needs a chance, and I'll know it when it comes. I have the patience to wait. Don't you worry about that."

He did, indeed, have the patience. He'd had it for a long time, carried it through long winters and short summers, through fleet springtimes and aching autumns. When he had nothing else—not food or shelter and only ravens to quarrel with—he had patience. Only days after one of those conversations over the jug, his long patience had been rewarded. He'd heard a little word drifting out of the forest to help him recognize his chance.

Looking into the Notch, into Qualinesti beyond, Brand believed that before long, the balance of power would shift in the borderland. It would tip in his favor, and the tipping would be sweeter than anyone might think, sweeter even than one-eyed Char might imagine, and the dwarf knew more of Brand's tale than most.

Chapter 2

~

There! There it was again.

Within the shadows of her hood, Elansa Sungold lifted her head. Tendrils of curling golden hair spilled onto
her cheeks and shoulders. Absently, she tucked them
back behind her long, tapered ears. Disturbed by the
motion, the small leather pouch hanging from her belt
shifted. The homey scent of dried herbs drifted, wolfsbane and chamomile and slippery elm bark, these and
more in little packets neatly wrapped and marked.
These were healer-herbs, the kind any well-versed
herbwife knew how to use.

Elansa cocked her head, listening for the soft slithering sound. She heard only the dull thud of hooves in
the dusty morning stillness of the forest. Before her
rode ten warriors, weaponed and lightly mailed;
behind came ten others. They were, she believed, a suf-
ficient force, for before the paths went deep into the forest, they wended round the stony lands along the edges
of the foothills of the Kharolis Mountains. There, in the
outlands, brigands ruled the roads, competing bands of
outlaws both human and goblin haunting the hills and
the stern mountains.

Elansa's mare snorted, tugging at the rein, impatient
with the slow pace. This one was bred to run in the
fields and meadows around Qualinost. She liked the
wind in her mane more than she liked the quiet forest
trails. A skilled rider with a firm seat and strong grip,
Elansa steadied her mount, then leaned a little forward

to whisper a calming word in the beast's ear. Like a child who hears her mother's voice, the mare grew quiet again.

The cool sapphire phoenix sometimes moved against her breast as she rode, or the silver chain slid on her neck. Here was her god, her Blue Phoenix, and what other god would she have than he who rises, falls, and rises again each new year from the ashes of the old? Once, a long time ago when she had been a girl, Elansa had longed to dedicate her life to the god, to become his cleric and live in his temple, but her father had other plans for her.

"The gods are gone, Elansa," he'd said. "We honor their memory, but let us not delude ourselves that it is anything more."

Against all custom, Paras Sungold had made for his only child a marriage to a prince of the royal house, to Kethrenan who was the youngest brother of Solostaran, the Speaker of the Sun.

"Marry the prince," he said, and they both knew he commanded. "Hurry to make yourself the mother of a child of his. Solostaran has sons, and they look to be fit enough, but it never hurts to be in place."

Indeed, thought Elansa then, and now. In place for what? A plague to take Solostaran's house? A rash of tragedy to sweep away her nephews, the elf king's children? She had not said so to her father, but she felt his greedy glance measuring her belly each time they met. As for Kethrenan, her prince, he had the patience to wait, and he didn't ever complain about the trying. Nor did she; he was an attentive lover.

Kethrenan, ah, handsome Keth. He had the wit and the skill to rule Qualinesti. Elansa, though she never hoped to love him, liked her husband well enough to know and understand him. She realized, as perhaps even he didn't, that given the chance Kethrenan wouldn't find it hard to summon the will to rule. Yet, with the Speaker's children so full of health, it wasn't likely that he would ever have the chance, and so all that wit and will Keth channeled into other streams. He was fiercely loyal to Solostaran, and in the Speaker's cause he spent his wild recklessness, determined to keep safe for his brother and his brother's heirs what he could not have for himself. In these days when the borders of the Qualinesti Forest were seldom crossed by elves, even less often by human or dwarf outlanders, Kethrenan was their dogged keeper. From Lauranost in the west by the Straits of Algoni to the abandoned fastness of Pax Tharkas in the mountains of the south and east, Kethrenan's warriors were a well-known presence, loved by elves, feared by all others.

Bronze leaves, fallen from autumn, whispered on the path as Demlin, Keth's serving man, walked beside Elansa, leading his own mount. The rusty gelding had come up lame an hour before, stumbling as they'd crossed a stream. A stone had lodged in the tender quick of the hoof.

"Not but a small bruise," Elansa had said, passing her hands over the injured hoof. "Let him walk unburdened for as much of today as you can, and he'll be right tomorrow."

She'd spat into her hand, added a small amount of dried root of wolfsbane from one of the packets in her leather pouch, and made a paste, which she applied to the hoof.

Demlin was content to walk until the horse could carry him again. "And it's not like anyone will be leaving me behind, Princess."

He looked up the trail, the stony way rising. Glimpses through the thinning foliage showed the first gleams of the snowy shoulders of the Kharolis Mountains. Dim in the sky, the two moons, Solinari and red Lunitari, early risers, hung like ghosts above the mountaintops. Between those mountains and into the woody border of Qualinesti lay foothills strewn with piles of boulders. So wide and tall were those piles that some individual boulders had been given names, long ago in the days when the borders of Qualinesti and dwarven Thorbardin marched side by side like two friends. Stone Castle, Granite Tower, Hammer Rock, Reorx's Anvil. In those years after the Cataclysm, the dwarves had pulled their borders closer to Thorbardin, but the names of the stones yet remained, known to all who traveled the steep rising trails at the edge of the Qualinesti Forest.

There! Elansa lifted her head. There, she heard the slithering sound again, like a snake winding through the leaves.

One eye ahead, another on the ground to avoid the mess the horses left behind, Demlin didn't seem to have heard what Elansa did. His face, plain and long, was a study in composure. To see him now, a stranger would not imagine he had another thing on his mind besides taking care to keep his handsome leather boots clean. Elansa, however, was no stranger to this man. She didn't think Demlin was deaf to what she'd heard.

Elansa lifted her hands and slipped her hood back, the sage-colored wool falling to her shoulders. High up in an oak, a jackdaw chattered, sounding like a kender laughing. Another joined in, and then a third. One of the horses ahead snorted, tossing its head so that the bridle rang.

Behind, one of her escorts murmured. A deep male voice chuckled, the sound low and comfortable. In the next instant, his laughter fell dead, killed by sudden silence.

"Listen," said the warrior to his companion. Then, after a beat, "Did you hear something?"

Demlin lifted a hand to take the bridle strap of Elansa's mare, the glittering of his long green eyes a warning. He mouthed the word, *Hush!*

A hawk's screech tore through the forest. Thus, the silence, Elansa thought, the wood was falling quiet, striving to become invisible in the face of the raptor. She relaxed a little. Demlin did not. In the pressing silence, Elansa heard again the sound of following, only now the slithering came not from behind. It came whispering from the right, from the left.

Elansa got a good grip on the reins but kept the pressure of her knees light so as not to frighten the mare.

A sword hissed from its sheath. The smell of lanolin and lamb's wool from the scabbard's lining tickled Elansa's nose. Pulse beating high and swift in her throat, she freed her legs of the length of her cloak. Through tight woolen trousers, even through the high leather boots, cold nipped. Demlin's hand tightened on the mare's bridle-strap, then loosened. He turned to look at Elansa, breath drawn, a word on his lips. In the space between one beat of her heart and the next, Elansa saw his eyes widen, and color drained from his face.

Demlin dropped his own mount's reins and leaped, grabbing Elansa by the arm. Yanking hard, he dragged her from the mare's back. Cursing filled the air. Something buzzed overhead as Elansa tumbled from the saddle. A warrior shouted, and another cried,

"Protect the princess!" Around them, a maelstrom of shouting and cursing erupted like the high, savage hooting of predators hunting.

Elansa hit the stony ground and the breath blasted from her lungs. Her left ankle wrenched, caught in the stirrup. In the moment she realized this, the mare hurtled forward. Stone slammed into Elansa's shoulder. Panicked, she tried to curl and protect her head. Another stone tore at her face, but she saw only the ground and the bright flash of iron-shod hooves, then two legs clad in blue wool and brown boots. The mare staggered, flinging and trying to turn.

Demlin sliced the stirrup from the mare's saddle. Elansa fell, at last, gasping to get her breath back. The thick scent of blood filled the air—hers and the mare's. She struggled to stand. Demlin took her hard by the elbows, yanking her to her feet. All around her horses swirled, bright hooves thundering on the ground and flashing sparks from stone. Her knees sagged, and pain lanced through her shoulder, through her ankle, throbbing in her head. Demlin caught her and held her up as cries of "Protect the princess!" filled the forest. Shouts and laughter followed. Out of the forest, like a dark tide, armed goblins overtook the trail. Orange-skinned, teeth filed to needle sharpness, they came howling like beasts, their weapons gleaming as they swarmed out of the shadows. One, and then another of Elansa's guard fell, some arrow-shot, others bleeding from sword cuts.

An elf screamed, and another. Elansa's stomach turned weakly. If she counted them by their death-cries, not but three of Keth's warriors remained. She cried out in grief and terror as another elf fell, an arrow through the neck.

17

"We mourn later, my lady," Demlin said, his voice low and shaking as he dragged her off the path and into the shadows of the wood. "Now we flee."

They ran through the trees, and each step Elansa took made her head rock with pain. She dared not slow; she dared not stop. The cries of goblins followed, a guttural speech that sounded like cursing. Goblins in the Qualinesti Forest—unthinkable!

Forest shadow closed out the sunlight, and Elansa tripped over a writhing root, stumbling to her knees on the stony, rising path. Before Demlin could drag her up, she staggered to her feet, feeling but never looking at the shredded and bruised skin on the heels of her hands. Her shoulder throbbed with pain, the skin raw, the sleeve of her blouse torn and bloodied. Lights danced before her eyes, bitter sparks from the fiery pain in her head.

The way grew narrow. On either side gray lichened boulders made walls that, as they ran, grew higher. With bandits behind and stone to either side, they could go only forward. The sounds of fighting grew faint, then vanished altogether. Death cries, battle cries, they were all silent. One rough peal of laughter rang out, then a sudden shout of anger and a swiftly killed cry of pain. Again Elansa stumbled, her wrenched ankle betraying her. Demlin steadied her, putting her back to a boulder.

"Take a breath, my lady, but we can't linger long. They know we're gone and—"

A twig snapped ahead of them. Elansa cast a swift glance up the trail, expecting to see a horde of bandits. She saw only one person, and this one was human. More, she was a woman. In the first glance, Elansa took in the cut of her—tall in hunting gear, her boots of tanned leather, the fringed shirt untied at the neck to show a **V** of golden skin. Hope rose, foolish and faithful. Surely here was no bandit but a traveler soon to be caught by the same ill luck that had snared Elansa and her party.

"Lady," she said, in a ragged shaking voice naming the stranger courteously. "There are goblins behind . . ."

The woman's lips pulled into a lean feral grin, like a wolf's, her long curling dark hair thick as a pelt, her gray eyes hard and without any light of mercy as she lifted her bow. "And there are bandits ahead, elf girl."

Demlin stepped in front of Elansa. She could smell sweat and the stink of his fear. The dark-haired woman laughed. "You're a loyal servant, but you make a puny shield. I think one bolt will pin you both. Want me to try and see?"

The woman's knuckles whitened, those of the hand that gripped the bow, and those of the one that held the arrow steady at nock.

"In the name of all gods," Elansa whispered, her voice threadbare as a beggar's hope. She put her hands on Demlin's shoulders. "Let my servant go."

The woman said nothing. Elansa moved Demlin away from her, gently insisting when Demlin refused.

"Let him go, please. He has nothing you need."

"He doesn't?" The woman looked at her long, her eyes glittering. "He has you, doesn't he?"

Again her grip on the bow and the nocked arrow tightened.

"Please . . ." Elansa said. "Let him—"

"Dell!" A man's voice, deep and rough, snapped the name like a command. "Hold!"

Without thinking, Elansa looked up, but she saw only the shape of a man, tall and thick in the shoulders, standing on the rock above her. Like the woman, he was human. The sun was behind him, so she saw no features, only his dark shape and a spill of sunlight along the edge of a sword's long blade.

"Dell," he said, a harder edge to his voice. "I said hold."

Dell hesitated another moment, then tossed her head in obvious disgust. "Brand, he's no use to us, just let me—"

"No. Go get Char and the others." He looked at her sternly. "And keep away from the goblins. That's for later."

Elansa let go a breath she'd not known she was holding. Turning and looking up into his shadow-hidden face, she said, "Thank you."

The man, the one the woman had named Brand, lifted his sword, stood a moment watching the sun slide on the blade, then sprang down from the boulder. The scent of him, woodsmoke and sour sweat and leather, made Elansa want to turn her head. She dared not risk the insult, so she stood straight and as tall as she could, though her head did not reach as high as his chin.

The man's eyes narrowed. He snatched her little knife and the leather pouch from her belt. For only a moment, his hands lingered at her waist. So close, she saw his eyes. In them she read hatred. Elansa's stomach clenched with fear, and her blood ran chill in her veins. He looked higher, hooked two fingers under the silver chain round her neck, felt the weight of the sapphire phoenix, and lifted it out from her blouse.

With one swift motion he took from her neck the chain and the sapphire phoenix. The weight of it was gone from her breast, the pulse of its magic vanished as though it had never been. It would not have beat in the hand of an elf who was not a woodshaper, and it did not beat in the human's hand. He held it as though it were only cold crystal as he stuffed it into the pouch at his belt, then shoved her own little pouch in on top of that.

Shaking and cold, Elansa moved to wrap her arms around herself to hide her trembling, then stopped. That gesture would have served only to call attention to what she wanted hidden, her fear.

"Sir," she said, surprised to find her voice holding steady as she accorded to an outlaw the respectful address she'd have given a lord among the Qualinesti. "I thank you for my servant's life. Please, will you let him go?"

"Let him go?" His voice sounded like winter's wind, cold and hateful. With the tip of his sword, he gestured to Demlin, who glared in outraged silence, a silence kept because Elansa's swift glance command-ed. "Isn't his life enough? You want his freedom too?"

Dry-mouthed with fear and trembling with anger, Elansa lifted her chin. "I ask for what I ask," she said.

The bandit took a step back, not a long one, only a half-pace. He, who seemed to like the slip and slide of light on his sword's blade, turned his wrist a little as though to see it again. Caught by the dazzle, Elansa looked where he did, to the silver shining, the light gliding.

"Very well," he said. "I grant what I grant."

The outlaw's sword rose, fell, and Elansa heard Demlin's cry of pain before she saw his blood. Demlin fell to his knees. Horrified, she leaped for him, catching him before he pitched forward. Holding him, his blood seeping into the fabric of her torn blouse, warm on her own skin, she saw what harm had been done. Demlin's left ear, severed, lay bloody on the stony ground.

"Beast!" she cried, turning, Demlin still in her arms. "Beast! You—"

The outlaw grabbed her arm and jerked her to her feet. He sheathed his blade and held her with one hand.

"Get out of here," he said to Demlin, his voice cold as steel. "Go back to your masters and tell them to find ransom for your lady."

Demlin, bleeding, managed to spit in disgust. "We will find ransom," he said, his voice ripped and ragged. "We'll pay it in steel blades—"

The outlaw laughed, a cold booming. "Now that's just what I'm wanting. Swords and knives, steel arrowheads and helms and chain mail." He kicked him, and Demlin fell onto his face. The gaping hole on the side of his head poured blood onto the stony path. "You see to it they pay in just that coin, elf, enough to fill two wagons. Tell them to bring it to the Notch, north of here and by Stagger Stream. Have it there by the rising of the full moons—two men, unattended!—and they'll find your mistress alive. Otherwise, they'll find her somewhere in the borderlands, dead when we've done with her."

Down from the rocks, spilling like shadows, came other outlaws, no more than ten, all human but for a dark-haired dwarf, one-eyed and hiding the lack behind a bright green eye patch. At Brand's word, the dwarf tied Elansa's hands behind her back, and others dragged her away up the trail. Demlin cried out, calling after her.

"Princess! We'll find you! Have faith!"

He said more, shouting to assure her, but his voice had the hollow sound of a memory only dimly recalled.

Chapter 3
ᖰ

In the sky, ravens swirled like storm clouds gathering. Their cries echoed, sharp as knives, in Elansa's ears. They quarreled at feast, vying for good places on corpses.

Names drifted through her mind. Wing-gloss, Oaktrue, Emberbright, Starglance . . .

These were the family names of Kethrenan's trusted warriors. Grief tightened round her throat, a necklace of pain.

Glimmergrass, Slenderbirch, River-reed, and Forrestal . . . all the names of bright and shining men and woman, all devoted to her husband, all pledged to keep her safe. All dead, surprised by goblins and outlaws in the home forest and murdered.

In her mind, Elansa recited their names over. She must remember them. She must be able to speak them like a litany of praise so she could tell her husband how they'd tried to defend her, how none of them broke and ran, how each stood ground until a goblin's arrow or blade snuffed out his life.

Elansa's stomach turned, sickened by the stench of the outlaws crowding her close, before and behind. They smelled of old beer and ale, of sweat and untanned leather. They smelled, she thought with bitter disgust, like humans. You'll never mistake the scent of them, an old elf wife had told her. "Humans," she'd said, "why the span of their lives is so short you can smell them dying."

Elansa's head throbbed with pain. Each step she took, stumbling and weary, seemed to drive the pain deeper, like a hammer driving a nail. She tried to look up the trail, the stony defile that grew more and more narrow. Lifting her head, she stumbled and fell to her knees. Kicked from behind, amid curses and laughter, she staggered up again.

Had they crossed Qualinesti's borders yet? The thought made her tremble. She'd never in all her young life been outside the forest. Since she was a child, thoughts of the world outside were images of howling wilderness, a place peopled by beings rough and strange. Godless folk—all but the dwarves of Thorbardin and the Silvanesti, those distant cousins of the Qualinesti. Wretched and fallen from sense, since the Cataclysm some of these were engaged in a wild and fruitless search for gods other than those who'd been forever known to the peoples of Ansalon. Seekers, these were called. You heard about them sometimes the way you hear about people's nightmares. Elansa shuddered. Others simply didn't care about gods, believing them to be fictions of the long-lived, superstitions and perhaps demonic agents of a magic they no longer understood. Into these hands she had fallen.

But not for long, she told herself. Not for long. Demlin would be on his way back to Qualinost. He'd tell his tale—his mutilation would scream it!—and Keth would come to fetch her home. He'd not bother with that absurd ransom demand. He'd not care about the orders of outlaws. He'd ride to the Notch with such a force of warriors as these miserable ragtag bandits had never seen. Keth would come to bring her home, and she need only keep herself alive and whole so she could watch her captors receive from the prince's hand what they had earned.

Elansa looked up, a brief glance, and saw only a hard bright sliver of sky, no sun to mark the passing hour. Ahead she saw nothing but the backs of outlaws, bent to climb, their leather shirts greasy and stained black with sweat. On each side, the stone walls grew taller, closer, and sometimes Brand, the most broad-shouldered among them, had to turn sideways to slip through.

Ravens swirled high above, like black ash drifting across the sliver of sky. Ravens feasting on the flesh of good men and women, in the forest reveling. Elansa shivered, as though she walked in winter. Did not the name Brand, in some old dialect of Thorbardin, mean Raven?

Climb now, she told herself, climb. Bend your back and climb. Bend and climb, bend and climb. This darker, more brutal chant drove out the litany of the warriors' names, overriding until it formed her only thought. Mindless as a beast, she climbed, and when at last the way before her cleared, bandits parting and moving right and left, she hardly understood what it was she saw, nor was she able to look at it long.

Noon sun shone overhead, the light darting and glancing from bald stone, a field of rock spread out before her. Elansa tried to lift her hands to shield her eyes. The motion dragged a groan from her. She fell, and it didn't seem to matter to anyone that she did. She lay with her cheek on stone, a princess who had never felt any pillow harsher than satin. A cool wind from the heights passed uncaring hands over her still form, tangling her sweat dampened hair. She opened her eyes and saw that she lay upon a high place, a barren table of rock. Ahead she saw no forest, only fields of stone and tall towers formed by a long-ago tumbling of boulders. Behind, she saw only the dark opening that led back into the defile.

Two hands grabbed her under the arms and dragged her up. A knife flashed, just out of the corner of her eye. She hadn't the strength to be afraid, not even the strength to be grateful when she felt the rope binding her hands fall away. Blood rushed back into her limbs, like blades in her veins, racing. She cried out, then forced herself silent.

Brand stood above her, tall and dark. He dragged her to her feet, grabbed her wrists and tied them again, this time in front. He attached a rope to the one binding her wrists, a long line as if she were a mule to be led. This he gave to Dell, who jerked hard so Elansa must follow. At the brink, she saw a vast field of stone spread out below, chunks of granite like the waste fallen from a sculptor's hammer, heedless as he worked. And the hammer, why it seemed she saw that, too, thrusting up from the stony field as though the sculptor had left it standing on its head, the haft pointing to the sky.

First over the edge was Brand, like a mountain goat as he leaped from stone to stone. Others followed, and now Elansa saw the full count of them. She counted eight bandits before Dell urged her forward. Then she looked at nothing but the ground, making her way by taking each stone right after Dell did. There would be no room for error, and she knew it. One stumble, and she would be dragged.

Thus they went, until at last the stonefield grew leaner, allowing for small trails between the boulders.

Brand chose one that seemed no different from the others, a winding way downslope. Always he kept the hammer-shaped rock in the center of the horizon. The ground leveled, the path wound between piles of stone, and the shadows of them were deep as night. High up in the sky, a hawk screamed.

Brand stopped, and all those behind him stood still. Nothing moved but the wind, and then, head back, the outlaw echoed the hawk's screech. A challenge had been offered and answered. Somewhere on the stony piles watchers waited. Dell tugged at the rope and Elansa stumbled forward, eyes on the ground again, until they came to the high pile of stone known to elves and dwarves and outlaws in between as Hammer Rock.

Brand took them into the shadows pooled at the bottom of the stone that made the hammer's shaft, and then the group disbanded, some going left, some going right. Only Dell and Brand remained. Too weary to look around or mark where she was, Elansa went where Dell directed, muscles aching, legs trembling now from exhaustion. They stopped for a moment before a gap in the stone that measured only a little wider than the breadth of Brand's own shoulders. He grunted something, a word of command, and Dell severed Elansa's bonds. Behind her now, she shoved Elansa forward, into the darkness, into the gap in the rough stone. They stood a moment in cool silence, like guests upon a doorstep.

As can all elves, in even the darkest place, Elansa saw the warm red outlines of life-aura surrounding all living things. She did now, looking down into darkness. People were down there, though folk of what kind or race she couldn't tell. She closed her eyes, then opened them again, letting them adjust to normal sight. Now she saw lights twinkling below, torchlight and camp- fires. People gathered around the fires, sitting or stand- ing, and several hounds wandered, looking for bones and bits of meat. A faced turned up, white and looking at the three on the ledge. One by one, the outlaws drift- ed toward the stairs.

Elansa looked around and saw that she stood not upon a doorstep at all, but upon a ledge of stone, like a gallery above a stony hall. Mute since she'd first been dragged away, she swallowed, trying to ease her dry throat, trying to find a word to speak. She managed one, "Where?"

Brand turned, and in that instant Elansa saw him decide not to hit her. "Shut up," he said, but no more than that.

Silent, Elansa looked out over the edge. The stone path dropped off, but gradually, winding round and again like a stair round a castle wall. No dwarf had delved this place. It had been born of ages when rivers ran and earth sank and caves were made. His hard hand on her neck, Brand shoved her forward, down the stairs.

She went, and anger stirred in her. Banked until then by weariness and fear, it roused again. She turned and, cold as ice, she said, "Take your hand off me, human."

Her words echoed hollowly in the well of the stony hall, and derisive laughter came howling up. Brand gripped tighter, the laughter swelled, and he did take his hand from her. With the back of it, he hit her. Crying out, she staggered, stumbling at the edge of the drop. She tasted blood. They sounded like demons at the bot- tom of the stairs.

"Get down there," said the outlaw, "or I'll kick you down."

She went, staggering down the stairs, into the dark depths of the place. Tripping on the last step, she fell hard to her knees. The crowd surged in, hooting and shouting. Hands plucked at her hair, at her face, her torn blouse. Crying out in Elvish, cursing them, she fought back.

Like thunder, Brand's shout. "Char!"

Hard hands grabbed from behind. The black-haired dwarf with the bright green patch over his left eye pulled her up and dragged her away. Shouts of protest and leering laughter followed.

"C'mon, Char! Share!"

"Pass 'er 'round, y' damn stingy dwarf!"

Elansa's stomach tightened, clenching in cold terror. Held helpless, her arms wrenched behind her back, she could do nothing but pray.

"O my Blue Phoenix—"

Char shoved her away from the others until Brand's hand gripped her shoulder hard, halting her. Char let her go, and Brand turned her to face him.

"Not a word out of you, elf, in any language. You don't want them paying too much attention to you, so keep your mouth shut." He pushed her toward the dwarf again. "Take her, Char. Her pretty hide's worth a fat ransom. See it stays on her bones."

Char did as he was told, grabbing Elansa by the wrist and pulling her along into the darkest part of the wide cavern. Some of the outlaws followed, curious or simply mocking. This the dwarf allowed, but not for long. With a growling word and his hand on the short haft of the throwing axe he wore at his hip, he sent them away.

"There," he said to Elansa, pointing into darkness where the only light was that reflecting thinly on lines of moisture trickling down a stone wall. "Settle in, girl, and keep yourself still and quiet. He's got the most of us willing to listen to him, our Brand, but some—" He cocked his head to get the sight of her with his one eye. "Some ain't so long among us and ain't used to heeding. Keep your head down, and you'll probably be all right."

Probably, he said. The word set Elansa to shivering— the uncertainty of it, the possibility of harm lurking behind it.

When the dwarf left, she collapsed, her legs giving way at last. I will not sleep, she told herself. I will not close my eyes in this place. Yet every muscle in her body ached, crying for sleep. I will not, I will not.

She tried to see out into the cavern, but all she saw were figures without feature. One was a woman, but she was not Dell. That one stood almost as tall as Brand himself, and this woman was shorter. For the men, some were tall, but most were thin as mongrels. She could spot Brand easily by the breadth of his shoulders.

I will not sleep. I will not. I will stay here waking, and never sleep until Keth comes to find me and kills every one of these vermin.

She reached for the talisman, the phoenix rising that had long hung round her neck, but that was gone, vanished into a robber's pouch.

O my Blue Phoenix, she prayed, ward me and keep me safe. Never let me sleep. Never let me relax my guard. . . .

* * * * *

The iron toe of a thick boot nudged Elansa hard, rolling her over. She woke with her heart thundering, the memory of groping hands screaming along every nerve. Scrambling back, she had no place to go. Stone stood at her back. She reached around in the darkness searching for a rock, anything to use to defend herself.

"None of that, now. Just sit still, I ain't going to hurt you."

The dwarf Char stood over her, a dripping tin cup in his hand. She knew him by the size and shape of him, by the reek of dwarf spirits, and because he stood over her bearing no light. He was a dwarf, and be they of hill or mountain kin, in dark of night or cavern deep, a one-eyed dwarf sees better than elf or human.

Awake now, she became aware of every afflicting ache and throbbing bruise. She heard other voices, gruff and snarling curses. Laughter rang in the stony chamber, harsh as a crow's. Char placed a battered tin cup of water on the stony floor before her. He never took his eyes from her as she reached for it, and she never took hers from him. She drank, the water tasting like finest wine on her lips.

"Is there food?" Elansa asked, watching him over the rim of the cup.

Char appeared to consider this, then nodded. "Up. On your feet."

Weary and unrested, still she managed to get up with some grace. "Lead," she said, the elven princess captured.

Laughing at the rag of her dignity, he led her toward the little lights and commanded her to sit.

Shuddering, Elansa sat before a low fire, a round of rock and flame in the shadow of the high stony staircase. Watched by Char and a few others, she tried to manage her meal. She ate out of a rough stone bowl, dipping her fingers into thin gritty gruel and spooning it into her mouth. The food tasted like a mixture of corn and barley with the barest flavoring of meat. Tiny globules of fat rimmed the bowl itself, so she knew someone else had lately used it. Her stomach turned, but turning, it also growled with hunger. She pressed three fingers together, made a hook of them, and scooped up more of the awful porridge.

Char watched her, not afraid she'd flee—afraid she'd be stolen out of his charge. So, that's you, she thought, gauging him. Given a charge and determined to see it through to its proper end. She didn't know what that understanding would do for her, but she was a princess, used to navigating the troublous waters of court life. She'd learned how to look at courtiers and servants and lords and reckon out the core of them, to know who was trusty and who was not. She'd learned, as well, that any insight gained was worth remembering.

Eating, she looked around, her glances small and not obvious. Though she wanted to see, she wanted less to call attention to herself. The place held little light. A few torches were tucked into stony niches on the walls, and one wide brazier smoldered in the center of the cavern. That might have flared high with fire sometime while she slept, but only embers winked in it now. The robbers' den, yesterday filled with people and noisy, was almost empty now, so quiet it seemed her breathing must echo. She heard the distant trickle of water, a spring she could not see, perhaps in another chamber. Other chambers there were, of this Elansa was certain.

Three dark gaps in the walls yawned like the mouths of tunnels or hallways leading to other places. Yesterday the bandits had split and some returned to the cavern by another way. Did one or more of these openings lead to those other ways?

A few hounds lay nearby, chins on paws, eyes half-closed and ears up. They all looked like they shared the same parents, long limbs, prick ears, short yellow hair and curling tails. This, she knew, is what dogs become when they are not under the care of kennel masters and breeders: tough and wild and far removed from their sires who might well have once lain at a hearthside or gamboled with their master's children. She looked past the dogs where a half dozen outlaws lay wrapped in their cloaks, sleeping. They were only hunched shapes, and Elansa had no way to know if they were men or women.

Behind Char, a lanky tow-headed boy stood talking with a pot-bellied elder. The boy had a sun-reddened face of one who'd been long outdoors. The old man's face was pale and pasty, his skin unhealthy and dry. The two cast covert glances at her, elbowing each other and leering. In the darkness beyond those two, another watcher lurked, red eyes glaring in the firelight. The figure moved, and Elansa's heart leaped with sudden fear as she caught a glimpse of a long slanted head, narrow eyes, and orange hide.

"That's the goblin," Char said. "Never mind about him."

34

Elansa looked away from the glaring eyes, but she didn't stop listening to the sound of the goblin's breathing, a hoarse, wet sound that made her skin crawl. She finished her meal, such as it was, and drank another cup of water. Then, because she could withhold no longer, she said, "Char, I want to wash and tend my needs."

The boy behind them snickered, and the old man said something in a voice so low that Elansa couldn't make out his words. One of the hounds picked up his head, and Char scratched his bearded chin, thinking.

"Well," she said, "there is a place for that, isn't there?"

Char allowed there was. "But I ain't sending you there unguarded."

The skinny boy's snickering became outright laughter. Elansa swallowed hard as Char's eye narrowed, a look she was getting to recognize as the dwarf considering. Then he slapped his knees and got to his feet. "All right then."

He rose, gesturing her to do the same. Behind, one of the hounds, a large raw-boned male, got to its feet to stretch and watch him curiously. "Follow me."

She did, and when she moved the dog fell in behind.

They went past the sleepers, some of whom stirred when they passed. One of the sleepers, snorting and cursing, cracked an eye and rolled over again. When he moved, Elansa shuddered. This one was an elf! How far had he fallen to find himself among this rabble? And where was he from? Not from Qualinost, she knew that much. No elf had been cast out from there in as long as she could remember, and none had left voluntarily. What elf would? Yet here he was among outlaws, a dark elf, driven from his home for some terrible sin or crime, forbidden the forest and communion with any of his race.

The dog trailing, his nails clicking on the stone, Elansa followed Char past the sleepers, past the place where she had slept, to the first of the openings in the stone wall. The sound of water came stronger now, splashing. They stepped into the darkness of the opening, and she stumbled a little when the ground dropped. Catching herself against the wall, she said, "I need light."

Unimpressed, Char said, "Too bad. Let your eyes adjust. They will. Fang," he said, naming the dog. "Keep." He hung back, saying no more, and the dog slipped in behind her, another guard.

She stood in the dark, trying to focus on nothing. The dog's aura was the only light she saw, his breathing sounded loud, hollow, and so she knew she stood in a narrow space. The music of water falling echoed, perhaps a small stream slipping down the stone. She stood still, waiting for her eyes to adjust. Soon she saw the smooth, level floor curving ahead. Following the sound of water, she walked until she came to the curve in the way. There the passage changed, dropping at the left. Looking over the side, she saw a series of three ledges like broad steps. These didn't look worked, they seemed like the craft of river and time, rough but not unlovely. Beyond the last, two streams ran, one narrow and slipping along the ground, the other a steady trickle of water issuing from a crack in the far wall. Someone had placed a basin beneath the fount to catch the trickle. She peered downstream, wondering if there was a way out. None, or not a very big one. The hound sitting beside her wouldn't be able to wriggle through the opening. Certainly a grown woman couldn't. It was the same upstream, only a little space in the stone from which the water issued.

Pale light drifted now from the distant ceiling. Elansa looked up to see a narrow fissure through which the light came. It looked like dawn light, gray and weak. I've been a day gone, she thought, a day and a night in the hands of outlaws. The moons would rise full in six more days. She smiled, a chill smile to contemplate what must come at the rising of those moons. In six days she would see herself avenged, and the blood of outlaws would paint the tale on the very stones of the borderland.

She found what she needed, a privy space at the running stream where waste would wash out of the cave, and cool fresh water from the crack in the wall with which to wash. The dog, clearly a long inhabitant of the place, crossed the stream beside her and lapped from the water fallen into the basin.

Clean, or cleaner, she watched the dog drink and, watching, she decided to test him. One small step she took, back from the basin. The hound never lifted his head, but his low warning growl gave a clear message. He'd been told to keep her, and keep her he would. When she left, he followed her, shadowing her steps, close beside as they came to the entrance again, the darkest place where the light leaking in from the fissure in the stony ceiling didn't reach. Char stood waiting, arms folded across his chest, head back, watching her.

"Fang," he said, never taking his eyes from Elansa. "Go."

The dog brushed past her, past Char, and vanished into the wider cave.

"Come along," Char said. He jerked his head. "There's something to see."

Elansa heard a rush of voices like the sound of a gale in the forest. One voice, a man's, cut through all others. Like a knife it slashed.

"The doing's mine, Brand! Not yours. *Mine!*"

Voices swelled again. Char shoved her ahead to the fires where many more men stood now than had before. Elansa tried to take a count and guessed at a dozen. They ranged in a semicircle round the bottom of the stairs. Char kept her on the edge of the circle, away from the light and the attention of the outlaws. Brand stood on the high place, the entrance like a gallery above a rough hall. He had the goblin by the scruff of the neck, and the cringing creature's hands were tied behind its back. Halfway up the stairs another outlaw stood, the elf Elansa had seen sleeping.

Cold fear washed through her, only to see that exiled elf, the dark elf whose name she would not speak if ever she came to know it. To see such a one was to see a dead man, lost to decency, lost to his kindred, forever banished from his kind.

The circling outlaws fell silent, so quiet that it seemed to Elansa all she heard was Char's breathing. Brand, up on his gallery, had the look of a soldier rolling the bones, a gambler reckoning his odds for greatest gain. Elansa's belly tightened, and her breath caught in her throat. A wave of excitement ran through the outlaws—shouts then sudden silence as Brand reached for the knife in his belt. With one swift motion, he turned the knife and offered it hilt first to the elf.

Behind Elansa, the dwarf said, "You see. You don't keep it all for yourself."

Shivering, Elansa thought his words made no sense. Keep what? She turned to Char and said, "What—"

The goblin threw back its head to scream, its orange neck thin and long. Like fire flashing, the knife in the elf's hand, and then that fire was quenched by dark goblin blood, the scream drowned to a gurgle as the elf kicked the corpse down the stairs.

Elansa's knees turned to water, and she groaned.

"Now," said Char, his voice quiet but not gentle, "that was a useless hostage. Took him a day or two ago, filled up his father's ears with the promise he'd get his pup back if his miserable tribe killed your escort in the forest. It was a good enough deal. They got the loot; Brand got you. Thing is, Brand never had a mind to send him back to his stinking little goblin town. Hates that goblin's da, he does. Hates him hard and reckons he's owed this killing and more. He wanted to do it himself, but Ley made his point. Ley had the better claim."

Char grabbed her and shoved her back into the darkness, into the little niche in the wall that had been her sleeping place. There she vomited onto the stone floor and the hem of her sage-green cloak. The cloak had been a gift from her father, she thought, her mind racing on mad tangents as her belly heaved. It had been made in the Street of Weavers by an elf woman of surpassing skill. The sweet scent of apple blossoms perfumed the cloak on the day her father had presented it to her. The Street of Weavers is lined up and down with apple trees. . . .

Shuddering, her belly empty of the thin gruel of her breakfast and giving forth only burning bile now, Elansa sobbed. The cloak had been her bedding, and she'd fouled it.

* * * * *

The elf ran like cloud shadows, swift over the stony ground. Leyerlain Starwing ran south with the wind at his back and a sack in his fist. The sack dripped blood, and the blood followed him in small spatters. In the sky, ravens gathered, for they smelled death and dinner. Leyerlain wasn't sharing, though. He had a use for what was in the sack.

He ran, finding paths in the stoneland that few would think existed. He knew the place as he used to know the shady groves of Qualinesti. He knew where to find water, even in these dry days, and he knew where to find caves if he had to go to earth to hide from an enemy. He'd long ago lost that stubborn elven pride that forbade a man to turn from a challenge or fight, no matter the circumstance. He'd lived a long time in this land, the dark dry realm between Qualinesti and Thorbardin, and so he knew the dicta of elven honor had little to do with how to stay alive outside golden towers.

He ran, and the ravens forsook him as he went up stony slopes and down, going southward and eastward. By midmorning, Hammer Rock lay far behind him to the west, the forest a misty line beyond that. He ran in the direction of ancient Pax Tharkas, but he'd no mind to go so far as that place. When the sun sat noon high, he slipped into a shallow defile, and a new flock of ravens came to see if he would die or let fall the dead thing he carried. He did neither, and now he stopped running and sat quietly in the shadows, the sack close to hand, between his booted feet. He drank from the leather water bottle hung from his belt, then settled. The ravens dispersed, the day grew long, and the light old. A chill breeze awoke, prowling down the defile. It carried the scent of smoke and meat cooking. That was goblin-town food, and he'd have sooner died of starvation than eat it. He sat in stillness until the day ended and the short twilight vanished. Not until darkness filled the defile did he move again.

Standing, he stretched and made ready to run. Most of the blood had leached out of the sack, but Leyerlain reckoned the sack and what it held would serve just fine. His way took him up now. He left the defile and ran along the ridge. The moons still below the horizon, the stars not yet awake, nothing lighted him on the height. He was but a shadow.

That's how they saw him in the goblin town, or how one goblin did. When the watch looked up to the ridge, an old fat goblin half-drunk and sleepy, he saw a shadow. He scowled, and he shook his head. He turned his back, looking for his jug of ale. Something hard hit him, like a stone right between the shoulders. Staggered, he fell to his knees, howling and cursing. He scrambled up again and turned to see what had hit him. He saw the sack.

"By every evil god," he snarled, cursing by deities nearly forgotten. A shadow ran on the ridge, tall and thin, and high keening laughter rang out to mock. The shadow vanished, slipping over the hill, and the goblin howled in fury, calling for his fellows.

He snatched up the sack, smelled the blood, and dropped it. Out from the mouth rolled a head, jaws gaping, eyes wide in the last terrified expression of dying. The headman's son had come home.

Chapter 4

Unlike their Silvanesti cousins, the elves of Qualinesti didn't think they were the center of the world—the best part of it, perhaps, but not the center. Thus, their maps were not like those of their cousins upon which the Silvanesti kingdom sat at the heart of Krynn, all other lands floated at the borders, pale and only minimally defined, as though they existed in some place beyond a misty border where nothing counted as interesting or important. A map made in Qualinesti showed the wide world around, named all the kingdoms still standing after the Cataclysm and the departure of the gods. Sometimes the maps named the kingdoms that used to be if those old borders could be determined upon the new face of Krynn. They had not been gentle in their leaving, the gods. It had, in truth, been a cataclysmic event, so violent it reshaped the world. But the Library of Qualinost was far-famed for its collection of maps, and so a keen-eyed cartographer could make out what used to be upon the face of what is. They made painstakingly accurate maps, those cartographers. Of course, because they were elves and, in their opinion not necessarily the center of the world but certainly the best part of the world, the forest kingdom of Qualinesti shone like a jewel on every map, all the world around a fittingly depicted setting for its beauty.

In the heart of the kingdom stood its capital, Qualinost of the golden towers, guarded by four spans of high bridges, shining in all seasons. The Jewel of the

Forest, so poets named the place. Its warden, Prince Kethrenan, had no such lovely image of the city. He was not blind to her beauty, he could enumerate all her charms, but it was and always had been that Qualinost and all the forest beyond was to the prince more than the sum of its glittering parts. This was the land of his fathers, defended in blood. This was the kingdom to which his mothers had willingly borne princes and kings. The blood of his ancestors made holy this forest.

None of these words would he have used to describe his feeling. He was no poet; he was a hard-eyed soldier. Still, he felt his connection to the forest and the kingdom as though all the blood of those distant fathers and mothers had watered the ground around his feet, and he himself had put down the roots of an oak, thick and strong. His brother the elf king had his court, his contentious senate, his lords and his ladies. Solostaran was welcome to all that. Kethrenan had his barracks and training grounds, his warriors. He had armories filled with swords and shields and armor, and every smith in the city his to call. These things he wielded for the good of the kingdom.

In the largest of the barracks rooms, the prince stood in the sunlight of a crisp autumn afternoon. A spare place, here Kethrenan loved best to be. One of a dozen like it, the barracks was nothing but a great sleeping hall for his soldiers with brackets for torches upon the walls and—as in ancient days—no hearth but a long fire pit on either side of which stood long trestle tables. He stood now, in the end of the day, leaning over one of the tables, shoulder to shoulder with his cousin Lindenlea. Cousin and the second commander of his brother's army, she was his most trusted friend, a woman who'd set out on the soldier's road at the same time he did, who'd taken her training alongside him, and who had risen in the ranks as a hawk rises to the sky, effortlessly. Outside the window soldiers practiced swordplay, and arrows wasped and thunked into the thick straw butts. Someone cheered, another jeered, and challenge crossed challenge, like sword blades. These things Kethrenan heard, but only vaguely. His attention he gave to the map spread out on the scarred table.

"Where is the last place you saw them, Lea?"

She pointed to the eastern edge of the kingdom where waterways ran whose banks were not, in this autumn season, too much troubled with water.

"Right here, just across the border. We're drier in the forest than we're used to being in this season, but out there they're dry as stones. The goblins will be crossing into the forest. If not now, soon."

Kethrenan grunted. "And this new leader?"

"An ugly brute, from what I hear. He's not a goblin. He's a hob."

The prince slid his cousin an interested glance. "We haven't seen a hobgoblin around that part of the border in years. What's his story?"

"I don't know. The best my scouts could learn was that he's come up from the south, or maybe the east. It's all wind and rumors. What's certain is that Golch is out and this hob Gnash is in. All our scouts agree on that, and that he's running things in the three goblin towns closest to our borders."

Kethrenan took that information in silence, returning to his study of the map. Down from the White-rush River, streams went branching, blue from the cartographer's inkwell. All had been depicted by the kind of careful line that comes from a tightly nibbed pen and a steady hand. Some had been drawn thin, some fat, some led into lakes, and others wandered through the forest, following the will of the world, growing or shrinking as Krynn herself dictated. The forest through which these streams went—these days slowly—was shown not in inked lines but dappled green brush strokes. Fair Qualinesti, sunny glades and secret shadowed glens, lay upon the map as beautifully as though it were seen in a still pond's reflection. The dab, sweep, and swirl of a brush depicted the wealth and wonder of elms and aspens, of steadfast oaks and, in the south near that edge of the forest that abutted the stony land between the elven kingdom and the dwarven, tall pines whose variety rivaled even that of the oaks. So hardy were those pines that when they did not grow on level ground, they managed to cling with gnarled grip to the sheer crumbling edge of the glens that scored the part of the borderland where the world was more stone than soil.

Without a word from her prince, Lindenlea pointed to the map again. "Here," she said, slipping her finger along the White-rush River. "And here, and here." She tapped the western part of the forest, right by the Straits of Algoni. "Here, and here. Right down to the Wayreth border, and of course all through Qualinesti and strong along the Kharolis Mountains."

This she said in answer to the unvoiced question: Where are your scouts?

Kethrenan nodded, satisfied. "I want reports from all the borders in the usual time."

He tapped restless fingers on the eastern border where the cartographer showed only dun reaches. The blandness of the color changed only a little to gray to indicate rising ground in the south and east. These were the foothills of the Kharolis Mountains. They held little of note but the old fortress standing a-straddle the gap between two of the northmost arms of that mountain chain. Pax Tharkas, fallen to ruin. Pax Tharkas, a reminder of better days when there was no wild windy waste between the two kingdoms. In those times, good roads had run through the foothills, kept safe by elf warriors and dwarf soldiers. It wasn't quite as the legends said, that a fair virgin could walk those roads with a sack of gold in each hand and reach her destination unmolested, but things were better then than now. In those days, goblins hob and small had seldom come out of their dark haunts in the deep mountain vales.

"Send word out that I want to hear from your scouts on the eastern border every second day."

Lindenlea nodded, a cool glint in her eye. "And if anyone comes across the hob?"

"Tell them to do what they do best, and don't bother bringing me back a trophy, just the news that it's dead."

"Yes, my prince," she said.

Outside, a cheer rose up, and other shouts in chorus. Swords clashed, the ringing martial music. Lindenlea glanced out the window to see the last light of day running like silver on a sword's blade. They didn't fight with blunted edges. They fought to the bone and the blood, and so good were they by now that mail and armor suffered, but flesh seldom did.

"They'll all be in soon for their mess," she said to the prince. "And I know they'd be happy if you joined them, Keth."

He grunted, his mind still on his map, counting his scouts, counting his borderland guard, and thinking about whether he wanted to send an extra force out to the border or lie back, waiting to see what would happen. Warden of the Forest Kethrenan was, but still at his very heart, he was a hunter. He understood the virtue of patience. By the time the hall began filling up with his warriors, two things had been decided: He would stay to eat with his soldiers, and he would wait to see what the new leader of three goblin towns would do.

* * * * *

Across the barren land a cold wind came up from the south, like word from a cruel land. Elansa woke shivering, her cloak damp with night-chill. Each night, for the past three, the air had hung damp. Never did rain fall, and in the gullies meant to shine with water the stones lay dry with only a thin thread of water slipping over. There was only the wind, and at night wolves howled in the stony reaches. Into that wind, for three days, Brand and his outlaws had traveled, Elansa in tow. They headed north, and though she didn't know for certain, Elansa hoped they were going toward the place Brand had called the Notch, the meeting place where ransom would be delivered and she would be returned to her people.

If Demlin had survived his journey. . . .

If word had been received in Qualinost in time for Keth to send the ransom. . . .

That would infuriate him, that particular demand— two wagons filled with weapons and armor. Kethrenan would find it easier to part with gold and jewels, to open the rich coffers in the tower of the Sun and pile up baubles. To have to part with precious steel . . . this outrage would burn his heart.

On the first day, Elansa had been forced to walk with her hands bound before her. On the second day, the ropes had been cut. This was at Char's suggestion.

"She's slowing us down, Brand. Either kill her or cut her hands loose."

Brand had looked at the moons, the red and the white like pale ghosts in the afternoon sky. They were five days from full, and he was reckoning time. He looked north, reckoned some more, and told Char to cut her loose.

"Keep that eye of yours on her," he'd said. "Lose her, and I'll kill you."

The dwarf had shrugged, but Elansa didn't think the threat was an idle one.

Now, on this fourth day from Hammer Rock, she woke and lay for a long moment still, trying to find the will to move. In the end, it was not will that helped her to sit. It was the groaning of the muscles in her back and neck, stiff from another night sleeping on stony ground. Sitting, she looked westward to the forest. She saw only a thin dark line sketched on the horizon, like a fading mark on an old, old map. There was Qualinesti, far away.

Here in the stony land, no dawn chorus sparkled, no lifting of birdsong to greet the new day. Here, there was only wind and, for Elansa, hunger and thirst and bruises. She was not always dragged to her feet when she fell. Brand insisted on keeping his hostage in condition to walk, but when he wasn't looking, or when Char wasn't near, Elansa was as often kicked to her feet as dragged.

She learned the names of some of the outlaws by hearing their rough voices, talking among themselves about her as though she were a dumb brute.

Kick 'er up, there, Arawn! Dell, drag that useless sack to her feet!

She learned other names that way, walking or stumbling. She heard their voices roughened by drink, by the cold, by the constant grit blowing across the barren land where only rocks and crows and wolves lived.

Ay, Swain! Y'keep lookin' at 'er like you think those skinny elven bones would warm y'up of a night. . . .

Chaser will have the warm of her before you do!

She heard the name Ley applied to the elf. She never heard the whole of his name. He seemed to have little to do with most of them. She'd only seen him speak with Brand and a tall, silver-haired woman whose name was Tianna and who had the look of both elf and human. Sometimes he spoke with Char, but the long silences between them seemed more the dwarf's doing than the elf's.

Brand's band numbered two dozen, among them all only two were women: dark Dell and bright Tianna. These two harbored no sympathy for the captured woman. Their laughter was as raucous as any man's when Elansa looked around for food or water and got none or little, when she fell and struggled up again. . . .

"Fine, fancy riding boots," Dell said once, looking pointedly at the thin-soled leather boots with the thick heel. "You'd do better, princess, to go barefoot."

Brand and Dell, Tianna, the elf Ley and the dwarf Char, Chaser and Swain and Arawn . . . these names Elansa learned, for these were often together, perhaps the core of the outlaw band. The names of the other outlaws she didn't know—surly, sullen men who ranged before and behind her, who drifted in and out of the shadows at night. These she knew only as a threat. These were the ones whose eyes looked at her from the darkness when the campfires were low, waiting for her to get up to relieve herself, to walk just far enough outside the light that Char or Brand wouldn't see. Then they followed, one or two or three, like wolves. After the second night, Char sent the hound with her, his long loping Fang, with the curt command, "Keep!"

Elansa looked around her in the chill dawn. The outlaws slept, dark shapes hunched under ragged cloaks. The embers of a campfire glittered nearby, and Brand sat stirring them to life with a burned stick. No one else was awake but the watch on the high ridge, Char and Tianna pacing. Brand looked up at her and then back to his fire making. Near his hand a cold chunk of meat sat, half a hare, furred in the ash of the fire. Elansa's stomach rumbled, hungry. She'd not eaten since the morning before. In exhaustion, she'd fallen asleep while a dozen lean hares brought down by slender arrows from Dell's quiver and Ley's still cooked over the fires. No one had waked her, and the several hounds who were Fang's companions dined in peace, without her hungry eyes on them. Elansa had learned the hierarchy of this brigand band: outlaws ate first, dogs next, the lone captive after. She'd learned to respect it quickly, for to complain was to go without.

She pulled her cloak around her shoulders and rough-combed her hair back from her face. Tangled and dirty, the knots pulled painfully against her fingers. Broken fingernails scraped against her cheek. The princess prepared herself for another day in the outland.

Brand looked at her again, then to Fang who came padding through the camp. He stabbed the hunk of meat with his dagger and jerked his head at the hound. They shared the meat, stripped from the bones, the outlaw wiping his mouth with the back of his hand, the hound's tail wagging in lazy sweeps. Elansa's throat closed up painfully, tears pricked at her eyes.

Yawning, Brand peeled off one more strip of flesh from the carcass, gave it to Fang, and flipped the bones, stringy meat clinging, to Elansa. The hound watched it tumble in the air, glanced at Brand, then at Elansa. Bones and pitiful remains fell in the dust.

"Go on," Brand said, to the dog or Elansa.

She didn't wait to guess. She took up the bones and gristle, and took what meat she could from the whole. The hound crept closer. She snapped a bone from the carcass and tossed it. While Fang's attention was elsewhere, she cracked a leg bone and split it for the marrow. This she did awkwardly, not so handy as those who did not eat from silver plates. Marrow, until three days ago, was no more than flavoring for what the cooks in the elf king's household liked to call a Hunter's Stew. Here, marrow was part of a meal, one she had learned early not to scorn.

All around her, outlaws woke, separating themselves from the earth and their cloaks. Two, Dell and Arawn, separated themselves from each other. Upon the ridge, Char and Tianna looked east toward the sullen dawn. Elansa licked cracked lips, looking where they did. Unyielding gray, the sky hung low, holding out the promise of rain that never came.

Swift and sudden, a hawk's screech ripped across the dawn stillness. Elansa's heart jumped. Outlaws stopped what they were doing and looked around, searching east. Hounds rose from the dust, stretching. Char and Tianna seemed to have vanished from the ridge. Elansa looked harder and saw them bounding down the thin path away from the height.

Brand snapped Dell's name like an order. The woman grabbed Elansa by the arm and dragged her to her feet. A dagger's gleaming edge pressed against the flesh of Elansa's neck. "Be still," the woman hissed. Elansa didn't breathe. The hare's carcass fell from her fingers into the dust, marrow dark in the cracks. The nearness of the delicacy broke Fang's concentration. The hound snatched the carcass and trotted away to enjoy the last of breakfast.

"Goblins," Char said to Brand, the first to return. "Tianna says about a dozen. I make it maybe less. Ten, likely. No matter the count, we both saw the shine of their weapons. We saw them come in from the west and turn north. Making for Stagger Stream, I'd guess. It's the nearest trusty water."

Brand heard this in silence, his eyes narrowed. The shine of their weapons, Char had said, and Brand had his hand on his own, the knife always at his belt. He cast a quick glance at his sheathed sword lying near the failing fire, then another swift look over Char's head. "Tianna! Get us going, girl! You and Ley think about east!"

Dell's hand gripped Elansa's arm tighter. "You're running? Brand, you're running from goblin scum? There's only a dozen, at most. You heard what Char said."

Brand turned as though she'd not spoken. He retrieved his sword, belted it on, and said, "Char, make sure there's no sign of us here for anyone to find. Arawn, you and Chaser in the rear." Then he turned to Dell, his eyes glittering. "You and Swain at the point. Let Ley and Tianna guide. We're heading east. You have a problem with that?"

Tension crackled between them, like lightning in a storm-sky. Her voice low and tight, Dell said, "I have a problem with running from an easy kill."

"Then get out of here. Take on the goblins if you like." He pointed to Elansa, his finger stabbing the air between them. "You," he said to her, "come here."

Held, she took a step but was not released. The knife's blade pressed closer to her throat.

Brand cocked his head, a slight gesture and dangerous. "Let her go, Dell."

Nearby, Char lifted his head, listening as he kicked out a campfire. In his hand Elansa saw the throwing axe that had, a moment before, been tucked into his belt. What Elansa saw, Dell did. Elansa felt it in the reluctant loosening of the woman's grip, the lifting of the knife.

"Touchy all of a sudden, aren't you, Brand?"

Brand shook his head, not to say he wasn't, to say she'd better not pursue the matter further.

With a rough shove, Dell pushed Elansa toward Char. "Here's your charge, dwarf. You know what to do."

The dwarf kept Elansa close as his own shadow while the outlaws broke camp. Each one stripped the meat from the night's leavings, stuffing it into their pouches, even marrow-bones. Char saw to it that campfire ashes were scattered, burned wood flung wide, the naked bones of last night's supper buried. In short time, two dozen outlaws departed the site of their night camp.

When she looked back over her shoulder, Elansa saw little sign that anyone had occupied that stony ground. She saw the thin gray line of the Qualinesti forest. It no longer ran beside her. Now it disappeared behind, swallowed as though the leaden sky had come down and eaten it. Throughout the long morning she thought of the goblin who had been Brand's hostage only days before. She thought of the killing, and how the goblin's severed head had made Brand's point to the leader of a goblin town: I despise you, and this is how much.

Should his quest for ransom fail, for whatever reason, would the outlaw send her own head back to Qualinesti, simply for the satisfaction?

Elansa did not doubt that he would.

* * * * *

They were twelve running north to find Stagger Stream. Twelve goblins, most of them orange-skinned, but one or two with that blue-brown hide that looks like rotting meat. They were, as Char had guessed, looking for water. Nearly every creature with any kind of sense of self-preservation was looking for water these days, but these traveled under orders. The goblin town to which they had belonged, which had lately become the headquarters of the hob they'd learned to refer to as the Great Gnash, had become too small for their new master's army. Goblins were moving into the place and drinking up the water in the puny stream that ran in the gully. Gnash wanted more water, he wanted more room, and he wanted a bigger goblin town from which to reign over the three he now ruled. He wanted four goblin towns and the seat of his power to be a new one.

Find a village fat for plunder. Find water.

Simple orders, and the twelve set out to do just that. They were the canniest scouts in Gnash's army, clever even for their savage kind. They would find what Gnash needed, and each one was certain great reward would follow. Not advancement, for goblins don't think that far ahead. Not one of them envies the position of whichever brute may be ahead of him in power or favor. Goblins envy weapons, treasure, and possessions. When they aren't fighting and killing, goblins like to have things to use and spend.

One of these twelve, a fellow with mottled blue-brown skin, was more eager for reward than the others. He wandered a little afield. He went a little east out of his way. He thought he heard water running, and he was right. A small trickle in a dusty gulch: water. And he saw the flung bones of what at first glance seemed to be some scavenger's meal. When he looked closer, he saw that the dead thing had been a hare, and the thigh-bone of the eaten hare had been inexpertly cracked for the marrow.

Looking around, the enterprising goblin discovered more bones, these buried in haste. He was a quick reckoner. By the number of supper-bones he found, he supposed there had been a dozen, maybe two, camping there. He thought he should call to his fellows, and then he changed his mind. He'd been south and had not seen two dozen men traveling. Off to the west, no sign, nothing in the north. Whoever had camped here had gone east. Curious and hopeful of gain, the goblin moved off in that direction. Soon he found signs to confirm his guess, the dark splashes on earth and stone to show where travelers had relieved themselves, scraped stone where boots had glanced. And only a little while after his fellows had discovered him gone, he saw a dim line moving across the stonelands.

He stood on a high hill. He couldn't count them or see if they were elves or humans or more goblins. The latter, he doubted. Goblins don't clean a campsite, or even try to. He went down the hill, slipping along behind in shadows until he came close enough to see who traveled.

Grinning, his sharp teeth glittering in the gray light of the overcast day, the goblin thought there would be great reward for him, indeed, if he took this news to Gnash. A whole tribe of human outlaws, that stinking troop with the elf and the one-eyed dwarf and damned Brand himself, was headed east and a little north.

Interestingly, they had a prisoner, and by the look of her gear she was not a woman from a rival band. Those boots were of finest leather, her ripped blouse of silk, her cloak woven in Qualinost or-near there. The goblin wondered what that meant—an elven prisoner marching carefully guarded.

Whatever it was about, he reckoned Gnash would like to know, and quickly. Not so much because the elf woman would be of more interest to him than anyone he could eventually sell down to Tarsis. He'd be interested because along with the army of the goblin Golch, who'd lost his son's head in a bad bargain, Gnash had inherited Golch's hatred of the outlaw Brand, the feud coming to him just as had the weapons, females, and house of the unlucky Golch.

Quickly, the goblin went back along his own trail until he came to a place where it seemed best to turn south toward the goblin town. This he did, and he ran swiftly, like the shadow of a storm-driven cloud, silent on the earth. In only a day and a night of running, he came to the goblin town, and what he'd hoped turned out to be true.

The Great Gnash was, indeed, happy to hear the news that Brand was on the move. He didn't much care to wonder why this was so. What interested him was that there were only two dozen of them, and he had a newly swollen army of goblins to try out. Some of them, it might be imagined, would be anxious to prosecute the old feud between themselves and the human, and Gnash himself hadn't killed anyone since he'd overtaken this goblin town of Golch's.

The thing that interested Gnash most, however, was that he'd have a chance to try out a weapon he'd found away south. He'd been carrying it around since he'd discovered it, secret and hidden far beneath the mountains. It had taken a bit of figuring out. He'd done all his conquering and killing in the goblin towns along the Qualinesti border with ever-reliable steel. Now, though, Gnash thought it was time to see if what he'd discovered in darkness might prove to be worth more even than steel.

Chapter 5

Restless, Prince Kethrenan walked, pacing the paths, the byways, and the fair roads of the golden city. His cousin took quick steps to keep up, for Keth stretched his long legs with every stride as though he must put as much distance behind him as possible. Not for the first time Lindenlea thought she and the prince were well matched in spirit but not in length of leg.

The song of bells drifted in the air, silvery and rhythmic, dancing to the jogging pace of a lady's pretty mare as she rode through the dark orchards. Her horse, up ahead, looked ghostly gray as the sky. Laughter pealed, and beyond a garden wall children chased the fat heavy flakes of snow drifting down. The first snow of the season fell upon Qualinost, sifting through the black sketch of naked tree branches. The city's graceful buildings, homes, shops, the far-famed Library of Qualinost, temples, and smithies would glow quietly, like faithful hearts beating. Even the barracks, stark and stern, seemed softened, if not by the quiet light, by the mantle of snow on their shoulders.

Beyond the buildings and the naked orchards, four tall watchtowers stood, each lined with burnished silver, each stronger than it looked. Slender bridges, spans which seemed so delicate one might imagine a fallen leaf would collapse them, sketched out the rough square bounds of the city by connecting the towers north to east, east to south, south to west, and west back to north again. Within those gleaming towers contingents of

Kethrenan's warriors were quartered, men and women who kept a strict rotating schedule of duty to insure that no tower ever went unmanned. Upon each of those arching bridges a regular guard walked its rounds. From the founding of the kingdom, the company who kept this watch was known as the King's Own, the guardians of his very walls. The names of past commanders of this guard decorated elven legend. These days, the King's Own was Lindenlea's to command. The honor was a considerable one for Kethrenan's cousin, and deserved.

The guard on the bridges, hard-eyed soldiers, looked always outward to the broad ravine surrounding the city. That cut in the earth, deep stone plunging down to rushing water, was the first line of Qualinost's defense. The second line were the troops who patrolled there, mounted squads whose first order in time of conflict was to burn the wooden bridges at the sight of enemies, whose next was to die to the man to keep all invaders away from the city itself.

Dark across the sky, crows sailed, their raucous shrieks damping the laughter of bridle bells. Kethrenan looked up, tracked them, and lost them in the snowy veil.

"What do you hear, Lea, from the watches at the ravine?"

"Only that it's quiet. 'Dull as dirt,' this morning's messenger said." She shook her head, for the messenger had been a youth, over-eager, untried, full of fancy and ancient songs. The first battle he saw and survived would disabuse him of the notion that a quiet watch was a boring one. "He'd be wise to be grateful for that."

Kethrenan agreed.

Lindenlea slid him a quick glance. "I don't think you're much different from that eager boy, cousin."

"Vastly different. I have a dozen more scars, have seen comrades die in battle. . . ."

She laughed.

"What?" he said, frowning.

"You. You sound like an old man. Old," she said, grinning, "and forgetful. Or is it really hard to remember the days when you used to long for the chance to fight in a battle and live to hear the songs bards would write about your adventures?"

Kethrenan snorted, dismissing a question flown too close to the mark. He could not dismiss her truth, though, and he didn't try.

Snow sighed, silencing the city. In windows, lights gleamed like eyes smiling for the warmth and the shelter. No birds flew, and few people were about, only the watch on the wall.

Kethrenan lifted his head and looked south, past the tall Tower of the Sun where his brother Solostaran held court, where he and Elansa lived. He thought about her, his wife, and he wondered how she fared out in Bianost. Did the snow keep her from her work? He didn't imagine it would. They'd had no chance to talk before her leaving, but he didn't need close conversation to know that Elansa had gone willingly, blight's enemy sallying forth in the golden autumn. No elf lived who didn't love the forest. So much could even be said for the Silvanesti kindred who tamed their wildwood into gardens. Yet to woodshapers it sometimes seemed that the trees of the wood were but another tribe of souled beings, the tribe breaking down into clans—Elm-clan, Oak-clan, Birch-clan, Rowan-clan, and Pine-clan. . . .

Woodshapers saw things differently than most elves. Elansa, his wife, was a stubborn girl who would not be put off by mere winter if her healing skills were needed. She would commune with her beloved trees as easily in snow as in sun. He pictured her walking among the naked trees, cloaked in fur, the snow glittering in her golden hair. The sapphire phoenix would sit heavily upon her breast, the stone glittering, the phoenix's wings spread as though the bird itself would leap from her and fly away.

Lindenlea's voice cut into this thinking, sharp through the muffling snow. "Keth, look." She pointed to the eastern bridge, to a runner jogging along the silver path.

"My lord prince!" he cried. He stopped, sketched a bow, and leaned over the parapet. "A messenger has come for you, Prince Kethrenan. He waits in the king's chamber."

Lindenlea's eyes narrowed, and Kethrenan could almost hear her thinking. A messenger waiting in the chamber of the Speaker of the Sun carried no word of little moment. In spite of himself, the restless prince's heart rose.

* * * * *

Voices followed Kethrenan down marble corridors, dry whispers ghosting in his wake. A servant spoke to a servant, women in the dun robes of the kitchen. Outside Solostaran's library, a scribe gestured to the quill-boy who'd come with a basket of freshly sharpened pens. In the shadows of the corridor, their blue robes seemed like deeper darkness as the scribe, her silvery hair the only gleam, leaned near to murmur. When they saw the prince, they looked away. That looking away spoke more and louder than any voice.

The skin prickled on the back of Kethrenan's neck, a hunter's hackles rising. He'd been feeling that since he'd left Lindenlea behind, sending her to make certain of all watches posted in and around the city. They had seen something in the attitude of the guardsmen on the bridges to make them slide narrow-eyed glances at each other. The nearer they came to the Tower of the Sun, the more alert the warriors became.

Servants melted away before the prince, slipping into chambers and alcoves, gliding silently out of his way until, at last, Kethrenan stood in the doorway of his brother's chambers. Silent, he kept himself in the shadow, observing.

Within, Solostaran stood like a candle's bright flame, king of the Qualinesti elves. He had his hand upon the shoulder of a thin, frail man. Beyond, two others stood close together, elves dressed in the rustic gear of one of the outlying villages. Kethrenan noted that they looked like kin to each other, and then he dismissed them.

Solostaran helped the frail man to sit in a deep, high-backed chair. They were an odd pairing, the Speaker and the man he helped. Tall for an elf, Solostaran was thinner than his brother. Kethrenan could see in him the blood of the great hero-king Kith-Kanan. It shone in the keen glance of his eye, in the strength that had nothing to do with brawn and everything to do with surety and grace. He was the flame of his people, their spirit incarnate, their heart and soul. But the other . . . the other looked like a beggar brought in from the gate, ragged and pale and sickly.

"Keth," said the Speaker, who knew his brother's step and didn't need to turn to see him. "Here is a sad homecoming."

In the shadows, the two strangers sighed. One glanced at the other. One slipped a hand into the other's. Brother and sister, Kethrenan thought absently. Upon the woman's cheek a small tear slid, drawn by the simple word, *homecoming*.

Kethrenan's eyes narrowed. He didn't know those two and he didn't know the man his brother said had come home. Surely that was a stranger leaning upon the arm of Solostaran as the Speaker helped him to sit.

The prince narrowed his eyes against the candlelight glinting off the black and white marble tiles of the floor. Here and there, in random pattern, one or another of those tiles was marked with the shape of a lily, white on a black tile, black on a white—the sign of some ancient king's love for a woman who, in her time, embodied scandal and who now only embodied a wisp of recalled legend. The Tower of the Sun was rife with such ghosts of older times, older feuds and hatreds and loves. It was part of the luxury of the place, a luxury of history, a luxury of fable. The place also reflected a luxury of design. An extravagance of glass wall brought the orchard and the city itself into the Speaker's chamber. Oftentimes, it brought sun pouring into the room, golden and warm. This day, that wall brought only gray gloom, and the apple trees and pear trees outside the window seemed like old men and women, gnarled and twisted and angry with age. It was left to banks of tall candles to provide light in the chamber, and torches in black iron holders. This light showed Kethrenan his brother's guest.

He was small as a youth, scrawny, shriveled, and wrinkled like an unfledged bird. His head bobbed on his neck as his hand lifted to pluck at Solostaran's sleeve, and the Speaker whispered something to the frail one.

Who is it, Kethrenan wondered, that my brother says has come home?

The man's face shone white against the emerald silk cushions of the chair. He turned—perhaps Kethrenan had made some sound at the door—and the prince knew him. Cold to the heart, he knew him, and he saw that he was maimed, the side of his head naked where his ear should have been.

"Gods," he whispered, crossing the room in swift long strides. "Demlin! Gods, what's happened to you?"

Solostaran looked up and gestured sharply. In his eyes was the sudden flicker of annoyance Kethrenan had known all his life.

"Easy, Keth," he said, his hand on Demlin's shoulder. "The man is not strong."

Demlin, greatly reduced, looked up at his lord, the man he had served all his life. Tears stood in his eyes, and Kethrenan shuddered with prescient chill. The pain of his maiming would never have wrung tears from Demlin. Something worse did.

Dull, gray light from skies the color of unloved iron crept into the room, and it seemed to Kethrenan that candles and torches could not stand before it.

"My lord," Demlin whispered, "I—"

"Where is Elansa?" Kethrenan's voice sounded like stone. "Where is my wife?"

"My lord . . ."

Gently, the Speaker of the Sun put his hand on the servant's arm. Demlin looked up and took the cup of wine his king offered. He merely wet his lips, not having the strength to drink that liquid fire, but even the small taste seemed to hearten him.

"My lord, Princess Elansa has been stolen."

In the far shadows, the two strangers, the elves who were kin, moved closer to each other. One sobbed, the woman. The other put his sheltering arm around her shoulders.

Demlin took a breath and said, "She is being held for ransom, and there are but two days for you to go and fetch her home before"—he tasted the wine again—"before she is killed."

Killed.

Solostaran glanced at his brother.

In Kethrenan's belly, coldness turned to fire. The fire raced to his heart and changed into fury. He was a man of battlegrounds, a warrior who knew what happened to women who fell into the hands of men unbound from the rules of law—soldiers in battle-lust, outlaws cast out from all society and virtue.

Solostaran knew it, too. "What is wanted, Demlin?" he asked. "However much gold, however many jewels, we will find them."

Demlin shook his head. "It isn't jewels they want, my king. They want . . . they want two wagons piled high with weapons. They want these taken to the borderland, that place known as the Notch. They want no one to go but the ones who drive the wagons. They will kill her, otherwise."

The outlaws wanted treasure, indeed, the one prize no sane man would ever grant them. Arm us, they demanded. Put your best swords into the hands of your enemies.

And yet, how could they withhold?

"Go," Solostaran said, and though his brother's cheeks shone pale with anger and underlying dread, Kethrenan heard the voice of a king speaking to his warlord. "Go, brother. Spare no man or woman. Spare no weapon. Go and bring home our princess."

* * * * *

Standing in the iron light of the hard day, Lindenlea watched as Kethrenan slipped on the shining shirt, the ring mail chiming as he settled it on his shoulders. He poured back the metal cowl as though it were a hood. He felt her regard, and her unvoiced question, as he reached for the tooled leather scabbard and slid it onto the broad black belt he wore slung low on his hips.

She wanted to say, "Cousin, how are you?" She said nothing, knowing he wouldn't answer. Everything he was, Kethrenan kept locked away in the coffer of his heart, doling out little pieces when it seemed fitting. It did not seem fitting for him to display what his heart felt now, the fear and the rage. No warrior should see that in her commander. She should never be given the chance to wonder whether he was truly in command of himself, lest she begin to worry that he could not command his army.

Kethrenan's hand loved the fit of the sword's grip. He loved the weight of the weapon on his hip. He was no archer; he was a bladesman, yet he'd become used to feeling the weight of his weapon low, as archers feel their quiver. Low he liked it, right where his hand fell naturally to grasp. The sword he fitted into the sheath, its sliding releasing the pungent smell of the lanolin from the lamb's wool lining.

Lindenlea eyed the sword and the gleaming grip. Diamonds winked on that grip. Sapphires shone on the hilt, and one baleful ruby eye. She leaned against the doorway of her cousin's bedchamber and said, "With the oldest sword you own, you go after her?"

"Yes," he said. "The oldest and the best."

He jerked his head at her, a silent command.

"Three troops," she said, her words clipped. Now she was a warrior reporting to her prince. "Sixty warriors, armed, mailed, angry as fire—and at your command, my lord."

Sixty. It would do. They would depart before nightfall, running out to the border and keeping themselves secret in the woods. No clanking army of dwarves, no trampling herd of humans, sixty elves, even geared for war, would go silent as the falling snow, slipping like wind through the forest until they found their hiding places. From shadows, in darkness, gray-cloaked, they would watch as two wagons of weapons rumbled into the Notch, as delivery of the ransom was made, and the princess was returned to her people.

Then they would fall upon those outlaws like terror. They would harry and slaughter, and they would leave nothing but corpses for the ravens.

Lindenlea would drive one of those wagons. Kethrenan himself would take the other. Gray-cloaked as the others, their shining mail hidden and their weapons at their feet, they would seem nothing more than drivers of the wagons.

Kethrenan looked around. His bedchamber was as much like a warrior's barracks as anything else. Spare bed, small chest for his clothing, his favorite weapons hung upon the wall to gleam and glare. When he was Lord of the Guard, he dressed here. When he was a prince in his brother's court, he would have Demlin fetch him glittering gear from the coffers in his wife's rooms.

Demlin. Another vengeance needed working. Kethrenan grinned a feral grin. It was as if he tasted blood in the back of his mouth.

He turned his head a little and looked out the window to where the curving wall of another chamber put a broad window eye-to-eye with his. A courtyard lay between, paved with sandy-colored brick in a pattern of Elansa's design. "We can meet," she had said, "here in the courtyard and no one will see us, so private will we be." So private—for the walls were high and draped in summer with wisteria, in winter with jasmine. There were other ways to meet of course, and one was in the bed of one or the other of them, access gained for a knock at the door which stood, never locked, between their many-roomed chambers.

"Come play prince with me," she would whisper at the door, and he would leave his stern chamber for the luxury of hers.

"Come play warrior-maid with me," he would growl, laughing at the door and holding it wide.

Kethrenan winced, thinking of his bed, her bed . . .

"No," Lindenlea said, seeing his glance. She stepped into the room. "Don't think about that, Keth. She's a quick-witted girl, your princess. She'll take care of herself, and she will be well when you find her."

"Do you think so?" he said, but he didn't care about her reply. He settled his sword in its sheath. Rough hands would touch. The hands of outlaws would paw. Humans might already have claimed a princess of Qualinesti. Kethrenan's mouth filled with the bloody taste of rage, hot and coppery. So strong the flavor that he moved his tongue around behind his teeth, wondering if there were truly blood there.

Lindenlea didn't offer more false assurances. He needed only to look into her eyes to see that she felt what he did: They would find Elansa, and they would avenge her. No matter if she were well and whole. No matter if she were defiled. Those gods-forsaken outlaws who had laid hands on her, if only to snatch her away and no worse, had earned their deaths the moment they touched her.

He did not doubt that Elansa would rejoice to see the blood of her captors run like rivers down the naked stone in the moaning lands where now she lay prisoner.

* * * * *

Elansa counted the days with difficulty. The iron sky made it hard to track the sun. No shadow lay on the ground in such even light. She saw no moons at night, and all her life had become a narrow torment of walking, interrupted only by the agony of a sleep that brought no rest. She no longer stumbled or fell. That had nothing to do with strength or with having become accustomed to traveling stony ground in boots whose leather soles were beginning to split at the seam. She would not fall, for if she did she knew she would not rise again. Brand would have to kill her and give over his scheme for ransom. She did not want to die. She wanted—more than she had ever wanted anything—to reach the ransom point, to see not two wagons filled with weapons but an army of elves geared for killing.

It would not matter if she were killed in the fighting as long as she lived long enough to see Kethrenan spit this outlaw Brand on his lance.

And so she walked, the joints of her ankles, her knees, and her hips aching. When in rare moments she could be still, she sagged against a boulder, head low and groaning, her muscles cramped in painful spasms. There was not enough water to drink. They rationed what they had in the rank-tasting leather water bottles, but no outlaw willingly shared with her.

"No sense in it," Arawn had said. "She's either soon back to her forest, or dead. Why waste the water on her?"

Char pointed out that here was another example of why Arawn wasn't known for long-headedness. "She dies before the ransom point, idiot, and what do we have? Blisters on our feet and a dead elf. She gets there, maybe more."

Grudgingly, Arawn admitted that was so. Nevertheless, he was not the first to share his water bottle. No one had found running water since Char and Tianna had spotted the goblins. In this more westerly part of the barren land it seemed there had been little enough water in good seasons. Now, there was dust.

Dust blew constantly, so that Elansa's throat burned, and her eyes felt dry as the earth itself. Her skin stung. Her cheeks and throat and arms were wind-scoured and raw. Her hair hung tangled and matted until, in frustration, she could have wept—had she tears.

After the second day, Brand called Tianna and Ley to him. They went aside from the others, talking quietly, and when he came back to the fire, he came back alone. The two went off into the night, loping across the ground as though full sun shone and they had a packed trail ahead of them. No one seemed the least curious, but Elansa lay a long time awake, wondering. She had not seen the gray line of the Qualinesti forest since the day before. She thought—she could not be sure, and so perhaps she hoped—that Ley and Tianna had turned west when they left the camp, back toward the forest.

Elansa looked at Char, sitting a small distance from her. It was, she realized, the distance he'd sit if there had been fire between. She thought she would ask him, "Have they gone to the forest?" But she didn't. He carried two leather bottles, one for water and one for dwarf spirits. His water bottle lay beside his foot, and the other sat upon his knee. He was not a good one to talk to when he'd been pulling at that bottle, sliding from surly to nasty to dangerous.

The night's cold fingers crept beneath the folds of her dusty green cloak. The hound Fang dropped down beside her, his breath smelling like blood and whatever he'd killed for his supper. Elansa curled into a tight ball of aching muscles and fell into what passed for sleep.

Before dawn had changed the dark of night to watery gray, Char's booted toe nudged her awake. Fang was gone, but only lately. She had the sense of the hound's nearness. Char dropped something to the ground beside her, a small strip of rabbit meat. His water bottle he set down more carefully, and it was that Elansa took first, drinking in quick greedy gulps before the dwarf's hand darted to take it back.

She noted two things in that moment. Char's hand was strongly scarred, as though fire had kissed it, and she had, in the last few days, acquired the habit of drawing breath to snarl when things were taken from her. She didn't now. She'd have gotten his boot the same way Fang might if he'd snarled. Still she felt it, the tightening of the throat, the instant when her lip would curl . . .

She thought, Who am I? She climbed to her feet, refusing to groan or even wince at the pain and the stiffness. Who am I? A woman who knows why a dog snarls.

* * * * *

The goblins on the east side of the Forest-Down-Around-the-Hammer-Rock-But-Not-Too-Close held mixed opinions about how lucky they were that the hob Gnash had come to take over things. Some puked up old legends about how living with that hobgoblin as master was a lot like living in the Abyss. There, they said, the only bird in the sky was the vulture, and if Gnash was a bird, he'd have been a vulture. Most, though, didn't go on with god-talk. Goblins had little to do with that, for gods—so everyone believed who wasn't an elf gone fey with age or a dwarf whose brains were calcified to stone—were no more than shadows. Most sensible people believed there were no gods now, just a bunch of stories you tell to children to make them shut up their babble and wail or they'd find themselves in worse straits.

For the most part the goblins who used to belong to Golch and now belonged to the hob Gnash took what came, and often enough it was booty from raids on villages and travelers foolish enough to go into the borderland without a strong escort. It was a good enough life. Goblins didn't mind waking each morning in their little hovels with the scraps and bones of their meals scattered round the ring of ashes that used to be the night's fire—as long as among the litter they could see the wink and gleam of weapons, the naked limb of a captured elf woman flung out in dream-tormented sleep from beneath a rough blanket, a human woman, any kind of woman not goblin. . . .

The goblin who had found sign of Brand's outlaws in the borderland was like-minded to the more accepting of his brethren. Ithk was his name, and trotting into the goblin town on the east side of the Forest-Down-Around-the-Hammer-Rock-But-Not-Too-Close, his breath streaming in the chill air, Ithk greeted guards and was passed through, recognized. As with all goblin towns, this one used to be a village where humans lived. Some had been hunters who took game out of the Qualinesti forest when they dared, some were farmers who scratched a living out of the stony soil, but the true value of the town had been its inn, a place known for the fineness of its ale and wine—some of that wine got from elven traders who didn't mind stepping out of the forest to do business—and the thickness of its feather beds. Travelers found that inn a good place to stop, and it became a favorite of traders and mercenaries and folk getting from one place to another. And so there were baker shops—two—and a butcher and a herbalist and even a chandler and a blacksmith. It had been a fine little village, as these borderland places go, and ripe for picking.

Ithk jogged down the street, his weapons ringing on him as he looked around in the frosty morning. The hovels he saw had once been trim houses and tidy shops set around a square in which one great house stood higher than all. This used to be the inn. Now it was where Gnash lived. He hadn't done the taking of this village, not him. Golch, father of Golch—the son murdered at the hands of those stinking outlaws out at

Hammer Rock—had done the taking back at the end of spring. Golch the father had lived at the inn, quite comfortably until Gnash came in, him and his army thrice the size of the one that Golch commanded. After his army overwhelmed this goblin town, he'd taken Golch the father and dragged him out of his house. Before all, he'd plucked out his eyes, cut out his tongue, then lopped off his head. Father and son, it turned out that they'd had more than a name in common.

Thus had Gnash declared himself the ruler here and taken all those who had belonged to Golch and made them part of his army.

Ithk banged his fist on the hob's door.

"In!" shouted the hobgoblin.

A wave of heat rushed out the door from a roaring hearth-fire. Burnished armor lay all around the front room, that wide space that would have been the inn's common room. The armor rose up in heaps—breastplates and greaves, shinguards and helms, all stolen from the corpses of the killed. Daggers and swords lay on the floor among the bones of old feasts. Among the broken crockery on the wide table, jewels glittered, ornaments pilfered from luckless travelers—necklaces from maidens who perished of fear or worse, rings from the fingers of matrons and piles of furs and feathers taken in the autumn from a barbarian Plainsman lost in the stonelands on his way to Qualinost. Atop one of these piles the hob sprawled, sucking his teeth and scratching for lice in places you don't like to get lice.

Standing on the threshold of this dire den, the wind blowing in snow at his heels, Ithk delivered his news, already imagining his reward.

"Master, the outlaw Brand is on the move."

The roar swelled up in Gnash's chest, rising from his belly like steam swelling in some dire invention of gnomes, something sure to explode and kill all those in reach. Piggy eyes opened as wide as they could, and the green-skinned hobgoblin bellowed, "Where?"

Ithk closed the door behind him. He looked once around, saw the scavenger dump that had once been a well-appointed inn, and shuddered. Over in the corner lay two corpses he hadn't seen before. Gnash had been busy, working or amusing himself.

"Out in the borderland, away down by the Notch. All of 'em from what I sees—the humans, the damned bastard lying dwarf, the elf, and the two women. But more women than that. They got an elf woman with 'em, and she looks like a prisoner."

The hob leaned forward. Things shifted around him, his pile of booty slipping a little as a knight's helm and three golden goblets rolled down the side of a bale of furs. It is the thing about hobs that they are more long-headed than their smaller kin. They have more room in their skulls for brains and generally know how to make that situation work for them. Gnash was, among hobs, a fairly intelligent specimen.

"How'd she look? Used? Beaten? Starved?"

"Hungry, but they all looked hungry. She was closely guarded, like something they didn't want to lose."

And what good, the hob thought, would she be to them with winter walking into the borderland? None. She'd eat food, drink water, and sooner or later they'd get tired of her. In winter, when it's cold and hungry and not much food to be had, you get tired of passing the prisoners around and would rather have the water they drink and the food they eat.

"Hostage," Gnash said, belching. He scratched under his arm. "For ransom." He twisted a cruel grin. "Ain't like that's not been done before, eh? Goblins been known to lose their heads over Brand's hostage-taking. We know what he got from Golch. I wonder what he's looking for from the elves?"

Ithk, who had been a particular friend of the younger Golch the Beheaded, did not reply.

Gnash slid from atop his hill of pilfered goods, big and green and warty, and he nodded to the little goblin. "Help yourself."

The goblin didn't move or even look at anything in the room. The last one to help himself too quickly was handless and about starved to death by now because no one could think of a reason to feed a useless, handless goblin. But when Gnash had left, gone roaring out into the streets to gather up a considered portion of his army, the goblin darted quickly to the heap his master had lately lounged upon. He snatched a fur from the top of the nearest bale, a bear's pelt with the head still dangling, and flung it round his shoulders for a cloak. Winter was indeed walking into the borderland, and Ithk had a bit of wit himself.

* * * * *

Gnash wasn't long at getting his army moving. He took only the little time he needed to look around his cluttered quarters for a thing he'd been carrying with him from one place to another since he'd first found it, a long time ago in the spring. It was a thing from the mountains, found in deep and secret places under the southern part of the borderland between Qualinesti and

Thorbardin. It didn't look like much. He might have walked right past it when first he saw it, but something about the crooked staff had called to him—not with a voice, no. It was more like a tickling in the brain that would have been the raising up of hair had that tickling been on the outside of his head.

He had a small talent for magic, did Gnash. Not all hobs do, but it isn't impossible to find those who have managed to make a magical device or two work. Gnash had done that, and he'd had a high time in the borderland, reveling in the destruction he caused in the process. He hadn't had to use the staff much to affect his conquests of the three goblin towns he now owned. Alas, he sometimes thought. But, after all, he'd needed the towns to house his growing army. He certainly couldn't kill too many of the goblins. That had left him with few opportunities to play with his weapon, but at last, here was one come right down the borderland to him.

And so, Gnash got his staff, and he got his army moving. It wasn't a great portion of his army, only a part, and these he didn't have to threaten or argue or cajole. They were afraid of him, doubly so when they saw that staff in his hand, the old gnarled wood. They'd do anything he demanded, but this he didn't have to demand. Best of all goblins loved fighting and killing. They were happy to go south toward the Notch and see what kind of blood they could spill. And they were goblins; they didn't care if they had to run by night and make their way under clouded skies. They rejoiced in the cover and ran harder, all the way down to just above the Notch. There they stopped, because their master demanded, and there they held. They made no camp, and they killed no animal for supper. They slipped into gullies and crevices and didn't complain. They knew all the places to hide—little caves, the abandoned dens of foxes, the gaps between boulders. One after another, the goblins made themselves invisible in the borderland and prepared to wait till the gods came back to Krynn, or until the Great Gnash told them to move again.

Brand was abroad with a hostage, one their master thought he was delivering for ransom. Some of the goblins thought it would be great fun to snatch the ransom from out of the human's cold dead hands. Those who'd once known Golch the father and Golch the son thought it would be very satisfying to have the ransom, but they thought the fun would come with the killing of Brand and all his scurvy band.

Even when they saw elves gathering, shadows at the edges of the forest with more substance than most, the goblins kept still, for Gnash warned that these must have to do with the ransom or some treachery. Gnash knew how to let things fall as they would and pick his moment at the proper time. It must be told, though, that Gnash's army had a hard time keeping still in such proximity to elves. The wind was blowing out of the forest, and it hung with the sick-sweet stench of Qualinesti, enough to gag a goblin, if any had cared to risk his own head at Gnash's blade for making retching sounds.

And, of course, he had that staff of his, that magic.

Chapter 6

Like the hound who guarded her, Elansa lifted her
face to the wind, the chill blowing not from the south
now but from the west. It carried the scent of pine trees
and snow. Fang pricked his ears, and Elansa filled up
her lungs with that perfume: the scent of home. Nearby
stood Brand and Ley. The elf had his back to the wood.
Past him lay a stony flat known as the Notch for its
wedge shape. Elansa traced the sketch of stone fences
that lay on the land. Someone had farmed here once.
Perhaps outlaws or goblins had driven them out.

Ley pulled up the hood of his cloak against the cold
and said, "We saw the wagons, Brand. North on the
road that runs alongside the edge of the wood. Two
drivers, teams of four stout horses. The wagons aren't
covered. We saw the weapons. Long sword-lockers,
and we couldn't see what's in there, but we could see
the shafts of lances and bows with the strings wrapped
round. We saw quivers stacked like logs, filled fat. No
place for warriors to hide in those wagons.

"We've been in the forest, and there's no one—birds,
saw some deer—just the forest. Tianna went in as far as
the glen—" He held up two water bottles, fat and dripping. "Plenty of that. I think they must have had some
good rain or snow."

Brand looked past the elf, away across Stagger
Stream. Not much water ran there, but Elansa knew
this stream didn't have its source in the White-rage
River. The head of this stream lay in the north, but

farther west in the stonelands. That, she had heard Brand say, must be blocked by rock-fall.

"It's all right," Ley said. "Just the forest and the wagons coming."

Elansa turned away, hoping no one could see the blood move to her cheek, the flush of hope rising. It might be the outlaws saw only two wagons and their drivers, but she knew—it had to be!—that Keth wouldn't simply trust the ransom and his wife to two drivers. He would be here. Somewhere he *was* here, waiting to take her home. And before he did he would kill every one of these bandits.

She looked around, but carefully, as though she were but casting down her glance, perhaps afraid. In fact, she looked to see where weapons were—the knife in the belt of Arawn, Dell's bow and quiver, Brand's sword, Char's throwing axe. On the ground, carelessly left beside the limping stream where it had been used to gut fish, someone's knife lay. Dull light wavered fitfully on the edge of the blade. In two strides, Elansa could have her hand on it. She didn't move. She simply marked it and looked away.

A small dusting of snow gathered white in the cracks between the rocks. The hounds that accompanied the outlaw band went with heads low, licking the stones. Over Ley's shoulder, Elansa saw Tianna standing. The woman faced the forest. Her hair blew back in the wind, a pale pennon of silver. Again, Elansa was struck by the elven look of her—the elegantly canted ears, almond eyes, silver hair. She stood taller than an elf, though, and there was something about her features, a lack of refinement perhaps, a coarseness that put Elansa in mind of humans. She looked away, as from someone's shame.

"Half-elf," Char said. He cocked his head, his one good eye narrowed. "Bother you?"

Wind blew, grit flew, and Elansa smelled snow on the air. She thought the question impertinent from a dwarf whose own kin did not like to see their blood mingled with other races.

"It is disgusting," she said, and she didn't care who heard her. Soon it wouldn't matter. Soon Keth would come and fetch her home. No one seemed to have heard her, or if anyone had, no one cared.

Brand snapped an order, a simple word— "Spread!"—and his outlaws melted away into the stoneland, their dun clothing making them nearly invisible. The hounds padded beside, and Fang kept close to Char and Elansa. She did not look at the knife. She did not look at Char. She walked, a step, another, the knife gleamed. One more step, and she fell, hard to her hands and knees, crying out and hoping her cry sounded no less hopeless or weary than any other the dwarf had heard her make.

Char never looked around. "Fang," he said, and the dog hung back to make sure she wouldn't bolt.

Neither did she, but beneath her right hand lay the forgotten knife, once used to clean fish. She slipped it quickly into the sleeve of her blouse. Making noises to sound like distress, she climbed to her feet, the dwarf and the dog none the wiser. At Char's command she went behind a tumble of boulders, great stones rolled out from the mountain a long time ago when the gods visited cataclysm upon Krynn.

"Stay," Char said, as he would have to the hound.

She did. From her vantage behind the pile she could see the road, rough and rocky. Upon it traveled two wagons, dust billowing behind. The horses struggled with the weight they pulled and the difficult road. Elansa held her breath, and she thought she heard one of the drivers call encouragement to the beasts. Gray-cloaked, she couldn't determine whether they were man or woman. That they were elves she only knew because they were her ransom-bearers.

Noiselessly, Brand slipped around the corner of the stones and dropped down beside Char. "Keep her here," he said, never looking at Elansa. "And don't trust her to the dog. Do it yourself."

"Aye, I got 'er. Don't worry."

The dwarf didn't have a hand on her, but Elansa could not doubt that should she try to break and run he'd drop her in her second stride, his throwing axe buried between her shoulders. She kept very still, feeling the blade of the knife against the skin of her forearm.

Brand stood, jerked his head, and Arawn stepped out from hiding onto the road. Together, the two walked toward the wagons, swords drawn, a fighting distance between them. Elansa's heart beat hard, her eyes stayed fixed upon the wagons and the drivers. The wind changed, and she smelled the horses. She heard Brand shout:

"Hold! Right there!"

Horses snorted, harnesses jangled. One of the drivers called in Elvish to her team or to her companion. Elansa shivered, knowing the voice. Lindenlea! Her every muscle tensed, ready to leap. One-eyed but quick-eyed,

83

Char grabbed her hard from behind, yanking her off her knees and onto the stone.

"Don't," he said. "Fastest way to die."

She sat still, jarred and clinging with awkward fingers to the hidden knife. As though in despair, she drew up her knees and buried her face in her arms. Beneath her filthy green cloak, she let the knife slide into her hand and closed her fingers round the bone handle.

I will kill you first, dwarf. In her mind, she snarled.

But when she looked up again, nothing of what she thought or truly felt showed on her face. She composed her expression into one of anxiety and fear, arranging mouth and eyes into flinching as though she were an artist sculpting.

Kill you first, she thought, turning her face, only briefly, toward Char to let him see what she wished seen.

Horses snorted. One whinnied. Another of the drivers called out, a curse that humans might think was meant for the poor weary beast. "Stinking bastards," is how that would have translated into Common. Elansa's heart beat hard again, slamming against her chest. That was how Prince Kethrenan addressed Brand and Arawn, though the two certainly did not know it.

The time had come. Now she would go free, now home, or—no she wouldn't think of the alternative. Now she would go free. Now she would go home.

In Common, Kethrenan called, "Where is your master, churl?"

She could not see them, prince or outlaw, but Elansa had been enough in Brand's company to know that he'd have shown no sign of anger at the address. In her belly fear slid like snakes. She had seen this man prepared to kill with no second thought, she had seen him hand over a goblin to death with no other consideration than to wonder whether he might take greater satisfaction doing the killing himself.

Soft, in her most secret heart, she prayed to gods Outlanders did not think existed. She prayed to soldier gods, and she prayed to her own Blue Phoenix.

Keep my husband safe. Hold him safe. Oh, take me home—!

"Get down from the wagons," Brand called.

Hidden, she saw nothing, and it seemed that all the world had fallen still, holding its breath.

"Get down!" She heard the rattle of shod hooves on the stony road and imagined the light leap of elves leaving the wagons. "Now, you—over there. You—the other side." A breath-held moment; someone didn't move, then: "Char! Show 'em what we've got!"

Char kicked her, hard in the small of the back. "Get up."

She stumbled to her feet, her hands still hidden. Char shoved her, and almost she turned, snarling. He kicked her to her knees. Char took a fistful of her tangled, tarnished golden hair. He yanked her head back, as Ley had pulled back the head and exposed the naked neck of a goblin soon to die. Her purloined knife fell from her grip. Laughing, the dwarf kicked it aside. Coldly, he pressed his own knife to her throat.

On the road, Kethrenan stepped away from the wagon. When he was told, he stripped himself of the knife at his belt and the sword on his hip. Lindenlea did the same, their gestures quick and careful. These things they handed to Arawn, and in the handing off Elansa saw the jeweled grip of Kethrenan's oldest sword. They had been wed with that sword as part of his marriage gear, polished and honed and gleaming in a tooled scabbard at his hip.

Brand gestured them farther from the wagons, splitting them up—Lea to the far side of one, Keth to the far side of the other. A great silence seemed to creep out of the forest, a stillness even of the wind. Char's blade pressed the soft flesh of her throat, too close. One thin warm line of blood slid down her neck.

"Dearest gods," she whispered, the muscles of her throat moving against the knife.

"Ah, hush that," the dwarf said, but not roughly. "He'll let y'go if yer man is minded to play fair with us. Brand doesn't break his word for spite. Just for good reason."

Brand jerked his chin at Keth. "Lead the teams forward, both."

Keth shook his head. "I was told this is to be a fair exchange, the weapons for the princess." He didn't look past Brand. He kept his eyes on the outlaw. "Bring her down."

"No. She stays where she is. Pretty much there's nothing you can do whether we hand her over or not, but if you hand off the ransom, I will hand off the woman. And don't bother asking how you can know if I will. You can't. I suppose you just have to trust me, don't you? Just like I trusted your master to have enough regard for his wife's life to send only two with the ransom."

Keth and Lea said nothing.

"Now," Brand said, his voice gone cold, "bring the wagons."

Keth did as he was told, like any hostler taking horses from the stable. The prince put himself between the two teams and took hold of the cheek strap of each of the horses on the near side. He led them, talking stable-talk, the language of whisper and the click of tongue against teeth.

The sound of a hawk screeched across the silence. The horses startled, and Arawn threw back his head a second time. His long dark hair was caught by a sudden breeze as he signaled the outlaws again. Like rocks come suddenly alive, they unveiled from their hiding places, coming out from behind boulders, rising up in their stone-colored clothing. Silent, they ran, men and two women used to the rough ground, leaping stones and rocks, making for the wagons.

Without looking away from Keth, the elf he thought was a prince's lackey, Brand snapped, "Dell, take one wagon. Ley, get the other."

All her muscles tense and aching, Elansa watched as Dell and Ley each took a team from Keth and climbed aboard a wagon. The clucking sounds they made to the teams, the rumble of wooden wheels on stony earth, shivered along Elansa's nerves. Char's hand tightened in her hair, but she felt the blade of his knife move a little away from the throat.

"Up," he said, low in her ear. "No nonsense, just get up."

She did, and as she rose his knife pressed against her side, tracing the tender space between two ribs to let her know where it was. "Organs in there, missy," he said. "Kidney or liver or spleen, eh? You don't want to risk those. Stand still."

She did, still as stone, and the wagons began to move. On the road, Keth stood alone, between the outlaws and Lindenlea. He looked at Brand, who nodded.

Char's knife moved, withdrawing.

Kethrenan took a step toward Elansa, and Brand took one to block his way. "No," said the outlaw. Behind his back, he gestured to Elansa: Come ahead. She stood a moment, trembling. Char pushed her, a hand in the small of her back.

One step she took, another, and suddenly all her muscles tightened to run. She held herself to tame steps, knowing that if she moved too quickly her running might be misinterpreted.

Keth lifted his head. His eyes met hers and held her gaze. She felt as though a tether stretched between them, a thin line to guide her home if only she went carefully and never let go.

"Come, princess," he said, speaking as though he were the lackey the outlaws imagined him to be. Lindenlea moved, a small restless shifting from one foot to another. Keth held out his hand. "Come to me, my lady."

Wagons rumbled on the road. Ley snapped long leather reins across the rump of one of the horses, and another of the team snorted. Eyes on her husband, Elansa walked, and all the while felt Brand's eyes on her. The skin between her shoulders itched. She wanted to turn and look at him, but she dared not. She felt it: He could snatch her back in an instant.

In the silence, every rustle of clothing seemed loud as wind in the trees. Out of the corner of her eye she saw the forest. Home. Beyond the Notch lay all the dark shadows gathering. No light dappled on this cloud-thick day, and yet it seemed the shadows were not all of a tint. Neither were they as insubstantial as might be thought. A dull gleam betrayed a secret, the slide of pale light on an ill-concealed blade. Elansa's heart jumped. Keth saw it.

"Come," he said again, gesturing now with his hand. "We're soon home, my lady."

And his eyes, gone suddenly cool and stern, said, *Come. Come ahead. Don't look around, just come to me.* She did, never taking her eyes from his, not even when she was but a reach away from him. His fingers touched hers, and she drew a shaking breath. In his eyes she saw cool command turn to fury as he took in the signs of her captivity—the hunger, the pallor of her skin, bruises and cuts, her ripped and filthy clothing. He lifted his head, just that, but she knew the gesture. She knew what Prince Kethrenan looked like when he was surveying his choices, picking his ground.

Home, she thought; I am going—

Every nerve in her body leaped alive, screaming. In her bones—at the very marrow—she knew an agony, both phantom and real. A scream wound from the forest, terrible and high. Another followed, and out from the woods an elven voice filled with rage and fear shouted, *"The wood is on fire!"*

In her heart, Elansa heard the agony of living trees as fire licked up their trunks, seared their barkish skins, and gnawed to the milky heart of each limb it grasped. In her woodshaper's soul she felt the anguished, burning echo. She had no voice to cry the pain, from her throat could come no sound that trees could make.

Shadows at the forest's edge sprang to life, full-voiced with elven war cries. Warriors armed with swords burst out of the wood, but they were only half of the prince's force. The others stayed behind, for they had expected to meet foemen in the borderland, but they had found enemies in the forest. Goblins, wielding fire and steel and shrieking like things from nightmare, fell upon the elves.

Seeing the elven warriors, seeing the goblins, Brand shouted, "Bastard! You set goblins on us!" Almost in the same moment, Keth roared the same accusation. Neither heard the other. Elansa heard them both, their voices small amid the death cries of trees.

"Arawn!" Brand roared.

Lindenlea shouted, "Warriors! To your prince!"

Battle-storm screamed around them. The howls of the goblins, the shrieks of the killed, and rage, rage. In one sudden moment of clarity Elansa saw that the goblins and the elven warriors were matched forces. She saw the outlaws and knew they would be crushed between them. She thought, Good! And she saw one of the bandits—Arawn it was, with his long dark hair blowing back—lift a sword to defend himself. He held Keth's sword, and Elansa thought, Let the goblins kill him!

Keth's hand tightened painfully on Elansa's wrist. He yanked her toward him, got his arm around her, and looked for haven for her. The forest was no place to go, and they could not follow the wagons.

Lindenlea shouted, "Keth!" and he let go of Elansa to snatch from the air the sword his cousin had flung. Not his good old sword, but a sword, lent by a warrior to a prince. Lindenlea laughed, a mad-minded war cry as she flourished her own borrowed weapon. She pointed north where four elven warriors broke from the rest, running to receive the princess.

They ran to meet the sudden escort, Elansa and her husband. It wasn't a far distance, and no one came near who didn't taste Kethrenan's borrowed blade. All around, elves let loose their war cries. Outlaws shouted curses; one screamed in death, another did, and a third. The stench of seared flesh mingled with the smoke of Qualinesti burning. The cries of elves and humans and goblins sounded like the cries of beasts in the slaughter pens. No one but Elansa heard the heartbreak of the forest, the death of trees.

On the road, Ley cried commands to horses, again the snap of leather on broad rumps. Dell shouted curses, and Brand turned, his hostage forgotten. He bellowed, "Ley! Dell! Stay with the wagons! Get them out of here!"

A pack of goblins came boiling out of the forest. No elves followed, no man or woman of the half of Kethrenan's force that had stayed behind.

The goblins ran, long eyes ablaze with killing lust. Orange hides and red hides, and sickly greeny-brown, all of them acted like a shield wall, swords high to protect the hobgoblin who ran in the middle of their pack. "For Gnash!" they yowled. And when they fell, their bodies filled with elven arrows, with shafts from an outlaw's quiver, others came and took up the cry. "For the Great Gnash!"

Gnash brandished a staff, an old, crooked length of bleached cedarwood. Unadorned, it looked too dry to be considered even for kindling. The hob howled a word like a curse, and fire shot from the head of the staff, a great gout of flame shaped like a long arm reaching. It grew a hand, as broad as a goblin is high. Orange fingers of licking flame closed around two fighting, an elven warrior and an outlaw. They burst afire, screaming as the flames that killed one fed the fire that killed the other. The arm divided, two limbs ranged out from the staff, and the sound of the hob's glee was the sound of madness as these reached out to grab elves and humans in fiery clasp.

"The hob!" Lea cried. "Get the hob!"

Hearing her voice, Elansa turned even as she ran. She couldn't help the need to look. Turning, she stumbled, staggering into Keth. As though Lea's cries were commands for the outlaws, one of Brand's men nocked an arrow to his bow and drew. He'd not got his elbow up before a goblin's dagger took him in the throat. But others had heard the order. Elven arrows buzzed, black shafts against the fiery wall of the burning forest, taking down one goblin after another. As quickly as these fell, that quickly did others appear, and the arms of fire reached and ranged, groping for the archers.

Keth dragged at her, pulling, and the four warriors waiting to receive her ran, swords out and ready. "Take her!" the prince ordered. "Keep her safe!"

It was on the lips of one to say the prince could count on them, he could know his wife safe. Elansa saw the very words forming as a sharp whistle pierced the frenzy, and something low and swift came leaping. Char's hound flung himself at Keth, eyes blazing. It sank its fangs into Keth's leg, then darted away as Keth stumbled. Fang raced back and leaped again. Great jaws closed around Keth's wrist, and Elansa smelled blood and the stench of the hound's breath. Despite his will, Keth's grip on his sword broke. Elansa stood alone between the hound and her husband who shouted,

"Run! Elansa! Run!"

Run! Run to the elven warriors—she didn't have to ask or wonder. She must run home. Running, Elansa saw a warrior's eyes go wide, his mouth open to cry out a warning too late. The weight hit her hard from behind, the breath of the hound scorched her neck, its teeth grazed the flesh of her shoulder even as Brand's big hand grabbed her and dragged her to her feet. He yanked her hard around, cursing the dog, cursing her, cursing. Swift, a blade flashed, again a honed edge pressed against her throat. He did not shout *Hold!* as he had before. He needn't have. At the sight of his blade against her throat, the elven warrior fell still.

He was Cressin Oaktrue. Elansa knew him and all his kin.

His eyes on Cressin, Brand grabbed Elansa round the waist and pulled her hard to him. On her neck, his breath felt like the hound's, steaming in the cold air and smelling of killing. Fang and his kindred loped across the stony road, the pack like five shadows gliding across the ground. From Fang's muzzle blood dripped, one, two, and three small scarlet spots blossoming on stone, a prince's blood. This Elansa saw as Char whistled again, calling off the dog and taking its place at Brand's back.

"Now you decide," Brand said, leaving Cressin to the dwarf and speaking to Kethrenan. "Prince, what do you want—the life of your little princess or the deaths of all of us?"

Keth's eyes blazed with fury.

Cressin cried, "Shame!"

The rumble of wooden wagon wheels on the south-going road sounded like low growling. The weight

93

they carried had increased: outlaws rode in the back of each. Outlaws ran jogging beside and behind. In this way the wagon filled with weapons rolled right out of the battle. If any elf or goblin saw it going from the battleground, none could do a thing about it, for they had engaged, the two forces, and would not disengage now.

"Like it or don't," Brand said, his voice filling with a dark kind of satisfaction, "we've got the weapons, prince, and we have a pretty shield to keep us safe while we take what's owed from the bargain."

Brand pressed his blade against Elansa's throat, better at it than Char had been. He drew no blood, but Elansa knew his knife-wielding habits. He'd slit her throat if he thought that would be satisfying.

Kethrenan, who knew how to look into the eye of a foe and reckon him, understood what Elansa did. As soon as she saw her husband know the truth, she knew herself lost. Again.

"Let him kill me," she moaned, the words hardly passing her lips, pressed back by the blade. "*Don't* let him take me, Keth!"

Kethrenan's eyes held hers, and it felt as if all the years of her life passed in that moment. He would not cause her death. He could not. Brand laughed, the sound of a gambler who has wagered well.

A cry rose in Elansa's breast, right to her throat, past the steel blade pressing. She let it die, unvoiced. To fling back her head and scream would have been to slice her own throat. She could not do it, for all she'd asked Kethrenan to let it happen. Neither could she whimper or plead. She was an elf. She was a princess.

And so the outlaw took her away. Brand of the stonelands had the princess once more. A cry did sound for her, though, against the rage of battle, the war cries and the death screams of elves and goblins, long and loud and filled with terrible rage. It followed her, winding through the barren land, the sound of Kethrenan cursing.

Chapter 7

Now began the season of lost things in the west part of Ansalon.

The seas lost their ships, all but those few brave craft that hugged the coasts of the New Sea and the Strait of Algoni, mostly fishermen and ferrymen. The winds of winter blew hard and swift from Ice Mountain Bay and around to the top of the world. Even those who lived in the warmer parts of Krynn, away north where there was naught but the mysterious Dragon Isles between them and no one knew what, complained of the cold. This cold blowing went on from H'rarmont and right through the beginning of winter, into the middle months, and looked to blow most cruelly in Rannmont. Out from Tarsis drifted terrible tales of people who went mad from the moan of the wind, the groaning and the unceasing sob.

It was said, at least by Rumor, that those mad ones did all manner of unspeakable things, and the least awful of the tales spoke of the man who murdered his family, insane and thinking they were ghosts come to steal away his soul.

"I have heard them moan!" he screamed, standing in their blood. "They were coming for me. . . ."

So often was that tale repeated, up and down from Tarsis to Palanthas, that people could be forgiven for thinking the whole poor city in the desert had been changed into a lunatic asylum.

All over, old people in all places, humans and elves and dwarves and even a few goblins proclaimed that there had never been such as winter, and that they didn't think they cared to imagine how much colder things could get.

Abanasinia and Solamnia lost the grassland green in the last month of autumn, all the tall waving grass gone brown and flat, and it crunched underfoot with as much voice as it has after a hard frost has lain upon it. In the woodlands near Xak Tsaroth and across the New Sea in Lemish, not much of gold or bronze or scarlet replaced the woodland green that year. It seemed that all in a night the canopy looked a bit thin, as it does when autumn is coming, and then refused to shine but fell, all the leaves as brown as oaks, whether the trees they flew from were oak or not. There had been no warning of this, so noted the folk in the mountains around Thorbardin. The birds had not flown away earlier, the hares and badgers and foxes did not go dressed in thicker coats than usual, and no one out calling his pigs from the forest claimed to have seen the squirrels and chipmunks any busier at the gathering of nuts than in years gone. It might be that a sign of the crashing winter could be the absence of goblins in the foothills of the Kharolis Mountains, both on the windward side and the lee. The great gathering of goblins to the hob Gnash had caused no end of woe to the little villages clinging to the foothills and the skirts of the Qualinesti forest. In winter, the raiding and the burning and the killing stopped. The humans did not pray much. They had no use for vanished gods, but they knew about gratitude, and though the winter dealt harshly with them, it did keep the goblins from the door.

They did not know that the winter silence of goblins meant that the hob Gnash had time to sit in his headquarters, that stinking pile that used to be a fine inn, and consider his possibilities. He did not count his losses to the elves in the abortive raid to steal a ransom. He used his goblins as though they were water from an ever-renewing spring. Almost, they were. The deaths of a half-hundred or more were nothing to him. He didn't even much care about the outlaw Brand. That was an old feud and not really his. Perching atop his treasure hoard or carrying out the occasional execution for the edification of his army and his amusement, he thought about how fine it was to wield fire. He thought about the finding of his fire-staff, and he began to wonder whether grander and better things were to be discovered that would make him not just lord of the borderland, but king of this part of the world.

They didn't know, the humans who lived in the borderland—or, for that matter, the elves of Qualinesti—that in Goblintown on the east side of the Forest-Around-Hammer-Rock-But-Not-Too-Close the hob Gnash was weaving plans.

* * * * *

In the season of lost things, Elansa Sungold lived beneath the ground. She saw again the cave beneath Hammer Rock where she'd watched the elf Ley slit a goblin's throat and hack off his head. She saw more caves than that—Brand and his outlaws knew more hiding places in the riddled earth than Elansa had imagined existed. They knew secret ways in and out.

"Not all," Char said one night as he sat pulling on his leather bottle, the one that held dwarf sprits.

It seemed inexhaustible, like a vessel from legend, something touched by gods and made to replenish itself after each sip. But Char did not sip, and no vessel is inexhaustible. He had his stashes, though—a keg here, another there, and woe the cave that had nothing to offer. Roundly cursed, it became a place the dwarf couldn't wait to leave, and his discontent did, some nights, poison everyone's sleep—the pacing if he waked, the groaning nightmares if he slept. Not that night, though, the one upon which he felt warm enough in the belly to become expansive.

"We got no notion of all the ways in and out of any cave we find, but we got me, little princess. A dwarf in the womb of the world . . . ah, he'd have to be deaf, dumb, and blind not to be able to find his way to anywhere."

They lived mostly beneath the ground. It was not the raiding season. It was winter, and no one traveled the roads. Brand didn't send his men outside the mountain but to hunt. He didn't like to stay too long in one place; he didn't like the idea of settling in. He had upon one hand elves who'd like to kill him for a kidnapping they felt was sacrilege. Upon the other hand he had a feud with a hobgoblin to prosecute. He had, too, a hoard of weapons to cache, a princess's ransom. This he took grim satisfaction in doing, storing swords and fat quivers and graceful bows in every cave that seemed secret enough to him. He conferred with Char, and he spoke in firelit plannings with dark-haired Arawn and the elf Ley. The outlaws who sat beyond their fire seemed content to wait, rolling the bones to gamble, kicking hounds that got too near a supper, honing weapons, and talking about those friends who'd died of a goblin's sword or a warrior's arrow. In low voices, they spoke of the hob and his fire-staff, but only to whisper. Like all the godless, these humans were superstitious, having no faith upon which to depend or to turn for explanation of things uncanny. They believed that to speak of such things as magical weapons, talismans, or any artifact from the days before the Cataclysm was to invite bad luck to the fire.

The work Brand planned was a great backing and forthing, the whole treasure of two wagons unloaded and piled in one deep cave, the pile of them reduced a little at a time by outlaws sent to bring forward what they could carry. They weren't so many as they had been before they'd been caught between Kethrenan's warriors and the hob's goblins. Their numbers were reduced to a dozen. Still, they managed to carry all they had, for they considered it good work, as miners consider working veins of gold good work. They broke up the wagons with axes, reducing them to splinters. The horses they set free to fare as best they could. At the end of the autumn, with the winds blowing harder through the stonelands than anyone remembered, no one thought the beasts would fare well for long.

In their caves, the outlaws were warmer perhaps than any creature outside could remember being. Four were warmer than most. There were but three women among them—Dell, Tianna, and captive Elansa. Dell and Tianna had long before proved with their weapons their right to decide whether or when they would share their nights. Tianna seldom took one of the men to her bed. Dell seemed well enough pleased to keep warm with Arawn. No one contended, not even Brand, though it was true that when Tianna could not be found sleeping alone, she was found sleeping with bearded Brand.

Those were two who could choose. Elansa was the third who could not. Upon her, men's eyes glanced in the day, at night they watched more closely, and she felt their dangerous hunger, their eyes like the glowing eyes of wolves circling beyond the campfire. More, she often woke feeling a hand out of the dark, the breath of a man leaning near, hot on her neck, wondering why he could not have what Brand had, what Arawn did. When this became distracting to Brand, he called them off as if they were dogs, saying there was but one of her and he wasn't going to lose another man fighting over her.

"No one gets her," he said. "Not now, anyway."

Arawn, for Dell was not near to hear, gave Elansa a long look, and his eyes narrowed in a way that made her shiver. He closed his hand around the hilt of the sword, the long elven weapon never far from his hands. This was Keth's sword.

"A prince's blade," he liked to say when he was in the mood to boast. "Whatcha gonna do with 'er, Brand? She's no use to us for ransom any more. We got that." He looked around at the outlaws, grinning. "Any other use she might be, you say no to."

Brand lifted his head, glancing from Elansa to the outlaws, who listened with various pretensions to noninterest.

"There's a use for everything, Arawn."

He didn't say more, but he told Char to see to it that no one fought over the captive woman. Char took his usual choice. The hound Fang kept near her in the day and slept near her in the night.

Yet, hound or no, Brand's command notwithstanding, the outlaws looked—young Chaser, Swain the old man, and Ballu, of indeterminate age and skinny as a scarecrow. She could hear Pragol breathing in the darkness, the firelight on his bald pate as he turned in his blankets to stare at her. She heard red-haired Loris whispering that Brand didn't have a right to say yea or nay to this.

"Spoils is spoils, an' ain't we each got a right?"

There were others—a man named Bruin, one named Kerin, who had hardly any teeth in his head even though he wasn't an old man. They watched too, with hungry looks. Only Ley didn't, and Char kept his distance.

She was not safe, no matter what Brand thought. She knew it, as women know.

In this season of lost things, Elansa lost sight of the sky. She lost the feel of the wind on her face, and she couldn't remember what birdsong sounded like. She forgot how to taste anything but food either burned black or not cooked enough. In the first weeks, she dreamed of scented baths and wisteria-hung gardens, and she woke forgetting those perfumes. Soon, she lost even the dreams.

Having lost sight of the sky, she lost track of days. Having lost the two moons, bright Solinari and red Lunitari, she didn't know how to track the nights, but she was, after all, a woman, and her body knew how to track the tides of time. One day, in the deepest part of winter, in a cave that might have been north of Qualinesti or south of it, she realized that a month had passed without its usual tidings. And then another did, and the news she got of her body made her weep. In quiet corners, far away from the outlaws with only Fang to watch, she wept to know that she was with child. In her womb had quickened to life the son or daughter of the Qualinesti royal house, Kethrenan's child.

She prayed, weeping, and she called upon the gods for strength, for courage. When she didn't know how she would find those things or accept them if granted, she begged for mercy. How would she carry a child, she a prisoner? How would she nourish herself and so nourish the life growing within? When she dared consider it, she wondered: How will I bear this child if ever it is brought to term?

And then, because this was the season of lost things, on a trek through the dark underground, in the womb of the world, she lost what she had lately found. In pain, with blood and weeping, her body cast out the child, the prince or princess. Then it was no hound who saw her sorrow. Then it was the half-elf, Tianna. She was not gentle or solicitous, but there was that about the look in her eyes, those almost-elven eyes, that suggested she understood.

One after another, they passed her. Dell, not looking to see what the prisoner and the half-elf were doing. She was a woman; she knew. The hounds went by, smelling loss, and the men went by, though most didn't look at her, not even out the corner of an eye. They knew, too. Only one stopped, just a moment hanging on his heel. Brand jerked his head at Tianna. She nodded. Some communication had passed between them that Elansa hadn't the wit or will to decipher.

Tianna put her hand on Elansa's shoulder, just a small touch. "You and I," she said, watching the others go by, "we can stay here a while. Until you can walk again."

Elansa nodded, and she crouched in the darkness, no more able to rejoice for the loss than she'd been able to rejoice in the quickening. When she finished her weeping, she cleaned herself as best she could and walked into the darkness, into the echoing womb of the world.

* * * * *

In the season of lost things, the elves of Qualinesti fared as the rest of the western part of the continent did. Their forest did not preen, their beasts did not warn, and the winds blew like rage-filled phantoms through the naked branches of oak and elm, maple and apple, and pear and aspen. It snapped the boughs from heavy branched pine trees so that the land closest to the stony reaches between the kingdom of the elves and that of the dwarves looked beaten. The forest had burned there at the end of autumn, set alight by a hobgoblin's magic, and while the fire had not jumped the gullies and glens and gulches that acted as a firebreak, it had done enough damage to make woodshapers mourn.

All mourned in the forest of the elves. They sorrowed for the trees burned in battle and the boughs stripped by winter, and most of all for a princess lost. Her story ran round the kingdom in low whispers. Someone made a song of it by autumn's end, and that song went with the bitter wind through the kingdom. In the villages and the cities they prayed for the princess who had gone out from her home to succor the ailing trees in Bianost, lovely Elansa Sungold stolen from her merciful mission and taken away by thieves.

Round the golden towers of Qualinost the sighs of the ladies and the maidens who had attended her made a gentler sound than the sobbing of the wind across the Plains of Dust, but no less a sad one. If some in Tarsis went mad from the wind, the folk of Qualinesti did not go mad with grief. They were elves, and elves have a way of feeling that isn't much like the way quick-hearted races do, or even dour dwarves (who are no less quick to kindle than any one else.) The fire of feeling runs in the elves, burns the heart, sizzles in the blood, kindles the soul. Those who think that isn't the case are mistaken. Sometimes they are mistaken fatally. It is with elves, though, that they don't much like to unfurl the feeling as though it were a banner to snap and sing and flourish in the wind.

And yet, there wasn't an elf in Qualinost, from the lowliest servitor in the humblest shop to the Speaker of the Sun himself who didn't think that their stalking Prince Kethrenan, who prowled the stonelands when the weather let him, who filled up the city with his own restlessness when even the mad would not brave the wild winds in that treeless land—there wasn't a one who didn't feel what the prince felt.

"He is as cold as winter," said one of the serving girls in the Tower of the Sun. This she whispered to her lover who had brought wine from the cellar one evening when the sky had been three days changed to lead, filled up with dark clouds that would lower but not release.

"In the temples they pray for our stolen princess, and they pray for our prince, and all our broken hearts. But I'm thinking they should pray for all the world, because when you look at our prince, you think, 'Why, it must be him brought this winter down on us all.' Him and his cold rage."

Her lover didn't argue. He hardly ever disputed her in any case. Things were much warmer, much easier, much more satisfying if he kept himself agreeable. But here he genuinely thought she was right. He thought the prince was indeed like some dire spirit of loss, a shade of winter.

Gods help us all, he thought later, as he poured for first the elf king and then his ice-eyed brother.

The hall was filled that night with Solostaran's glittering guests, lords and ladies, the members of his senate, those contentious representatives of the Houses of Qualinesti who liked best to jockey with the king for power when it seemed there was a chance to exercise some. They did not tonight. No power was to be had there, in that public hall whose walls and floor were of marble as stark and cold as the winter without, not when the matter of a kidnapped princess hung so coldly over the gathering, the sorrow unspoken, ever-felt.

One of the senators looked around her at her fellows, at Solostaran and his children, young Gilthanas and Porthios, for this gathering was made to celebrate the anniversary of the birth of Gilthanas. He was still a romping lad, as his brother, but he managed solemnity this night. It hadn't been difficult for either, for they grieved the loss of their aunt as everyone did. Not a senator had occasion—as in times past—to look at another, raise a brow and say quietly, "They are boisterous, those boys. One hopes that will pass. . . ."

This senator who had raised her brow in times past admired the decorum of the boys now. She was the Head of House Cleric, a woman who regularly bestormed the gods in their temples with prayer for the sake of the stolen princess. She watched the wine-server fill the golden goblet set before Prince Kethrenan. She thought, gods help us, for we will live in a land colder than Icereach itself and live there forever if our Princess Elansa is not found.

But then she saw the color come to the prince's pale cheek, just a quick flash of blood beneath the skin as a servant, maimed Demlin, whispered something to him. Kethrenan looked up and caught the eye of his cousin seated halfway down the table. Lindenlea stood, murmuring something to her dinner partner. She had dressed herself in flame-colored silk and whitest ermine. For tonight's dinner she'd hung earrings of amber from her ears, piled her hair upon her head, and held it there with diamond-crusted combs and golden pins. Yet when she rose, the rings on her arms and the necklace she wore rang a little, reminding the cleric of the chime of a mail shirt.

Beside his brother, the elf king leaned close and blood leaped to his cheek as well. Anger, the Head of House Cleric wondered, or hope? Solostaran gestured, a quick wave of the hand. *Go!* And Kethrenan did, with a nod to Lindenlea, who followed at once.

Like a sword, thought the Lady Cleric as she watched the prince leave. He's like a well-honed sword leaping suddenly to hand. She thought that was a good image, for she was a poet. Like a poet, she felt the truth of it in her bones.

Someone had just brought word to cause a weapon to be drawn forth, and that weapon was Prince Kethrenan.

* * * * *

"Listen," said Lindenlea, her hand on the prince's arm to still him. All his restless energy filled the barracks, crackling. "I'm not telling you not to do this—" His sudden sharp glance did not frighten her. She knew him, and so she simply quirked her lips in wry challenge. "I'm only saying, don't trust him, Keth."

"I know what you're saying. You've been saying it since we left the Tower. But you also tell me Demlin's seen him, and he thinks I should listen."

Demlin, indeed. Lindenlea didn't say anything to that. One-eared Demlin was a man of single purpose, well matched to his master. Neither Keth nor Demlin thought about much other than the recovery of Elansa. If in the Tower of the Sun they said the prince was driven by his vengeance, in the servants' quarters they knew Demlin was obsessed by it. Master and man, they shared a kindred grief. First one and then the other had been forced to let the outlaw Brand take away the woman they were sworn to protect.

Kethrenan and Lindenlea stood in an empty barracks, a deserted mess. Wind howled outside the windows, and the dark finger-bones of skeletal apple trees scratched against the panes. They'd smelled snow on the air as they'd walked from the Tower of the Sun to this realm of soldiers. Lindenlea had said it was strange that for all the cold and the wild wind they'd endured this winter, they had seen little snow. Kethrenan wasn't interested in how strange that was. The cold kept him out of the borderland. The wind would freeze an elf's skin in an hour and sap the strength from limbs. What matter if snow attended or didn't?

"Where is he?" the prince asked. He was no less finely dressed than his cousin, though perhaps not as brightly. He went in black and red, and his cloak was steely gray—the colors of a blooded sword. He paced the deserted room with a measured stride, as though he tried to reckon out the length of it. Once or twice, he dropped his hand as though to touch the hilt of the sword he had belted on. It was not the one he would have worn this night. That one was in the hands of an outlaw.

As was his wife, in one way or another.

Kethrenan tasted blood, as he had since first he'd learned of Elansa's kidnapping; as he had when the recovery had failed and the only satisfaction he'd had of that day was that his warriors had killed half a hundred goblins. Even that was a lean satisfaction. The hob had gotten away, he and his burning staff.

A sharp voice called out suddenly. Kethrenan knew the tone, if not the man. He didn't stop his pacing or look around. On the heels of that cry came another. Upon the silver spans hemming the city, guard called to guard. *"Avrethe!"* they shouted in Elvish to the full guard, to all the city. *All is well!* In Qualinost, folk marked time by those calls.

Avrethe!

A sharp rap of knuckles on the stout oaken door turned Keth from his pacing.

"That's him," Lea said. Her eyes went from the prince to the door. "Be careful, Keth."

Be careful. He could be lying. Be careful. It could be a trap. Be careful. . . .

Kethrenan jerked his head at her, a wordless command, and she opened the door. Wind whirled brittle leaves into the room. A pennon of torchlight streamed ahead of the bearer. Lindenlea stepped back, gesturing the two elves in. Necessarily, the gesture included their companion. Wrists tied and led by a thick rope round his neck, the third one might have been better termed a prisoner.

"Now why," whined the goblin, his blue-brown skin looking like spoiled meat in the torchlight, "why is it I'm all the time hearing about the famous hospitality of elves, and this—" He looked up at the elves, tall above him. "This is what I get? I've not come to do harm. No, I've come for other reasons, and—"

The prince turned his back on the whining creature. At this feigned royal disinterest, one of the guards hit the goblin in the back of the head, staggering him.

"Shut up, unless you have something more than complaints to give the prince."

The prisoner righted himself with difficulty and whined a little more when his fur cloak slipped from his narrow shoulders to the floor. The barbaric thing, naught but a bear's scraped hide, hit the floor hard, the head of the dead beast making a dull, empty sound on the wood floor. He bent to retrieve it, smoothing the fur back from the head and staring a moment into the empty eye sockets. When he looked up again, he didn't flinch. He didn't wince to meet the eyes of the elves, not even those of the prince.

"I got more," he said, a honed edge to his voice. "I got news he wants, an' if he treats me fair, I'll tell him."

Lindenlea lifted a hand, fist tight as though she were ready to follow the guard's cuffing blow with another.

"Hold," the prince said. When Lindenlea let her fist open and her hand drop, he nodded to the goblin. "What do they call you?"

The goblin seemed surprised. It isn't a question often asked by elves of goblins. "Ithk," he said. "Ithk of Goblintown on the east side of the Forest-Around-Hammer-Rock-But-Not-Too-Close."

Kethrenan raised a brow. The goblin had spun out that name as though it meant something.

"Isn't that where Gnash the hob rules?"

"Him," said the goblin Ithk, not allowing himself to be baited by elven scorn. He adjusted his fur carefully till the bear's head sat between his shoulder blades. "Ain't no good thing in my mind though. I quit him."

"Did you now?" Keth glanced at Lea. "Why?"

"Hates 'im. I *hates* 'im. He's no good. Took our Golch's army and his goblin town but ain't got the guts to do more than talk about our ancient feud with Brand of the Stonelands."

Our ancient feud . . .

The words caused a warrior by the door to snort sudden laughter at the thought of this creature naming contention between outlaws and goblins a feud, or even ancient. Kethrenan silenced her with a narrow glance.

"Go on," said the prince to the goblin.

His eyes darting from Kethrenan to the others, suspecting mockery, Ithk nevertheless went on. "Bastard Gnash killed Golch, saw the son's head come back in an outlaw's sack, and *did nothing about it.* Says he gots better things to do than chase a handful of humans. Says he gots an army to grow. Hates 'im."

Kethrenan was grateful Ithk didn't say Gnash had shamed him, for if he had, the prince himself might have laughed at the idea that one of these wretches could speak of shame.

"And you're here—why?"

"I want to kill that whoreson bastard Brand." The goblin's lips pulled a nasty grin. "I'm thinkin' you do, too. I know how to find him."

The warriors looked from one to another. The torch in the hand of the elf woman cast streaming orange light and shadow all around the room. In that running light and shadow, Kethrenan took one long step. Swift, he snatched the goblin's shoulder, his long fingers gripping hard.

"Tell me," he said, no pretense to amusement in his voice now. Ithk yowled like a kicked cat, struggling to get away. Keth gripped harder. "Tell me where they are and how you know."

"I know," the goblin whined, "because I looked. Ain't me can kill 'em by myself. Ain't Gnash going to do it. I'm thinkin' you want to know where he is. They're nowhere in the light, but I know how to find 'em, and you want to know, so maybe you'll pay me good—"

He twisted in Keth's grip, the bear-headed fur falling to the floor.

"My prince," Lindenlea said, her hand on Keth's arm, "don't break him. Let's see if we can determine whether he is telling the truth."

Kethrenan found her suggestion sound, though he'd have liked to break all the bones in the goblin Ithk for the sheer effrontery of the creature's thinking he could come here to bargain. He ordered his warriors to take the goblin to the Temple of Solinari, the moon-white marble hall where, in secret chambers, mages kept a lovely necklace of golden links from which depended a stone of indeterminate nature. Sometimes it shone diamond clear. At other times, it shone red and burned the flesh like a fiery ember.

"See if the creature is telling the truth," the prince said to Lindenlea. "If he is, come tell me. I'll be in the Tower."

"If he lies?"

Kethrenan shrugged. "Kill him."

The prince's cousin did as he ordered, and for a time a high screeching could be heard echoing through bright Solinari's temple. It rang strangely in that place of peace and prayer where the air smelled always of rain-washed midnight. The screeching didn't go on long, and in the end the clerics had to say to the Lady Lindenlea that they didn't know what to tell her about how the Stone of Truth judged the goblin's tale.

"Sometimes the stone showed clear and bright, sometimes like a liar's bloody hand. You'll have to make your own judgment, my lady. If you think the prince is served by killing the creature, kill him. But don't do the killing here, and get some of your warriors to dump the body outside the city if you don't mind."

Lindenlea took this news to her cousin. Walking back through the city, watching the first fat flakes of snow drift down from burdened skies, she thought things had turned out as she'd feared from the start. They would be offered the risk of trusting a goblin, there would be no surety, and Keth would consider the possible gain worth the risk he'd take.

"What fee does he want?"

Lindenlea shrugged. "Brand's head. He says he wants to be the one to kill Brand."

"He can't, but he doesn't need to know that. Tell him what he wants to hear."

Lindenlea did that, and she left the goblin in the care of warriors, well guarded in a cell until he was needed. Ithk raised his objections, but not too loudly. It seemed he was disposed to be cooperative.

Grimly, Lindenlea left him. Restless, she strode the streets of Qualinost, a tall figure in flame-colored silk and whitest ermine making for the shining lights of the Tower of the Sun. Faintly, strains of sweet music drifted on the snowy air. They had started the dancing in there, the elf king, his kin, and his senators, celebrating a young prince's birthday. Lindenlea did not doubt that Keth was there, that sword of a prince ready to begin his search again.

And soon, too. It must warm up to snow, and she could feel the temperature of the air changing even as she lifted her face to the falling snow. There would be a snowfall, and then there would be a thaw. Kethrenan would ride out from his brother's city and go again in search of his wife. Lindenlea would, of course, be with him. He was her cousin and her prince.

Her boots were the soft boots of the court—thin-soled, buttery leather with fur trim useful for drawing a man's eye to a shapely calf. They were not meant to carry her across any terrain rougher than thick carpeting or polished floor. Still, none of the guards on the four spans who saw her doubted that here was a warrior, back straight, stride long, her hand moving like it wished to grip a sword.

Now began the season of hunting lost things.

Chapter 8

⁓

"Here is what I know about how to live," said the princess to herself in the dark reaches of the earth while winds moaned without and snow fell, the hissing of it heard at the mouths of secret caves.

I know how to mend my clothing with needles of bone and thread of clumsy sinew. I know how to recognize the smell of good water and foul. I know to watch the dwarf when we are walking—he never puts a foot wrong. I know I am beaten if I fall, and I am kicked up again. I know how to eat fast, though I am the one who eats last. I know how to keep quiet in shadows, and I know it is a blessing that I no longer dream.

I know to keep my eyes low. I know to speak to none of them. I know there are some who watch, some who wait. I hear them breathing, occupying other shadows than those I cling to. I hear them.

What is it they wait for? They are like hounds themselves. They wait for chance. Hounds. I know to keep near the hound. I know to share my food with Fang so he is willing to be more with me than with Char.

These things Elansa thought, often and over, for they were the new rules for how she could live. Sometimes, when she sat a long time in her shadows at night—or what she imagined must be night—Elansa sensed two pairs of eyes on her more strongly than others. They held her in tension between them, the eyes of Arawn,

Dell's handsome lover, and the eyes of Brand. Brand would watch her thus even as he lay with Tianna asleep in his arms. He didn't like it that dark-haired Arawn wouldn't let go the matter of the disposition of the prisoner.

Sitting still, barely breathing, Elansa would think of what Char had said, a long time ago on the night the goblin was killed under Hammer Rock.

"You see," he'd said, his breath sour with drink as he watched Brand hand over the goblin to Ley. "You don't keep it all for yourself."

In some way Arawn had come to believe that Brand, by declaring the prisoner off limits to his men, was keeping her for himself, if not for the nighttime, then for some other reason. More and more, it became clear that Arawn didn't like the idea or seem to consider a stolen elven sword a fair exchange for nights with a stolen elven princess.

"Char," she said, one night when the first snow of winter fell softly upon the breast of Krynn, when the people in Tarsis wept for joy because at last the wind had fallen, and in Qualinost a warrior in ermine and fiery silk brought a goblin to Solinari's moon-white temple. "Char, why did Ley want to kill the goblin, back at Hammer Rock?"

The dwarf shrugged and reached around him for something, the skin or a last bone of stolen goat for gnawing.

"The usual reason." When she shook her head, not knowing the usual reason, he said, "Golch's da killed Ley's woman. Not so long ago, either. Maybe a moon's turn before anyone laid eye on you. Ley's still in mourning."

Coldly, she said, "And he thought the killing would help?"

Char sat back, the skin on his knee fat and full. He closed his hands around it, cradling it tenderly. "Y'do what y'do."

All these things Char said looking into a far corner of the cave where the roof sloped down to the ground and made a private place. Elansa looked where he did and saw the silver spill of Tianna's hair where it flowed over Brand's chest. With his look, not his words, the dwarf told her something about Tianna and grim Ley, a thing Elansa would not have guessed. And yet, knowing, the truth seemed inevitable. The half-elf had the look of her father, more than the shape of his eyes or ears, more than his elven grace. It was the way she glanced keenly around her, her careful tension, the tilt of her head, even her rare laughter, that gave her kinship to Ley.

"Leyerlain Starwing," Char said, unstopping the skin with his thumb. "I guess that makes her Tianna Starwing."

Elansa looked away. Of course the woman would not be granted her father's name in such a shameful circumstance. Of course she would be given some other name if Leyerlain Starwing's family knew his shame. Something made up for decency's sake if they were moved by compassion, or she'd simply be known as half-elven.

Elansa withdrew into her safe shadows, calling the hound to her. The sound of the dog's nails on stone caught the attention of Arawn and of Brand. She hung again in their tension, and it was a long time before she could sleep.

These things, these cautions, these fears, they made up the borders of her life now, even as she moved through a world without borders, caverns and tunnels running beneath the face of Krynn, lands no one had ever claimed.

* * * * *

Horses snorted, dancing in the cold and tossing their heads. Riders spoke calming words. Kethrenan left them, guiding his mount close to the lip of the drop into the stonelands. He pulled his helm from his head, tucking it under his arm. On his forehead, sweat turned to ice. Wind whipped his hair back from his face, scouring his skin red. Before him, out across the stoneland, lay the formations known since the Cataclysm as Stone Castle, Granite Tower, Hammer Rock, and Reorx's Anvil. Ravens sailed around the lower piles, while rooks lived in the highest. Between the Hammer and the Anvil, two eagles soared, winding down the chill sky. To this place they'd ridden, and all the while dark visions had haunted the prince, like dark wings clapping. At night, when he lay wrapped in his cloak apart from the rest, sleepless till most of the night had worn away, it seemed he heard Elansa's voice on the wind, wailing, lifting up to beseech the gods to have pity on her suffering.

Kethrenan lifted his hand to shade his eyes against the sun's glare. Far away in the south, he saw the gleam of light high up. Those were not the snowy peaks of the Kharolis Mountains, not so near. What he saw was, perhaps, the glint of light on the ruined towers of Pax Tharkas.

Here was Qualinesti's sternest border, once the

land that lay between the elves and their allies, the dwarves of Thorbardin. In times past, roads had run through this bitter plain, made by friends and connecting the underground kingdom of the dwarves, the forest realm of the elves, and the western kingdoms of humans, all running out from Pax Tharkas.

But that was a time ago, well before the Cataclysm changed the face of Krynn and rewrote all treaties, and no one counted on roads running through the stony plain now. There was a new clan of dwarves, the Neidar, made from those who'd broken from their kin in the hard years after the Cataclysm. They called themselves hill dwarves to make it clear to all they had nothing to do with their mountain-dwelling kin. The mountain dwarves, who in the main had been the allies of the elves, now delved only in Thorbardin, seldom coming out into the sun. In Qualinesti elves kept to their forest glades. Sundered, the erstwhile friends had not fallen so far as the humans had. Whatever must be said of them, elves and dwarves, they did not deny the existence of gods. An old dwarven proverb said, "The man who denies the wind because he can't see it is an idiot." Elven wisdom murmured, "Who fails the gods with lack of faith, fails himself."

Humans, short-lived and lacking in the patience of those races whose life span can be two hundred years or more, had turned from whatever lore of gods they'd once possessed. Turning, it seemed they had changed themselves into beggars and thieves, godless wretches who saw in the visible marks of the anger of the gods reason to decide no god existed at all.

And they, who promoted the blasphemy of unbelief all across Krynn, had down the long years managed to forget that it was one of their own race who caused the

Cataclysm and the withdrawal of the gods. They chose not to remember a Kingpriest gone mad in Istar, who had declared himself a deity. Not many of them liked to admit it was a human who had enraged the true gods, causing them to hurl down upon Krynn a fiery mountain to remind mortals who was divine and who was not.

Into the hands of these his wife had fallen.

Kethrenan swallowed, savoring the phantom taste of blood in his mouth, salty and warm. He did not bleed, not in his body. He did perhaps bleed in his soul, as though the rage living in him were fanged and gnawing from the inside.

"Demlin!" he snapped.

Maimed Demlin spurred his mount, a fine gelding out of the prince's own stable. Winter had reshaped the servant. His long face, once alight with congenial good humor, was now the face of a man who'd been hollowed and filled up again with bitterness. He covered his maiming with a square of black cloth tied as seamen and pirates do. It gave him a dangerous look, lean and not very warm in the heart.

Demlin did not come alone. Tethered to the pommel of his saddle, upon a long braided plait, the goblin Ithk jogged beside.

"Where?" said the prince.

Ithk pointed down the hill to the stony slope of Hammer Rock.

"There's where he took her, your woman, in the fall. Can't say he's still there. Wouldn't be. But sign is he's been since, maybe twice since he took her."

The hard blue sky glared down. All the world below was a whirl of snow running in white devils. In the sky, the moons hung like pale ghosts, the red and the silver, risen early or lingering late.

"Prince!"

Kethrenan looked over his shoulder and saw Lindenlea point north. He looked where she did. A dark plume hung low over the earth.

"What's down there?" he asked.

Lindenlea shrugged. "A village or two—human, most likely. Maybe a goblin town in the making by now. That doesn't look like a gathering of hearth fires."

Ithk move restlessly. Demlin kicked him quiet as Kethrenan squinted, trying to see. In the end, he could discern only smoke. Human village or goblin town, it didn't matter. They were outlanders, not even to be accorded the grudging respect granted such former allies as dwarves.

"Your word, my prince?" Lea asked.

"Follow Demlin."

Demlin kicked the goblin again, and Ithk set out down the slope. Tethered, he leaped from stone to stone, and he had enough slack to keep him from tripping over himself or Demlin's mount, but no more than that.

Lindenlea called the order, her voice sharp as a blade's edge on the icy air, her breath streaming back in frosty plumes. Side by side, the lord of Qualinesti's warriors and his cousin sent their mounts plunging down the steep slope. They ran like quicksilver, madly galloping their horses over treacherous ground. Sunlight leaped in bright darts off their helms and mail shirts and shot from the tips of their lances.

Before all went maimed Demlin and Ithk. All the way down the hill, the goblin ran as though he feared the horses would trample him, and when he reached the floor of the little vale, he stopped and scrambled onto a pile of stone high as a horse's shoulder. Quivering with cold, Ithk looked around, his head swiveling on his scrawny neck. His skin color changed to a gray hue.

Demlin cried, "My lord prince!"

Something hunched up from the snowy ground, a burned body. Kethrenan swerved his mount in time to miss another such lump, and then they saw bodies all around.

Every corpse was a goblin's corpse, and Keth guessed they'd have starved in the winter if they hadn't been killed. Killed they had been, though—some with arrows and swords, some more cruelly than that. Snow covered them, but not wholly, and Keth saw that some had been beheaded, others had had the hands cut from their wrists or their feet from their ankles. The stretched jaws showed that the severing had happened before the killing.

Across the snowy ground they saw hands thrusting up from the drifts, clawing as if reaching for the last of life. Faces stared up, eye sockets empty. Ravens had feasted, and all around the gore of a great massacre lay frozen, glittering with ice crystals like diamonds on ruby fields.

"Dear gods," Lindenlea whispered.

"It's Gnash's work," Ithk said. He pointed north where smoke hung dark on the sky. "It's him. He's makin' another goblin town his own." His mouth, lips so thin as to seem nonexistent, twisted. "These didn't like the idea, and Gnash didn't like their not likin'."

"What did he do," Lea said, "kill every one of the goblins in the town?"

Ithk shook his head. "Nah. Half these are his. Gnash, he's got the fire, and he's got the belly for killing. He does what he does. Me, I does what I does." He jerked his head toward Hammer Rock. "Brand, he been in there, first when he got yer woman, again not long ago."

Kethrenan's blood quickened. "You know this, how?"

Ithk's eyes shifted right, then left. "I know," he said, and only that.

Horses snorted, not liking the death-smell, the goblin-stink. All around, the wind moaned low, having slid down the hillsides as though in the wake of the elven band. To Kethrenan it sounded like the voices of ghosts. Close to the pooling shadow of Hammer Rock, the prince dismounted and tossed the reins to Lindenlea.

"Wait here," he said. He pointed to Demlin and one other warrior, Lathal, a mage of the Birchbright clan. "Come with me."

With tethered Ithk, they walked into the shadows beneath Hammer Rock, and they found the way in. Lathal lit a torch, and they took the stairs.

"I smell old fires," Lathal said. He held the torch higher, and the light spread out through the darkness.

The scents of old fires became embodied in the rough rounds of stones marking long dead cookfires. In the dim light, the elves breathed and smelled, faintly, the greasy scents of cooked food and the clinging scent of rough wet wool. Guided by the goblin, they walked around the dark smudges of campfires on the stony floor. They found niches in the stone walls and burned brands scattered. Kethrenan prowled among the campfires, and he looked like a dog trailing a scent.

"My lord prince!"

Kethrenan turned to look at Demlin, the servant's white face gleaming in the torchlight. Long eyes shone bright, and in the shadows his mouth looked like a dark gash in his face. He held up a strip of cloth: the green hem of a cloak.

It's hers.

The thought rang in Kethrenan's heart, even before his fingers closed round the cloth, before he felt the satin underlay and saw the careful, tiny stitches running the length. Hem-stitches, lovely, for each was shaped like a tiny elven rune to signify health and luck. They were proud of their work, the tailors of Qualinost. The one who had made the cloak from which this piece had been torn had likely been very proud indeed. He'd been working for a princess.

Blood stained the scrap of cloth, a darkness soaked into the fiber, rough as a scab. The prince ran his finger over the stain and scraped it with his nail. Rusty flakes fell away, but most of it was long soaked in.

He felt it again: the coppery salt-taste at the back of his mouth, as though blood seeped thick and warm near his throat.

Ithk said, "Come with me. I'll show you what else I know."

They went through the cavern and into a narrow passage where the sound of trickling water became loud in their ears, bouncing to echo off the close stone. The little passage turned, then widened, and the torchlight threw their shadows ahead, long and dark. When the goblin looked back, his eyes glowed as a dog's eyes, eerie and orange in the dim light.

A little farther they went, until the way opened and the glow of the light glinted on running water. Here they smelled a foul combination of odors—lantern oil, perhaps, wet wool, body waste . . .

Demlin shot a glance at his master, and the prince shrugged. Lathal came forward past the prince, past them all. His torchlight bobbed in the air, floating; its beams illuminated a running black stream and spangled the surface with silver. The ground dropped down in two ledges like broad steps. Across the water a small trickle slipped out of a crack in the far stone wall. So long had it run that it had hollowed the rock into a shallow bowl.

The goblin trotted along the edge of the stream on Demlin's leash. The elf lowered his torch, for day's light shafted down from the far ceiling. The roof of this cave was not solid, and upon some of the stone higher up snow had sifted in. Hemmed by silent stone, with only the voice of water and the breathing of elves, the goblin turned his back on the stream and the small fountain. He pointed toward a niche in the wall behind them, a hollowing as though a god's hand had smoothed and indented the rough wall.

"There."

Demlin's breath hissed between his teeth. Others murmured in surprise. The faint streaming light fell upon a weapons cache. They were not fools, whoever had hidden this hoard. Oiled woolen cloaks wrapped the long blades of swords and the beaked faces of axes. None of the precious steel would rust for lack of care, even here in this damp cavern.

Ithk said, "Some o' what Brand got off you, eh?"

Demlin yanked on the tether. The goblin staggered, but the sly light in his eyes didn't falter.

"Some, but not all. He's got it stashed all over the mountain. Some here, some other places . . ."

Not prepared to believe the answer, Kethrenan said, "You know them all?"

Ithk shook his head. "I know all the ones I know. Found six stashes just like this one. None north of here, all south."

All south. Brand would keep close to them. He'd be sure to stay within range of his weapon caches. Kethrenan walked round the little hoard, the small part of what Brand had stolen. He snorted, a humorless sound.

"Steel's not all they store here."

He nudged something small and round near the edge of the hoard. What he kicked had a wooden voice. The faint odor of dwarf spirits mingled with the stink of oil-soaked wool.

He circled the hoard again, then slipped a throwing axe out from its oily wrapping. The oaken haft felt slick in his grip, but he wasn't going to need it long or do any precision cutting. Wordless, he struck the keg, splintering the wood and loosing the liquor in gurgling flow. The goblin sighed. Demlin and Lathal shared a mirthless grin.

Turning on his heel, Kethrenan left the others to follow. He took the stone stairs upward two at a time. Still clutching the hem of his wife's cloak, he strode out into the bitter brightness of the day. His sight dazzled, he saw only shapes and shadows. No matter, he knew them, his warriors.

"Prince?" said Lindenlea, the word a question.

He held up the strip of bloodstained green cloth, waving it like a pennon.

"She's been here!" he cried, not to her but to all. His words echoed from the dark stone of Hammer Rock.

"Our princess has been here, but now she's gone. They are all gone, but here is the bloody hem of her cloak to say that she left this stinking hole alive!"

Their voices rose in rage, elven men and women clashing swords against shields and shaking their lances at the sky. One, a woman with eyes as fierce as a wolf's, shouted above the rage and the roar, "We will find her, my prince!" and others took up her cry. "We will find her! In the name of every god, we will take her back! We will bring home the princess!"

The force of their vows ran like fire in Kethrenan, and he would not kindle to it. He could not. This was not a season for fight. This was a hunter's season. He had seen what the goblin wanted to show him, and he knew Ithk was not going to lead him to Brand's doorstep. Ithk didn't know which of the hiding holes kept the outlaw now.

A slow grin tugged his lips. It was the hunting season, and he could be a hunter.

"Lea," he said, "take the warriors and find a clean place to camp, out of the wind. We have some planning to do."

* * * * *

By the light of a high, hot fire, they looked at the small map. It was roughly made; goblins aren't skilled at that craft. Drawn on the back of a scribe-made map from Kethrenan's broad leather wallet, no ink to define but only soot from the fire, it showed six caches, each marked by a wavering triangle. They all pointed generally south, as Ithk had said. They didn't make a straight line. Brand had stowed his war gear in places that, when connected, made a triangle. The broad base of it lay in the northernmost part of the goblin's map, where the largest part of the load of stolen weapons had been stored. The narrow head of the triangle lay farthest south.

Almost, Kethrenan thought, pointing at Pax Tharkas.

"That," said the prince, laying his finger on the point. "That was the last cache he made."

Lindenlea said she didn't know how Keth could know that. Demlin, maimed Demlin, said the answer was obvious.

"They had two wagons to unload and not so many men to do the work. They stashed most of it along that line—" He traced the base of the triangle, smearing it a little. "And they took the rest as far as they could go."

Lea considered, and she nodded. "Likely they've been living within that triangle all winter, close to their weapons. Smart."

"Wolf cunning," Demlin said, unwilling to give the outlaw more than that.

Keth let them bat it back and forth, his cousin and his servant. He listened a little, but he had his eye on the mark indicating the farthest cache. *Wolf cunning*, indeed. He sat back, feeling as he did when he knew exactly what must be done to bring the prey to earth.

He explained it to them, quietly and clearly, while the high wind moaned around the hills and the voices of his warriors played quiet counterpoint. Lindenlea didn't like the plan. She listened respectfully, but she didn't doubt that her cousin knew what she was thinking.

"My lord prince," she said, her voice stiff with disapproval, "this isn't how I would manage it."

He nodded. "I know. You would fly in with troops and burn down the mountains with your fury. And you wouldn't find them that way, Lea."

She shook her head, careful not to speak as she would have were they alone. Alone she'd have said, *Cousin, you're not thinking! Keth, you're a fool to trust this goblin!*

She had said it before, in Qualinost. She believed it now, and, she supposed, there was no need to shout it.

He knew. Here in this cold camp, they were commander and warrior, not cousins. She did not speak her frustration; she spoke her warning.

"My prince, I don't know why you trust the goblin. You can't really believe that story about how much he hates Brand and what a coward Gnash is. Gnash is no coward, Keth."

"I know. I've seen Gnash in action, and I've seen what he leaves behind in the wake of his ambition. Gnash is blood-hungry. If he's not going after Brand, it's because he considers him small fry, something to be dealt with later. Me, I don't consider him that."

Kethrenan looked past her and past Demlin, who was rolling up the map. He looked at the goblin, guarded and pretending to sleep. It was a strange thing—something he wouldn't say to Lea or to Demlin—but he believed the goblin. He believed he wanted revenge on Brand. He knew what that looked like, the hunger.

"And him? I'll trust him till I can't. Then I'll kill him."

Lea frowned. "Remember what we saw in the temple, Keth. We heard him howling when the Stone went red. He's hiding something, and I don't trust him."

"Aye, well, it's not you who has to. You, cousin, are going to clean out this weapons cache, then you'll take this troop back to Qualinost. You're going to commission a better map than the one the goblin has made. While that is being made, you will take warriors and put them thickly on the borders, because I don't like all the goblin activity I'm seeing here. After that, you will send troops out to the other caches and empty them. I don't care what you do with the weapons. Break them if you can't carry them back. Just be sure to leave nothing for Brand."

"And you?"

The prince sat back, smiling for the first time in a long time. It was no cheerful smile, nor was it warm. He sat that way, still, for a long moment. When he looked up, Lea thought his eyes were frightening: cold and without the softer quality that might lead a person to think him capable of mercy.

"Demlin and I—and Ithk to be sure—are going hunting. I know the outlaw's territory now. It used to be all this wild borderland. It's been shrunk a little now. Wherever it is he's gone to ground, he won't be far from one of those caches, and from time to time, he's going to have to put his head up for food. When he does—" He slammed his fist into his palm, startling Lea, startling the horses. "When he does, I'm going to take that head off."

Chapter 9

Tianna said, "It's a good day when you see the sun."

Just those words, no more, and Elansa couldn't have said the half-elf sounded wistful or wore any trace of sun-longing in her expression. She simply stood at the mouth of the cave, bent her bow to string it, and settled a full fat quiver on her hip.

"I'm not going alone," she'd said to Brand when it was decided it was her turn to go above and hunt. "And I'm not taking any of those damn men with me."

Over this dark season she'd grown a dislike for most of them, hungry-handed men who now and then tried their luck with her. Luckless hungry-handed men, but Elansa saw that the half-elf was getting tired of making her point. Tianna was, Elansa thought, getting tired of them all. It had been a while since she'd shared the sleeping furs with Brand. She spoke to no one but her father, sometimes to Char, but only if she was of a mind to flatter him for a drink. She looked beyond the fire a lot, like someone who was thinking about moving on.

Brand had said he didn't care who Tianna hunted with. All he cared about was that she come back with supper. And so she'd looked around for Dell, who could not be found. Neither could Arawn be found, and that answered that. Tianna announced she was taking Elansa and no one was to worry about her escaping.

"If she tries, I'm just in the mood to shoot her."

Tianna tested her bow's string, liking the tension. She slipped an arrow from the quiver. Fletched all in white

but for a green cock-feather, it was a beautiful shaft—
straight, with sunlight gleaming on the golden wood.

"Not a bad day, either, when you feel the wind on
your face."

Her words caught Elansa by the throat, like grief.
How long it had been since she'd seen the sun or tasted
the wind! How long? She didn't know. Greedy, her eyes
took in all she saw, and that was not much. Stonelands
stretched as far as the eye could reach, a dun earth
brushed here and there with shadow. On the shaded
side of the hill, little crevices and cracks between rocks
held dusty snow, but the air was warmer than she
remembered it being the last time she'd felt it moving
on her skin. No matter where she looked, she saw no
sign of her forest. It was as though the horizon had forgotten the green and the gray and the way the lines of
trees could soften its line.

She had lived below ground with the outlaws for a
time she didn't know how to reckon. In the sky the two
moons hung, faint and weary from the night. A trick of
the light made it easier to discern red Lunitari. She hung
full, and so must her brother Solinari. Full, but how
many times had the moons turned since Elansa had
been taken? Her body had twice missed its cycle, two
months. A month later, she had lost the child. She'd not
caught her rhythm back yet, and she hadn't been able to
discern the patterns of the other women. As best she
could estimate, all the winter had passed since Brand
had taken her away.

The wind shifted, coming down from the warmer
north. She thought she caught the scent of green things
growing. Tears welled and dried at once. She did not
weep now, or ever. It was a sign of weakness, and she

could not afford that, not in the day, not in the night.

Why didn't Keth let me die?

Came the accusatory reply: Why did you stop him?

Across the sky, a raven went winging, its cry like a curse in the silence. Another followed, and then more. Tianna nudged Elansa and went leaping down the stony slope. Elansa followed, springing down the hillside with the same confidence as the half-elf. She had been walking inside the mountain for months, and the way was no easier on the inside than out. Lately, since he'd decided he wasn't going to kill her out of hand, Brand had seen to it that she fared better with food. She ate before the hounds did now, and that almost doubled her fare. She grew strong with the food and the hard walking. She did not take this as reprieve from the threat of killing, though. It was just that she had to be able to move as quickly and strongly as anyone else.

The wind, the sweet wind, did indeed smell of green. Tianna stopped at the foot of the slope. She looked back, marked the dark slit in the side of the mountain that was the way back, and then watched the ravens, the dark flock growing thicker.

She jerked her head at Elansa. "Come on. They're following something minded to do a killing—goblins maybe. No place we want to be."

So saying, she turned in the direction opposite from where the ravens were going.

Elansa followed, but once when Tianna wasn't looking, she cast a glance at the sky, then along the dun land behind. She saw nothing, but the birds flew high and they saw more. For a moment, her heart rose, and she thought, Do they see searchers? Do they see Keth?

Or does he think I'm dead?

Wind moaned lonely in the empty land, sounding like lost things. Elansa ran to catch up with Tianna, and she walked beside her around the base of the hill and north into the warmer wind. They went that way for a while. She was not a hunter, this stolen princess, but she had become a watcher. She knew, almost before Tianna stopped, that she would. Something in the way the half-elf's shoulders squared, a thing about the way she moved to settle the quiver on her hip.

"Wait," Tianna said, not whispering, but low.

Elansa had already halted, and she was already smelling what had warned Tianna. Blood and smoke, and something so foul she could not name it. Bleating, like the cries of goats, sounded against the hill, echoing.

"Ogre," Tianna said. She looked around. Nothing in her countenance seemed like panic, but Elansa felt the urgency as though it were a spark leaping from one of them to the other. Tianna grabbed her shoulder and turned her around, pointing uphill to where tumbled stones made a pile as high as the women were tall. "Up there! Go!"

Goats cried again, then one made a terrible screaming and fell silent. Laughter, harsh as daggers, bounded around the stone as two more death cries cut the air. Someone—or something—shouted in a language Elansa couldn't identify, neither Dwarvish nor Elvish nor Common. All the words of it—if words there were—sounded like calls to murder. She ran, scrambling, her heart thundering in her breast and her mouth dried up with fear. She fell once, pushed herself up again, and bent her back to run. She ducked behind the stone and had no time to catch her breath before Tianna pulled her to her knees. Long elven eyes widening, she mouthed one word: *Quiet!*

She need not have warned, and yet it seemed to Elansa that her own breathing sounded like stormwind. She forced herself to take small silent breaths.

The ogres, three of them, came up the defile, and each carried a dead goat slung across its shoulders. Sunlight gleamed on scabrous, yellow skin. Tiny, mean eyes darted here and there. Thick ropes of saliva hung and dripped from keen fangs. Taller than any elf Elansa had ever seen, taller than any human in Brand's band, they covered the rough ground as easily as ever Elansa had strode through a marble hall.

Tianna mouthed a curse, eyes glancing this way and that, looking to see if more of the horrible creatures would follow or if these would meet with others. The three came closer, and the stench of them made Elansa's gorge rise. She clapped her hand to her mouth and willed the bile burning up from her belly to stay behind her teeth. Her eyes watered from the pain, from the stink, and the three walked by, goat's blood dripping down their backs. They shouted back and forth to each other, not caring who heard them.

One stopped, adjusted the load of the goat round its shoulders. It lifted its head, sniffed the wind, and went suddenly still. It shouted something, and the others stopped.

Tianna mouthed, *Do not move.*

Elansa could not have. Her heart slammed against her ribs, and sweat broke on her brow. She became aware of her own smell—sweat and skin and hair not washed, the leather of her broken boots, the wool of her cloak. Please, gods, don't let the wind shift!

One ogre shouted to the lingerer, who moved on.

When they were gone, the two women breathed

again. Tianna slapped her shoulder, as she might have the shoulder of one of her fellows, a half-friendly gesture assumed to be understood.

"We're out of here, girl. No hunting for us."

Elansa rose, looking at the way back, but Tianna shook her head. Wind caught her silvery hair, and she brushed it back. "We're not going back in the way we came. I know another way."

She did. Of course she did. And the way took them along the defile, back the way the ogres had come. They walked for a time, following the scents of smoke and death, and came to a rare place in the stoneland, a place of water where tough grass grew around the stream and the little pond. Like broken skeletons, the fire-blackened beams of two buildings that might have been house and barn stood starkly against the dun earth. Goats wandered, lost and bleating. Beside two nannies little black-footed kids skipped. In the middle of what must have been a dooryard, a man lay sprawled, his neck broken, one arm ripped from the socket.

Elansa turned from the sight. "Who would live here?"

Tianna, looking up the slope for a way back into the mountain, answered absently. "Humans do mostly, like him. Sometimes dwarves. Don't bother asking why. There's as many reasons as there are fools who try to live here. Outlaws like Brand, outcasts, stubborn folk who don't like the towns or the company of their own. Sometimes people live here because they remember that before the Cataclysm their long-ago fathers did. They claim the land, though the gods long ago made it useless. Fools, all."

Elansa said nothing.

"Ah," Tiana said, pointing up-slope. "There it is. Come on. Climb. And don't get tired of it, there's going to be more walking before the day's done. We'll be moving right out, count on that. Those ogres look like they're searching for a good spot to set up. That'll be inside, and no one I know is crazy enough to stick around when there's a chance ogres are moving in."

So they climbed, hunters with no gain. The way in to the outlaws' cave opened halfway up the slope, a narrow passage behind a boulder. Elansa never would have found it. She didn't imagine anyone could who didn't know it existed. In the shadowed place between the inside and the out, she paused and looked back. She didn't look north to where the murdered goatherd lay dead. She looked south. No raven flew in the sky, and she said to Tianna that she thought those dark wings hadn't been following death. She thought they'd been fleeing ogres.

Tianna said she supposed so. "No one ever said they were stupid birds."

Elansa would not have said Brand was a stupid man, no matter what else could be told of him. No sooner did he hear Tianna's news than did he call his men sharply to order.

"We're gone," he said. "Ogres are outside and looking for a way in. Pack up and clean out."

Elansa worked with the rest. She knew the way. They broke the fires and scattered the stones from the rings. They took all the bones of old meals and tumbled them down into the darkness of a crevice that seemed to have no bottom. Stone leaves no track, so they had nothing to do but be certain no sign of them lay behind, forgotten—no leather thong cast away from a boot-mending, no scrap of cloth, no sign of their waste. This they managed in a short time. They were very good at leaving nothing but shadow behind.

Through all the work, Elansa noticed something no one else seemed to pay much attention to. Dell and Arawn did not work together, though they always had before. They worked far from each other, doing different tasks. Elansa looked around from her bone-gathering, and she thought something had changed, something between the two lovers. She saw it finally, something in the mood of the whole band of outlaws. It was the kind of indefinable change you feel in the forest when the wind drops and the whispering trees have nothing to say. Still, you know what they're thinking, those trees: *Storm coming.*

"You," said Brand, who never named her. "Come here."

She did, her hands full of bones. He looked her up and down. His eyes had the sharpness of calculation. The cave had grown dark. Cookfires were gone, and torches were sputtering to life. She couldn't see him well, just the outline of him—broad shoulders, head back, the red firelight edging the thickness of his beard.

"Listen," he said, and it was the voice he used to give orders. "Get rid of all that, and come right back. Once we're going, you be sure to stay near me."

She didn't understand until she passed Char on the way to dump the bones. The dwarf knelt beside a flickering torch, carefully filling his leather bottle from the last of a stout little keg. He looked up, head cocked to give his good eye the sight of her.

"Do what he says," the dwarf warned. "Arawn, he ain't got no woman now."

* * * * *

Six captains each took a troop of warriors out from Qualinost. Each captain had a finely drawn map on supple parchment, the bold lines in broad strokes of darkest ink. Each map resided in a tooled leather scroll case, safe against the elements and the grit that plagued the borderland. Each captain had the same order from Lindenlea: "In the prince's name, clean the weapons caches."

Proud warriors, they heard those orders and set spurs to horse, riding through the great gates with the sound of thunder. It was not the best order. They imagined a better one that sounded like, "In the prince's name, find the princess!" No warrior lived in Qualinost who didn't feel the burning shame of having had the stolen princess within reach and then losing her. None of them didn't dream of killing the human scum who had twice taken Elansa.

For now, though, these must content themselves with knowing they would take weapons away from the outlaws, and that was good work. They ran out to the border and there found more of the prince's soldiers, a great line of them ranging the stonelands from the Notch where they'd lost the princess and north to the edge of Darken Wood, south to the place where the Qualinesti Forest became the Forest of Wayreth, that old land of mages. They made a wall, bristling with swords and lances. Their encampments were not secret but plain for all to see.

"It would be nice to have the chance to spit a goblin or two," Lindenlea had told them, each commander she dispatched. "But that's not the mission. The mission is to keep them in the borderland. There will be no crack in the wall between Qualinesti and them. Engage only if you must."

Those were hard words for winter-weary soldiers, but they were orders and so not to be questioned. Small, shining outposts of Qualinesti set up on the border, and no one traveling by, not human or goblin or wandering hill dwarf thought those encampments would be friendly places to stop.

But the six troops setting out across the borderland thought the sight of all those warriors was a glad one. Their hearts rose to look back and see the brave pennons flying, the sun on burnished shields, on plumed helms. Stern faces, hard hands, these were elves trained in battle, elves whose hearts turned to only one need: Protect the kingdom.

It's a good day, thought one of the warriors, she who was bound with her fellows to clean out the easternmost cache along the base of the triangle that formed the outlaws' territory. It's a good day to pull a wolf's fangs.

And that's how they saw it, all the Qualinesti, watching or riding. They saw it as a scouring of wolves. No wolf of the goblin-kind would do mischief on the border, and those human wolves in the mountains would soon find themselves toothless and hard-hunted.

Indeed, a good day.

* * * * * *

Today the way was up, the passage narrow, and the floor rough. In the womb of Krynn, the change of days was judged to fall on the far side of the longest sleep.

Elansa had been counting, and she counted three days passing since she and Tianna had seen the ogres and found the dead goatherd.

The outlaw band went along passages and tunnels she recognized. In these months she had threaded many of the underground ways and had learned to see landmarks here as she would in the forest. In some ways, the picking of landmarks was little different. A grouping of stalactites was like a grove of birches. One recognized a shape, a configuration, and strove to remember it. In some ways, it might have been easier. Sooner will a grove of trees change than a grove of stone.

She knew the way they took on the first day. She even knew it was an easterly way. They were walking toward a weapons cache.

"Not for a take," said Brand when the boy Chaser asked about that. "It's on the way, and outside of there is some good hunting."

That word, *hunting*, ran back along the line of outlaws in whisper and echo. There would be a day or two of existing on jerked meat, smoked lengths of juiceless hare so tough that nigh-toothless Kerin would be gumming it for an hour to be able to swallow it. No one was happy about that, and Elansa would have imagined Kerin the least of all of them. The loudest in his complaint, though, was Arawn, who said to Bruin and Swain and anyone who would heed that he would have set out hunting sooner than Brand had roused himself to do. If the thing had been up to him, when they'd had to move out, they'd have had better to eat on the way.

This he said, and other things, and Elansa heard it all, slipping careful looks at Brand as she walked. She thought of Kethrenan and his warriors. She thought that such talk as this would have gotten a Qualinesti soldier so severely disciplined he'd be wondering whether he needed to find another profession. Brand, however, let the talk go, though it wasn't to be imagined he didn't hear it. So close to him did she walk that Elansa saw the muscles tighten in his neck when Arawn questioned him. She saw the bristling of his beard as his jaw clenched.

Walking and taking great care not to stumble so she would not be kicked back to her feet, she wondered why Brand held his peace.

"It's not a weakness," Char said quietly when they'd stopped to rest. The day had not passed, only some hours, and this moment to be still would not last long. "It's not that. It's a kind of strength. Arawn knows that. Or so far, he does."

Elansa eyed him keenly, the dwarf who seemed to know all these men and their various tales: Chaser the orphan, Kerin who lost his teeth in a fight with a troll—"Proof the boy's not too bright"—Dell who became an outlaw because she would not become a whore, and the tale of Ley and Tianna. There were other stories to tell, and he knew them all, often drunk in the shadows and hearing things people wouldn't have imagined he'd had a dry wit to understand or recall.

She thought, watching the dwarf now, that he would tell the tale of Arawn and Brand, and she would understand why this outlaw lord tolerated what he did. But Char only said it was time to get going again, and she should take good care not to lag behind Brand.

On the next day, they learned the weapons cache was empty, and the men began to mutter about the loss of their hoard. It had not been stolen by ogres. The place was clean, no sign of their filth. Not even a rag of the oil-soaked cloths meant to protect the steel from rust remained—only the faint scent of the oil and the wet wool. Further, they saw that the way out of the mountain had been blocked by a tumble of stone, the dust of the fall still gritty and fresh on the floor of the cave.

"Our treasure," Swain called it. Nigh-toothless Kerin agreed that the gleaming swords and fine axes had been the due of them all, now stolen. Chaser nodded but said nothing aloud. The one Elansa had expected to complain was silent.

Arawn stood quiet on the outside of things, watching. He did not watch the grumblers or even seem to care about the plundered cache. He stood with his hand on the jeweled grip of Kethrenan's sword and watched Elansa. She felt his eyes on her, and Brand's. She was again held in tension between two men.

A long moment she stood so, breath held.

"You," Brand said, his voice hard and sharp.

He meant her. She fell in beside him, keeping pace with him as they left the cave and never lagging behind. They walked many long hours, and not even Arawn complained about this. Their cache had been discovered, their way out blocked. It might be chance, a goblin's luck to find the cache while sheltering against the cold. But he was no fool, Brand, and so he sat a while with Char and Ley. They discussed the next closest way out to good hunting, then he sent Dell, Tianna, Loris, and Pragol ahead to be sure the rest of the caches were secure. A meeting place set, the four slipped away into the darkness, soon parting from each other.

"He doesn't send Arawn," Elansa said to Char.

The dwarf shook his head, his lips set in a grim line.

He said nothing, though he had the look of one who knew the answer to her implied question. He would not give it, though, or even look at her as they walked.

It was not until they grew too weary to go on that Brand let his band stop for the night. During that night, he grew impatient of crossing glances with Arawn. So that he would not have to cross swords, he settled the matter of the disposition of his captive. In the ruddy light of failing fires, he called Elansa to him and nodded to the place apart where he'd spread his sleeping fur.

"Your choice," he said. "Me, or Arawn. And when he can't hold you, soon all the rest."

Slowly, like a draining, the feeling went out of her body. She did not turn cold. She did not flush with shame. It was as though all sensation had fled, or perhaps she had herself flown from that complicated structure of flesh and bone and blood that was her body. She did not feel her heart beating, and when she noticed that, she wondered whether it were turning to stone.

Behind her, voices went still. A hound growled somewhere, then fell quiet. In that perfect silence she heard two things: the sound Char's leather bottle made as he unstopped it, and the long breath in-drawn he always took when he was about to enjoy himself for a time. The breath, though, the breath taken was not Char's. Brand took it in the moment he knew he was going to be able to make his point to Arawn easily and, doubtless, pleasurably.

In the silence, she went to him, for no matter what he said about it, Brand had given her no choice at all. When he told her to, she undressed. Perhaps she shivered in the cold, but she didn't feel either thing, the cold or the shivering. When he gestured, she lay down, and when he touched her, his hands callused and rough, she did not protest or fight him. She would not give the watchers beyond so much as that. She lay silent beneath him. She let him make his case to his outlaws and make her off-limits to them. She was, in the end, grateful for one thing. She was grateful he didn't kiss her or even try to.

Chapter 10

A red-tailed hawk screeched across the sky, the sound the first thing Kethrenan heard waking. He lay watching the rosy gray, the cloudless sky, waiting. He lay, breath held, for that is just what hunters do, even when prey is so far away no breath of theirs can be heard.

He knew how to wait, did the prince. He knew how to watch for a bird in the sky. No good to lie with his eyes darting all about. You miss the motion then. You miss what you're looking for. He lay still, and he became aware of a similar stillness across the camp-fire—Demlin, on his back, watching for the hawk.

They were good hunters, the two. It was a thing the prince hadn't known about his servant. Until lately, he'd known Demlin to be a good pourer of wine and a good man to pick the right clothing for a state dinner. He'd known him to be a congenial fellow and conscientious. He'd not made him part of Elansa's escort, all those months ago in autumn, for his battle skills. There had been warriors for that. He'd included Demlin in the party so his wife could have someone of the court to talk to on her way, someone witty and amusing.

Events had turned the courtly servitor into a hunter, hard-eyed, keen to kill, and with the wit to know that he who keeps still has a good chance at the prey that will soon walk past him.

The hawk sailed in the high gray sky, wings spread to catch the currents, tilting a little, circling, then climbing.

Queen of her skies, she sailed and paid no attention to the elves on the ground. What were they to her? Nothing. She sailed out of sight, rounding away.

Demlin let his breath go. He got to his feet and went around the fire to where the goblin lay curled in a ball against the cold air. He toed Ithk. The goblin had not been sleeping. All the while he'd lain watching the hawk, Kethrenan had known that because he knew what it sounded like when Ithk slept. That was a noisy undertaking.

"Up," Demlin said, toeing the goblin again.

Ithk whined, and he whimpered. Poking up the embers of the night's fire, Kethrenan thought that if he never heard another goblin's whining voice, he'd be a happy man.

"Let him eat, Demlin," he said, "and see he's quick about it.

They had a way to ride today, south toward the last point on Ithk's map of caches. By now, he knew Lea's bands had emptied all the others and sealed the entrances. By now Brand would know it, for these were his ways out, and no one could live underground forever without coming up for food. He would find one way sealed, and he would perhaps find another. He would soon learn the rest when he sent men to see for themselves. He would know he dared not range the northern part of his territory now. He would know—he was no fool—he must go south.

Kethrenan grinned, as wolves do. He would know himself hunted, and he would not know who hunted him, which of his enemies, the hob or the elven prince.

For a moment, the thought gave him pause. It always did when he wondered how Elansa would fare if Brand guessed the face of his hunter.

"They will keep her for hostage, my prince."

Kethrenan looked up. Not only had Demlin become a good hunter, he'd become an uncanny diviner of his master's thoughts. Long face pale, never scrubbed to color by the wind, maimed Demlin nodded.

"She's his shield, my prince. He won't throw her away."

And why, after all, should it be strange that Demlin could know his thought? Maimed Demlin, Demlin the sudden hunter . . . he and his master shared the same will. Why not the same thoughts?

Beyond the fire, Ithk gnawed on the cold leg of a lean hare. Hunched against the cold, his bear-headed fur over his shoulders, his eyes darted from one to the other, master and servant. He said nothing though. He sat very still. Perhaps he was thinking, but Kethrenan doubted that. Goblins were not known for thinking.

*　*　*　*　*

Brand's outlaws made a dark wandering now, for reports had come back to Brand that the three caches that ran in a line—like the base of a triangle—were plundered, the ways in and out from them stopped with stone.

"It might be goblin-work," Dell said. "Someone knows where they are, Brand. You know Gnash was ready to steal the hoard when we got it. Might be him."

A little, for a moment, Elansa's heart stirred, warming to hope. Perhaps this was the work of the hob, perhaps the work of someone else. Perhaps a prince was taking back what was stolen. Swiftly, she killed the hope and begged gods to protect her from ever showing it again. She feared that if Brand suspected Kethrenan was responsible for this, he'd kill her.

What would they do? Dell asked it. Tianna did. Others wondered, and the tide of their voices was an anxious one.

"We go south," Brand said as he got to his feet. He commanded the camp struck, then called Char and Leyerlain to him. They conferred for a space, the elf arguing some point Brand wasn't granting, the dwarf silent. Rolling the sleeping furs, which now she carried, her unwanted bed on her back, Elansa heard them. The goal was to find a place to hunt and to go on from there.

"We go south," Brand said when others asked. "Before anything, we find food."

It was the right thing to say, for if they were not hungry, they were weary of jerky. She might have learned more, once in the time before she became Brand's bed companion. She might have learned from Char what Brand's idea was for going south. He used to tell her things, but he never looked at her now but over the lip of his bottle, never with anything but great contempt.

She had not looked to him for that. The dwarf had treated her with a rough and grudging kindness sometimes. In the absence of it, she realized, she had wrongly thought of him as a potential ally.

"Ah, he's finally pickled his wits," Dell said, seeing what Elansa did. "Don't worry about him. One night he'll make enough noise sleeping that someone'll slip a blade between his ribs to shut him up."

She did not say so to jest.

Elansa was becoming used to the stillness of lying in the darkness, Brand's body between her and the others, listening to the sounds of others sleeping—the small whimpers, the sighs, the groaning. One wept in his nightmares, not always, but sometimes, and he was the dwarf Char. Usually a quiet sleeper, now he was like a disturbed ghost, moaning. Most of the outlaws granted him the grace of acting as though they didn't know or hear or see his night-hauntings. It was a courtesy among those who must sleep back to back and walk side by side.

One did not grant the grace, and he was Arawn. He watched the dwarf, a cold, reasoning look on him.

* * * * *

"Up!" cried Brand, his voice almost cheerful. "Up! Let's go! We'll be hunting supper soon."

Though he'd spoken more from hope than certainty, he was not wrong. That day, Char, always the guide in the darkness, found a way out the outlaws had never mapped—an easy way, a smooth slope and uncomplicated by twists or turns.

The hour was early, night only lately faded from the sky. Still, this much light was more than she'd seen in a long while, and it dazzled. A breeze touched her skin, and Elansa watched as three archers left the mountain, running downslope and bounding like spring goats let out from the dark confines of winter's byre. Among them was Brand, and they were not long away, for this was a good time for hunters. It was Brand himself who brought back the two small lambs, neat-footed offspring of wild mountain sheep. He carried them back up the hill, one slung over each shoulder, to the cheers and laughter of his men.

Seeing him, Elansa shuddered, for he reminded her of the ogres. They went past her, hunters with long strides and bellies soon to be filled with good food. She stood a moment, looking out, her hand upon stone. She was startled by the wild wide stretch of the world without. How far the borders of that outer region, where the horizon bound the stony waste to the sky never-ending?

In the brightening sky, something moved, something wide-winged and dark. It sailed in circles, drifting low, soaring and circling again. The freedom of it took her breath, the simple ability to change direction, to form a will and carry it out. In her, tears rose. She refused them and refused to feel the tightening of her throat. These things she never allowed herself. These things she did not risk, for to allow one feeling was to allow another, and another, and soon there would be others she could not permit. Instead, she treasured her numbness, almost calling it holy.

She lifted her arms as though they were wings, unknowing, unaware of what she did.

A hard hand took her wrist and turned her. Brand pulled her close, and she saw his eyes were alight with the triumph of the hunt. He smelled like the wind, like the wider spaces he had run in. He took her chin in his hand, but not in rough grip. A little his fingers moved against her neck, a caress. She did not turn, and she tried not to see him, though she looked right at him.

"Come inside," he said, and his mood was good. The command sounded more like a request.

It was, of course, no such thing. He took her to his stony bed while others went out to find wood for fires and cleaned and cooked the kill. He did not command her to undress. He did that for her himself, slipping her torn blouse over her head and taking off her ragged trousers. When he moved to take off her broken boots, she stopped him and did it herself. They had been of finest make, good riding gear once . . . she would not think of that or feel his hands on her. Still, she noticed he was not so peremptory this time. It was not a matter of satisfying himself or underscoring his authority with his men.

He touched her gently, and once, his lips against her neck, his beard on her breast, he said, "I saw you try to fly."

He sounded amused but not angry.

She dared not respond to that, the care he took to be easy with her or his amusement. She lay beneath him as she always did. She let him do what he willed, as she always did. Once she wished she could kill him, but even that she did not allow for long. She must not feel, not even that.

When he was finished, he turned away from her. He didn't sleep. He lay staring at her. She closed her eyes, but neither did she sleep. She listened to the outlaws, the mingled voices of women and men. She smelled the blood of lambs, the sudden sharp bite of Char's dwarf spirits, and smoke and leather and unwashed bodies. When she opened her eyes at last, she saw Brand had a pouch in his hand, the one that hung always from his belt. He jogged it a little, and something rang within.

Her eyes grew wide, and her pulse raced suddenly. It was her stolen phoenix! Her Blue Phoenix! When had the thought of it, the memory of its magic, been chased from her heart? Almost as soon as she'd been taken. Almost the very day she had entered this wretched captivity. She had been hemmed by need on every side, the hundred needs of survival, and they had crowded out all else, narrowing her. Thoughts of her phoenix, the magic and the beauty, had long ago flown out of that constricted existence.

"You remember it," he said.

Elansa swallowed, trying to find her voice. "I do."

Brand uncinched the pouch. He spilled the silver links of chain into his hand and tumbled the sapphire phoenix atop them all. How lovely it was! Firelight gleamed on the sapphire, the whole stone shaped by gods, never by the hand of a mortal. He looked at it for a long moment.

She remembered how she'd noted that none of the outlaws had spoken of the hobgoblin's fire-staff but in low whispers, their voices shrouded in superstition. What would Brand's reaction be if he knew the true worth of the sapphire?

Brand slipped the silver chain over his head. The look he gave her as he did this was a complicated one, but Elansa had been long away from her feelings. She could not intuit a meaning.

* * * * *

To the surprise of his men, Brand did not head for the last cache, though they did go south. Whenever they would stop he consulted with Char, quietly in corners. They had a plan between them, the dwarf and the human. They were long-time schemers, these two who had arranged a plot to steal a princess.

"Put it to you this way," Brand said to all of them gathered. "Someone's found our caches. Someone's blocked our ways out. I'm thinking whoever it is knows where all the hiding places are, and he's expecting us to run to the last."

The outlaws muttered.

Ley lifted his head, a sharp gleam in his long elven eyes, and said, "I expect even Nigh-toothless Kerin has better sense than that."

They laughed, even Nigh-toothless Kerin who'd had the bad sense to fight with a troll. The mood among them eased.

"Even Kerin," Brand agreed. "So we're gonna be keen witted. We're going south. North or east doesn't seem like a good idea, and west is out of the mountain. I like it better in here." He waited for them to murmur and mutter and sort their own agreement out among themselves. "South for us, and something good and grand."

They liked the sound of that, all of them. Even Arawn. Yet it wasn't long before Arawn's mood changed. A day of walking, a short night of rest, another day of walking, and his became the voice most often heard on the way through the torchlit gloom.

"A mile above is like three below," he said at the start of another day's march. "Be getting tired of it now. Tired." When he said that he looked not at Brand. He stared right at Char as though the distance were the dwarf's fault—a turn missed, a road mistaken.

Char slid Brand a glance, and Brand nodded. When Elansa looked back along the line she saw Dell's head up, her hand upon the hilt of the sword at her hip. The tall woman was but a dark form in the darkness, yet Elansa knew that if she could see Dell's face she'd see it shaped into lines of wariness.

"Come on," Char said, his tone heartier than it had been, almost encouraging. "The way gets longer the more we linger."

The voices of the outlaws welled in the cavern, mingling with the whisper and hiss of torches. Elansa thought some of those voices had more of Arawn's mood in them today—discontented and restless. It was not the same kind of restiveness she'd sensed in Tianna on the day they saw the ogres. This had more discontent in it, a dangerous edge. She was not alone in sensing this. Brand went like a hound who'd caught a bear's scent, head up and keen.

They had a practiced order for marching: Char and Brand in front, Elansa right behind. Dell kept the rear. Her eyes were no better than any human's, but she had a sense of hearing as keen as a cat's. The others had places between, and Fang and the hounds ranged freely up and down the line. They made good time, for the way was smooth for a long while, the ceilings high and the walls wide. The torch bearers kept their fire high, the flickering glow illuminating a floor that seemed to have been worked not by nature but by craft. This didn't last long. Char took a turn into a narrower passage, one that required him to bend low.

"Down," he called back, bending at the waist.

His companions dropped to all fours, Elansa among them. She crawled on stone, scraping her hands and leaving behind little prints of blood. Behind her, men cursed, Arawn the loudest, and Char's voice came back in scornful challenge.

"Come on, ya' whining babies. It's not that far!"

Knee to hand, knee to hand, they followed, some bleeding, most cursing, until at last they could stand again, stretching cramped muscles and wiping blood on the sides of their trousers.

Brand stood at the entrance to the taller passage and watched each man pass him. To every man he had a low word to say, sometimes a joke, sometimes commiseration, sometimes praise.

Elansa, standing to the side, saw each one of them respond. Even Arawn responded when Brand nudged him and said, "Up on your feet now, Arawn, before we mistake you for a dwarf."

The sullen lines of Arawn's expression eased a little, and he crooked a grudging grin.

They have traded such, the joke and the grin, before, Elansa thought. Why, at some time they must have been good friends.

Following Char, they went into caverns where wind moaned like ghosts, and into others in which the air didn't stir at all. These last, Elansa liked least. Their stillness was like something trying to steal her breath.

Through all the winding ways, though the humans lost all sense of direction and time passing, Char assured them he knew not only the way south, he knew the hour and time of day. And true enough it was that he was able to predict the flight of bats out from a cavern at sunset, the rush of their return at night's end, and this when not even the grayest gleam of light could be found. He knew all the passages and tunnels as though he'd played in them since childhood.

"Come ahead," the dwarf said, when weary men lagged. "I'm thinkin' it's time we got some water for the bottles, eh?"

"Water?" Arawn laughed. "And where will you find that for us, dwarf? Know a pretty little glade we can lay ourselves down in while the water runs by the banks?" His voiced dropped into bitterly cold regions. "Or maybe a fountain springing dwarf spirits to lull you to sweet dreaming sleep?"

Silence settled all in the darkness, a crawling unease. With the suddenness of wind lifting, the murmur of voices swelled, louder it seemed, and undercurrents of fear ran beneath.

Arawn snickered. Dell, coming up from the rear of the line, stood tall between the dwarf and his heckler. With a chill, Elansa realized some line was being drawn upon which the outlaw band was invited to choose position—Arawn on one side, Char, Dell, and Brand on the other. Feet shuffled again, and the band began to separate, to choose.

"Enough," Brand snapped.

No one moved. All along the line the murmuring fell still, yet the tension didn't ease. Unvoiced questions hung in the air. The choice that Dell meant to force breathed like something hidden in shadows, alive yet unseen.

Char stepped away from Dell and turned from Brand. "Y' can all stand around here if y' want," he said. His tone said he was not warmed by Dell's show of support, or Brand's. "Or y' can follow. Up to you."

Dell moved back down the line to take up the rear guard. In silence, Brand and Elansa followed Char. One by one, the others fell in behind, some with a will, others uneasy now where only an hour before they had trusted.

A countless time of walking later, the dwarf stopped. Not looking around, he said to Elansa, "Lift the torch higher."

She did, illuminating what lay ahead. Like a small doorway, one all but Char would have to stoop to pass, the opening looked into a vast hall, wider and higher than the cavern under Hammer Rock. Soft, silvery illumination filled the opening, and beams of light shot down from high above.

"There are openings," Char said, "so high up you can only see the shafts of light but never the gaps in the stone roof. It comes down very far, that light, and that's why it's so pale."

Doubtless that light would indeed seem pale when compared with the light of the outer world, yet it seemed glaring in this place where utter darkness reigned. Squinting against it, Elansa lowered the flaring torch. Over Char's head, she saw a wonder beyond.

From the ceiling hung stalactites, some as thick as a human's chest, others as fragile as the first icicle of winter. Up from the ground a forest of stalagmites reached, some not as high as Elansa's shoulder, others so tall they touched the distant ceiling, making arches through which the outlaws could pass. Looking to the left, she saw, far along the wall, an opening to match the one behind. Another series of tunnels and passages ran behind that second entrance.

"The Hall of Reorx," Char said, his voice low with reverence as he spoke his god's name.

"Is it?" she asked. "Did the god make this?" Elansa looked at him curiously. "Is there lore among the dwarves about this place?"

Behind them others pressed. Elansa and the dwarf moved forward into the hall and out of the way.

"No," Char said. "No lore."

He walked ahead. She followed, and the light

pouring down from above showed a floor that sloped gradually down in one smooth flow, as though a god had indeed crafted this place, shaping and burnishing the stone. Moisture glistened on the walls, on the stalactites and stalagmites, and this caught the light and enhanced it. Elansa saw glimpses of color in the stone—blue and red and pearly white, striations of black and green . . .

Char cocked his head, looking at her keenly. He seemed to relent, a little, of whatever grudge he'd conceived against her.

"No lore, but y' can't think a god didn't have a hand in this."

She could not, and it seemed that those who followed, godless though they claimed to be, could ascribe the work to no mortal hand or even the craft of time. They trod carefully, following Char and Elansa. None remained untouched by the beauty around them, this place that made their old robber den seem like a fox's hole. One after another—even sullen Arawn—spoke oaths whose meaning till now had never been felt.

By the gods' good grace . . .

In the name of Reorx . . .

By Paladine's shining glance, have you ever seen the like of this?

Elansa took a deep breath of cool air. Breathing, she tasted water. Somewhere a stream ran, chuckling over stone.

"I hear water, Char, and you promised us we could fill the bottles fat."

In the crowd, Arawn muttered something, his voice twisted and sour.

Like a whip-crack, Dell snapped, "Shut up and keep moving."

If Arawn said more, Elansa didn't hear it. Char had stopped between two columns of stone, thick stalactites reaching nearly to the floor.

"Look," he said.

Breathless, she stood at the edge of a series of stairs winding down. And these were stairs, not the chance shaping of time and rivers. Someone had made these steps. Someone had carved them, as steps had been carved in the robber den, but these were broad and shallow. They reminded Elansa of the gracious flow of steps leading into Solostaran's banquet hall. At the foot of the stairs ran a broad silver stream, its voice magnified by echoes.

Impulse took Elansa, and she ran down the steps as though she were traipsing into the elf king's feasthall, a princess bejeweled and silken gowned. She paused, she turned, and in the dim light on one of the risers, she saw the mark of a lily such as is found in some corners of the Tower of the Sun. Craft, indeed! With good cause did these steps remind her of home. That mark alone suggested the maker of these had done work in the Tower of the Sun a long time ago.

Others followed, and Brand came last. She bent to the water and then knelt on the stone. Making a cup of her hands, she scooped up an icy drink, the water so cold it hurt her teeth. Nonetheless, she drank her handful and then another. She splashed her face and neck and looked around longingly, sighing for a place to wash off the stink of long days and nights unbathed.

She turned, for she felt the touch of familiar eyes on her. Brand looked at her, his head back like a man considering. "If you want," he said, "I could—"

She stood and walked past him, but she never looked at him. If she wanted, he could arrange for her to bathe. He could find her a private place. She knew those words were on his lips, and she knew the bath would not have been so private as she'd liked. He would be there, guard or company in the water.

As she brushed past him, she heard him say, "It would have been what you wanted."

Later, when she thought about those words, later with him asleep beside her and the light of campfires gleaming on the links of the chain that held her Blue Phoenix, she lifted a hand to touch it. Ah, lightly, lightly, she didn't want to wake him.

It quickened to her touch, her lovely Blue Phoenix. She was to have banished a blight with the help of the magic in this talisman. She was to have healed trees in Bianost and made them whole again. The sapphire pulsed just beneath her fingertips. Brand stirred, sighing in his sleep. His face eased a little, the hard lines of it softening.

She wondered if he felt the magic in the stone.

He turned onto his side, his face hidden.

Chapter 11

~

Elansa felt Brand's eyes on her everywhere she went. They tracked, they followed, and when she turned or lifted her head to look at him, he did not look away. He was thinking about her, and she knew he was weighing something, perhaps her fate. He watched her eat, and she did not challenge. She drank from the stream, slipped away into the privy place, and came back. He watched her leave, he watched her return, and she did not challenge.

Elansa pressed her back to cold stone and rested her head against the wall. Brand stood talking to Char, the two a little apart from the others. The dwarf gestured, sometimes broadly, sometimes subtly.

Quiet as a shadow, Tianna dropped down to sit beside her. She took a broad-bladed dagger from her belt and a whetstone from a little leather pouch. In silence, she made stone and steel sing, honing the weapon. Little sparks flew, dancing in the dim light. She lifted the blade, touched it lightly with her finger, and found it keen. She turned it and, not looking up, said, "What are they talking about?"

The question surprised her. Elansa shrugged. "I'd be the last to know."

At this, the half-elf looked up. "You should be the first. You sleep with him."

Elansa watched the sparks fly. "Not by choice. There is no pillow talk, Tianna. There is only . . ." She shook her head. There was only command. "You had a better chance for that than I will or want."

Elansa studied her face. Tianna had a lovely face. Her lips were wide, and her eyes were not so long as an elf's but lovelier than a human's. She had bathed, somewhere in privacy, as did Dell. They could. They had long ago let their male companions know how they would enforce their privacy. And so her hair, clean and shining, was the brightest thing not afire in the cavern. She wore it in a thick braid, and a widow's peak framed her brow.

Tianna looked up, and her long eyes gleamed with humor. "He can be a good lover," she said, low. "I didn't get tired of that."

Elansa ventured a question. "What did you get tired of?"

Tianna looked around, at Brand and Char in their animated conversation, at Swain and Ballu and Chaser rolling the bones, at Dell sleeping and Arawn brooding. Her glance swept past Nigh-toothless Kerin, Pragol, Loris, and Bruin, whose hair was the same color as a wolf's pelt. She looked at her father, the elf who spoke very little and not to many of his companions.

She said, "I'm tired of this. Tired of moving and tired of all these men." She sighted along the edge of her dagger, the tip of it glittering. "I won't be leaving him now. There is too much shifting and change in the air. One of us goes, and it could all come down."

"Arawn would like that."

"He acts like he would. No matter. I'm here for now. When we get where we're going . . ." She shook her head. "Brand'll be getting where he's going. Me, I'll just be going."

They sat a moment. Chaser crowed in triumph, and Swain grumbled about ill luck.

The silence settled in again. Tianna slid Elansa one swift sidelong glance and whispered, "You'll want to keep an eye on me, princess."

Elansa understood that the words weren't warning but suggestion. Tianna got to her feet and strode away. Elansa, for months a prisoner, had grown used to living as a captive. She knew how to keep her feelings close. As though the half-elf had said nothing at all, she settled back against the wall, feeling the cool damp stone against her shoulders.

She looked around her. A grander cavern, still this little forest of stone was a robber's den. For this time, these brief hours of rest, the outlaws had fallen into old patterns—gambling, sleeping, and quarreling. She knew all their voices. She could pick them out with her eyes closed. She heard them each night in her sleep. She stretched out her legs and stretched her arms up high. She was cold and cramped and weary. The light shafting down from some high crack in the stone ceiling grew fainter, paler. Day was ending. Perhaps moonlight would soon reach down here.

Ah, for the smell of the outside air, the freshness of a quickening breeze! She thought of the red-tailed hawk, winged and free. Secretly, behind the mask of her face, she thought of Tianna's words. *Keep an eye on me, princess.* They sounded like wind in the sky. They sounded like hope.

She felt his eyes on her—Brand's keen glance. Wrapped in her cloak, as much against his regard as against cold, Elansa lay down with her back to the wall. As she had long ago learned to do, she slept, but she didn't sleep peacefully. For the first time since her capture, Elansa dreamed.

She dreamed about being watched. Eyes were upon her—Brand's brown eyes, weighing her, judging her. She dreamed she did not suffer that. She dreamed she allowed it, and in her dream, she looked into those eyes and spoke as a princess speaks, in the full confidence that her station was her shield, her rank her defense against all who would harm her. She was, after all, an elf among these half-savage outlaws, a princess of the royal house of Qualinesti.

She said, "Look, Brand, as deeply as you dare, and see if I am afraid of you."

In her dream, she was not.

*   *   *   *   *

Elansa felt the shadow of the hand before she felt the flesh and bone. Cool, sliding over her flesh, she felt the shadow gliding. Her heart slammed up into her throat. She stiffened and jerked away. Too late! A hard, callused palm clamped across her mouth, another grasped her wrists, her two slender wrists in one broad-handed clasp, prisoned as though by ropes again.

Elansa's blood pounded in her temples. It seemed the whole dark world beat to the rhythm of her sudden terror. Her breath snagged in her throat, pressed back by the hand across her mouth, and she struggled, trying to find flesh to bite. Her teeth came down upon the pads of the palm. Her captor grunted, and she tasted blood even as he gripped harder. Eyes wide, she saw in the pale moonlight the flaring red outline of a man bent over her. By that dim light she saw his eyes, wide and white, and his mouth opening. His breath reeked of spiced jerky, and he stank of sweat and smoke.

"Hush," he whispered.

Brand.

A little, Elansa relaxed. Her muscles eased, the tension drained.

Brand's grip on her hands loosened. In one swift motion he pulled her to her feet. "Quiet, and come with me."

Shaking and wrapping her cloak around her shoulders against the chill of the underground, she stood in barely broken darkness. Faint light suffused the cavern—the light of the two moons gone pale for all the dark distance it had to travel to find them. Brand stood close, his beard bristling against her face.

"Come," he said, and his breath touched her cheek.

She heard no threat, no danger in his voice. He turned, assuming obedience. Following, Elansa walked carefully past the sleeping forms of Brand's outlaws. Char and Fang, master and hound, each twitched in sleep. Passing those two, she smelled the scents of hound and dwarf spirits all tangled up. She walked around Dell in her corner. Arawn and the others were hunched and unmoving as stone. Four were missing. She saw them in the distance, darker forms against the darkness, standing watch near the entrances to this stony forest.

Elansa looked across the stream to the stony wall, at all the pillars built up over centuries uncounted, minerals dripping down from the roof to form accretions on the floor, age after age growing tall until this wonderful forest of stone lived beneath the earth, illuminated by thin shafts of moonlight and pale blades of sunlight. This was the work of gods, or the work of the world itself. Yet here in this wonderful place someone had

fashioned steps, the breadth and height carefully measured, the stone beautifully smoothed and polished, and
her feet knew those steps as well as she knew those in
the elf king's hall.

Elansa and Brand walked to the water, right to the
edge of the stone where the stream was noisiest. When
he stood farthest from his men, Brand put his back to
the water and turned to face her.

"Now, tell me something," he said. Here fell a broad-
er shaft of mingled moonlight, so she saw how bright
his eyes were. "Tell me what you know about Pax
Tharkas."

"Pax—"

"Hush!"

He warned even as she heard her own voice begin to
echo. Behind them, someone stirred, then stilled. Over
her shoulder she saw Swain at one of the entrances turn
his head, then turn back to his watch.

"Pax Tharkas," she whispered. "I know much about
it, or what it used to be. Why? Hasn't Leyerlain told you
about it?"

"Never cared about it till lately. Tell me what you
know."

Curiosity pricking her, she said, "Pax Tharkas has
long tales attached to it. In the library at Qualinost we
have a whole room devoted to the histories of the place.
Our greatest king commissioned the building of it—"

"Kith-Kanan."

"Yes," she said, surprised to hear that name on
human lips.

Brand shrugged. "In the Stonelands, you hear
things." He cocked a curious eye. "You kin to him?"

Coolly, she murmured, "No. My husband is

Kethrenan Kanan, and he is kin to the ancient king."

But his attention had wandered. He was not impressed. "Ah, well, married to kingly kin, that's not so bad." Again, he quickened, his eyes glinting with barely suppressed eagerness as he returned to what most interested him. "Now. Pax Tharkas. Tell me."

Low in the air of the cave, torch smoke drifted through the faint beams of moonlight that arrowed down from a ceiling they could not see. Two hounds growled over a bone. Char dreamed again.

"Pax Tharkas was, a long time ago, a monument to friendship between elves and dwarves and humans."

She looked past him, to the black-and-silver stream running, and warmed to her story, telling him that for a thousand years and half a thousand more the fortress whose name means Peace of Friendship stood inviolate, guarding all the land about in three kingdoms. The rich Tharkadan Iron Mines were there, safe behind the great walls and guarded by the two tall towers. From there came the iron and steel that had, before the treaty, been the cause of wars between dwarves and elves and humans. With the treaty and the building of the fortress to seal it, trading pacts were made, and wars became the stuff of history.

Then came the Cataclysm and the withdrawal of the gods from Krynn, the withdrawal of the elves to Qualinost and the dwarves to Thorbardin, the scattering of the humans. . . .

In those hard times, the very face of Krynn was remade. Seas shoved out of their basins, and the climate across the face of the world changed. In the ensuing years, kingdoms fell like toppled sand castles, and the wealthy became poor, and poor people became desperate. Pax Tharkas became the sole property of the mountain dwarves, the far western outpost of Thorbardin manned by clans grown suspicious of outsiders. Old alliances fell to dust, old treaties were forgotten, and the names of old friends went unspoken as the elves of Qualinesti and the dwarves of Thorbardin grew eager to turn inward where the godless could not come.

"Pax Tharkas was many long years in the making, and few deny it is the finest craft of dwarven hands," Elansa said. "It's built astride a south-running mountain pass, an enormous fortress of stone with two tall towers and an outer wall no enemy has ever breached. Kith-Kanan, the first king of the Qualinesti, our first Speaker of the Sun, is buried there in a fine crypt, and his Royal Guard lies near."

"Have you ever seen it?" Brand asked.

"The crypt in the Hall of the Ancients? No. No one alive has. It's guarded by dire magic. And I've never seen Pax Tharkas itself." Her voice dropped low. "But I think we are near Pax Tharkas."

Brand's eyes lit with amusement. "What makes you say that?"

She pointed to the step upon which they stood. "Dwarf-made, don't you agree?"

He didn't disagree. How could he? He'd spent years in the outlands of Thorbardin. The mark of dwarves was everywhere to be found and not in the least noted in the ancient stonework in the robber-hall under Hammer Rock. Cunningly worked columns lay shattered beneath the ledge where his men had long kept watch, as though some great temple had once stood, then fallen. If one didn't see mountain dwarves much outside Thorbardin, one often saw the ancient work of their hands.

Elansa took his silence for agreement. "I believe the dwarf who made these steps must have been in the Tower of the Sun. I'm sure he saw the steps these mirror. This work is ancient, and so are the steps in Qualinost. He was, I think, one of the designers of Pax Tharkas."

Brand snorted. "A step's a step."

She bent to one knee, tracing her fingers along the riser until she felt the mark that made her case. "Look." She lifted her head and looked into his eyes. "Put your hand here and see the proof of what I say."

He bent, and she guided his hand toward the mark she wanted him to feel. So close to him that she felt his breath on her cheek, she knew his surprise when he touched and traced the lily-mark.

"That is the mark a dwarf made upon those steps in the Tower of the Sun, in the feast hall, and that hall was commissioned by a woman whose name, in Elvish, means Lily of the Night. Why would her sigil be here in this place if the maker of these steps hadn't had to do with Qualinost and Ashanlilana, the Lily of the Night?"

"An elven queen," he said, "marked there and marked here."

Color rose to Elansa's cheek. Ashanlilana hadn't been a queen in Qualinost, though for a time she had been queen in the king's bed. The Lily of the Night had managed no official status for herself, though her mark, her lily, remained in several chambers of the ancient Tower of the Sun—on tiles, stair risers, and in bas-relief on two of the colonnades that led out from the tower and into the royal family's private gardens. She had, in her time, had great influence on the heart of the king.

"Tell me this," Brand said, pulling her to her feet, "who lives in Pax Tharkas now?"

"Why, no one." Did these humans know nothing? Did they roam between the Tower of the Sun and Pax Tharkas as though they'd been dropped down into foreign lands? "No one lives there. The dwarves held on to it for nearly a century after the Cataclysm, but they lost it during the Dwarfgate War. Now the only things living there are ravens and wolves and rats and—"

"Ghosts. You call it Pax Tharkas, and dwarves do. The rest of us call it the Fortress of Ghosts."

That was a dark enough name for a place meant to stand as a monument to friendship, but it wasn't the name that made her draw in her breath. Sudden understanding and wonder filled her, and she looked over her shoulder to the place where she saw Char and his hound.

"He led us all this way, so close to Pax Tharkas, with no sight of sun or moons or stars."

"He's a good guide when he's not drinking. None better in the hills around or even here in the belly of Krynn."

"I don't doubt he is. Arawn doesn't seem to agree."

"Arawn's a fool," Brand said. "He's looking for trouble, but Char won't give it to him."

"Why do you keep him?"

"Arawn or Char?" He shrugged. "We're long-time friends, me and Arawn. Me and Char, too. They have their faults. One drinks a bit, the other . . . he has a hard time with things sometimes. Arawn doesn't like it when things change. Makes him feel like he's got to shove up against me to prove who he is." Brand combed his fingers through his thick beard, and his lips quirked in a mirthless smile. "I won't kill him unless he makes me."

The moment had an odd clarity, a strange stillness, and Elansa realized that the observation Brand had just made might have been one Kethrenan might have made. Not couched so roughly, but they knew their men, these two. They knew what moved them, how far to push them, and when to stop.

Caught in the disjointed moment when she saw her husband and her captor in a similar light, she spoke with perhaps more softness than she had in months. She said, "Brand, why are you going to Pax Tharkas?"

He scratched his beard. Head cocked, he looked at her, deciding if he should say. In the stillness, she saw the gleam of silver around his neck, the glinting of the sapphire phoenix on his chest. He reached to touch it, the god-figure, and Elansa thought, He doesn't know what he's touching. He doesn't feel the magic.

"Do you know the Notch?"

How could he ask?

"Sometimes I used to stay with the farmer and his family," Brand said. "I liked their daughter. She liked me for a time. They were friends. They'd feed me when I needed it, shelter me if I wanted that. I gave them things—sometimes steel, sometimes just a brace of hares. It was a good place to be, a little fastness in the border to keep them."

But it hadn't kept them. It had burned, tumbled down, and been deserted. Elansa had seen it.

"What happened to them?" she asked.

Brand's eyes narrowed, and his hand fell from the phoenix. "Got raided."

"Goblins?"

Whatever warmth she'd seen in Brand's expression was gone.

"No," he said, and his eyes touched her, cold. "Elves. Too close to your precious border, that farm. They took a deer or two, hare or pheasant when they could without going too far in. Took too much." He jerked his head. "The little fastness couldn't stand against your husband's will. And I moved on, back and forth, building me a feud with goblins. But I remembered them and their little stone fastness that stood true against all but an elf prince. I thought I'd find a fastness of stone for myself. One that would stand against anyone. I'd sit there in the mountain, stash weapons all over the inside of this place, and never a goblin or elf would stand against me."

But the goblins had got a hob for a leader now, Gnash whose army swelled daily, or so it seemed. And the elves. . . . well, that hadn't worked out well, either.

"What will you do in Pax Tharkas?" Elansa asked.

He lifted his head, rough and shaggy. He looked at her long, and she saw that his nose jutted like an eagle's beak. "I have enemies. I will hold the place against them, and they will not take me."

The boldness of his reply astounded Elansa. His dozen outlaws grumbled against this journey daily, they grumbled against each other, and one threatened to break the band asunder while another planned to leave. Yet Brand spoke as though he were a general in the field, and all his troop loyal to the last heart.

I have enemies, and they will not take me.

Is he mad? She wondered. It might be he is.

A sudden cry shattered the moment—Chaser's shout of terror. Elansa turned but didn't see what hit her, what crashing weight bore her to the ground. She didn't know it was Brand on top of her till she smelled his breath and felt his beard on her neck.

The cavern erupted in a howling so terrible she thought the stone would break.

Chapter 12
∽

In the darkness, Char's voice bellowed, "Ogres!"

As though the warning cry had conjured it, the stench of ogre filled the cavern, the reek of rotting meat, filth, and unwashed flesh. And blood. Under it all ran the thick coppery smell of blood. She didn't see Swain anywhere, but Chaser lay flung against a stone wall. He looked like a broken toy, his neck twisted and an arm ripped from the socket. Blood poured from where his arm had been, running like a river. The high keening Elansa yet heard in her ears was the echo of his death scream.

Cries of rage filled the cavern. Brand dragged her to her feet as arrows flew, bowstrings twanged, and a thundering voice roared in a language Elansa had never heard before. Ogre-speak, words that made her think of oaths and curses and ugliness, raged around her like a storm.

Unarmed and defenseless, Elansa looked around. She searched for a place to run to, a way out. Four ogres, hideous creatures half again as tall as a human, had the ground between the outlaws and the entrances to the cavern. They seemed to have no weapons but clubs, and those looked like no more than stout tree limbs. A fury of hounds stormed around the knees of the ogres— Fang and his brethren tearing at the legs of the monsters. One hound died shrieking, and another flew through the air and smashed against a wall, its bones broken. Ah, but the rest held, furious and changed into creatures as fierce as wolves. Five harried one ogre, ripping calf muscles, exposing veins to bleed their turgid greenish blood. By the time the third hound died, the ogre was on its knees, laying about with its club and screaming. An arrow pierced its neck, and another followed so close to the mark that they vibrated against each other, shaft and shaft. Thick greenish blood sprang from a tapped vein, and Elansa heard Ley shouting, "Again, Tianna! Again!"

The half-elf shouted a gleeful war cry, and two arrows flew as one. Now four pierced the ogre's neck, and the great creature wavered on its legs.

All this Elansa saw in the instant of her panicked search for a way out. Ogres before and behind an icy stream and a stone wall. . . .

Where to go?

"Nowhere to go," Brand said. "Nowhere but where you are. Only crazy people fight ogres, or desperate people."

Brand thrust a dagger into her hand, and her fingers closed round it as though she'd know how to use it. In his own right hand Brand held his sword.

"Defend yourself," he said as the curses of ogres and the oaths of humans raged in the cavern. The stink of blood and bowels loosed in death fouled the air. Brand leaped up the steps, the lily stairs, and Elansa followed as though pulled.

"Fight!" Brand roared, his voice like thunder bounding off the stone walls. "Fight to the tunnels!"

Arawn swung his sword above his head, whirling it in a silver wheel of light, calling men to him. Brand did the same. As though they'd done this a hundred times—had they not?—the outlaws sought a comander.

Half went to Arawn and half to Brand. In this way they divided the two remaining ogres.

In the middle ground, the outlaws engaged, and they were like hounds themselves, harrying the foe. The light of the distant moons glinted off steel blades and the polished iron of arrowheads. Cold as a pitiless glance, the light slithered on blood-slick stone. Into this Elansa plunged, clutching Brand's dagger as though it were a lifeline. She'd not gone three long strides when something hit the ground at her feet, something that sounded like a cabbage flung down.

Her gorge rose, and bile burned a fiery path up her throat. A broad hand fell to the stony floor, severed at the wrist, fingers spread as though to grip. When she looked up, she saw Brand. Wearing his own blood and the blood of an ogre, his eyes blazed, his face contorted with battle rage. Just in the moment their eyes met, someone hit her from behind, and she fell to her knees onto hard stone. Her elbows crashed on the ground, and her fingers went numb as outraged nerves refused to feel. The dagger—useless metal!—flung from her hand, skittered over the ground and got lost in the darkness and the fighting. The breath jolted from her, Elansa tried to rise. A weight bore her down, the two hands of an ogre closed around her, squeezing as it lifted her from the ground. Muscles screamed, and she felt her ribs groan from the pressure of its grip. Stinking spittle dripped into her hair, onto her neck. Breathless, her heart crashing against ribs, her sight began to fail, to fade at the edges and turn black.

Elansa had no breath to scream, hardly the sight to look for help.

And then, the ogre's blood spilled out of its neck and onto her arm and her hands. It burned! Like acid, like fire, it burned her flesh. She fell from the ogre's grasp and hit the floor.

"Get up! Get up!" It was Char shouting at her, the dwarf just pulling his axe out of the back of the ogre's neck. "Get up and run!"

But where? The battle had surged to the walls where the passage out gaped. In between, the cavern was littered with the dead—one ogre's corpse, the bodies of five hounds, and poor broken Chaser.

She moved, stumbling, and then flung herself aside. Char shouted something, and through the madness a yellow blur launched.

Fang!

Slavering, the hound hurtled past Elansa from the side, eyes like fury. He sank his great fangs into the ankle of an ogre, then changed grip and leaped to clamp on the monster's wrist. The ogre stiffened, reeking foully of pain. With its other hand it grasped Fang's neck, thrust a thumb through the hound's windpipe, and flung the beast against a wall.

Running, weeping, Elansa lost her footing on blood-slicked stone, and she fell. She scrambled up again, and only when she saw what had tripped her did she stop. Brand lay on his side, motionless. She saw him, and she saw—in one bright moment of clarity—the sapphire phoenix spilled out of his shirt.

She could have healed a blight with that phoenix. She could have called up the power of the god who is the ruler of all nature and all the world around would have become as a living being to her—earth and sky, fire and wind and water. She would have spoken to them as she would to kin.

Elansa reached down and took the sapphire phoenix in her hand. It throbbed beneath her fingers. It knew her. How not? In her veins ran the blood of the generations of woodshapers who had used this talisman to heal.

"My Phoenix," she whispered.

Brand groaned, his eyelids flickering as the stone hanging round his neck quickened, as the blood in Elansa's veins began to sing. He opened his eyes, and it seemed to her, looking into the brown depths, that he saw her from a far place, as though they stood with a vast plain separating them. The roar and the rage of battle faded, and she knelt in a quiet place. Not a place of safety, no, not that. Danger howled all around, but now, for this moment a sheltering wing had dropped between her and death.

In silence, she began her prayer. *O my Blue Phoenix, give ears to the earth to hear me. Give wit to the stone to know me. Give courage to the rock to break and fall and—*

A fiery energy shot through her from her knees to her neck, screaming in her every nerve. Here was the pain of the world breaking, of stone falling and rock shattering.

She screamed, and screaming she would not let go the flashing energy running through the stone. She did not know magic from pain. Ah, but this was not different from taking in the illness of trees to change it to strength, making an alchemy and transmuting sickness into health.

In her heart where all her prayers were born, Elansa cried, "Habbakuk! Phoenix, my strength rises!" And like the Blue Phoenix rising up out of the ashes, wide-winged, powerful and alive, strength flared in her.

A voice—hers!—shouted, "Run to the tunnel! Now! Run now!"

She shouted looking at Brand, at the outlaws as though across a wide plain. He opened his mouth, and her own words came out, like an echo. The echo shattered the image, and the world she returned to was breaking apart.

The walls shook. The stony floor of the cave trembled. From the ceiling, stalactites hung by gods creaked and fell. The forest of stalagmites trembled as though in a storm's own wind. One cracked at the base and tumbled, crushing an ogre.

Someone screamed, "Earthquake!"

And someone else shouted curses and howled, "Magic!"

Brand grabbed her by the arm and dragged her up from her knees. He staggered, bleeding from a head wound, but he was strong. All her muscles buzzed and burned. Her head seemed filled up with fire. No matter where she looked, she saw the phoenix, and it seemed it no longer hung from Brand's neck. She saw it in shadows, on the floor as she ran; she saw it in the space where a tall pillar of stone had stood, in the gap between splitting stone.

Brand shoved her hard, pitched her into the darkness of the tunnel. The roar of the roof falling drowned out his shouting, but she knew he shouted at her, some question, some desperate plea.

"Make it stop!"

The plea screamed in all her bones, in her blood, in the deepest part of her where she felt the agony of stone breaking. *Make it stop!*

With trembling fingers, Elansa reached for the sapphire. Brand pulled back, and then he held. He suffered her touch, and she saw that wasn't easy for him. When her fingers brushed his skin as she took up the phoenix, she felt him flinch. Still, he didn't back away, and he stood very still when she whispered her prayer, giving her thanks to the god who had heard her.

Then, the silence of the earth. The quiet of stone. The weeping of water, a spring loosed into the cavern. In that silence, Elansa heard the ragged breathing of outlaws, the groaning of someone wounded or amazed. Brand's fingers touched hers, then pried them one by one from the sapphire phoenix. She thought he would surely take the talisman from his neck, perhaps throw it away in fear. He did not. He took it back, and he tucked it into his shirt.

And how not? Would he put such a weapon into the hand of a prisoner? Of course not. He would hold it, if not to use, then to keep her from using it.

Char went past her, very carefully, and looked back into the cavern.

"Y' brought down the world," he said, his voice hushed with awe. "Girl, y' brought it right down on their heads."

All around her Elansa heard the breathing of outlaws caught in the dark. Humans, none could see her but Ley and Tianna and Char. The dwarf had the best sight, and he looked at her as though he were seeing something fair and foul.

"Char," Brand said. "Do you know where we are?"

Char grunted.

"Is that yes or no?"

Again, the dwarf grunted. "That's no. The way we took into the cavern is all choked with"—he snorted—"all choked with what she did. There's another, but . . . well, it ain't where I was thinkin' to go."

Fear pricked along Elansa's neck.

"Don't worry about that," Brand said. "That tunnel go south?"

"So far as I can see."

"All right then. You just lead on, and don't turn aside from any water you find."

The dwarf said nothing, but he did as he was asked.

* * * * *

Lindenlea stood in a field of black and dun, on grass-less earth littered with burned buildings, charred beams and foundation stones scattered. The bodies of the slain lay untouched by any who had survived. It had been the same in every little village or luckless farmstead the hobgoblin had taken his army through. He'd been active in the last weeks, but his pattern had been strange.

No, she thought, looking around her. The strange thing was that there should be a pattern at all. He'd burned and raided in a determined line, straight along the edge of the Qualinesti border, but never close enough to draw the attention of the elven scouts stationed along the edge of the forest. She'd kept her forces strong and alert, riding the length of the border herself, spending no more than a day or night at each camp and making certain the bright wall of elven sol-diery kept to the letter of her command. It did not matter what the hobgoblin did beyond the border of the forest, and no one was to mount sorties against him. As long as Gnash knew how the elven border bristled with blades and hard-eyed warriors, he would keep his distance.

And so he had. The progress of his raiding traced

against the sky, seen in smoke. Only days before, Gnash had deviated from his pattern. The hobgoblin had turned east within sight of the first bright peaks of the mountains. The deviation had piqued Lindenlea's curiosity. A scout had said that he'd seen a burning deeper into the borderland and not along Gnash's usual line.

At the head of a troop, Lindenlea had ridden out to see what she could see. They had found this place, this broken and burned place that had only days before been one of those stubborn little villages clinging to a crossroads, remembering, perhaps, older days when travelers came through to eat at the inn or trade goods from Abanasinia or Tarsis. Not many did come—these were not hospitable lands—but those who could afford armed escorts did, and they came to this place. Lindenlea thought the name of it was Well's Cross.

Or had been Well's Cross. There was nothing left worth sticking a name to now.

Her soldiers had scoured the place looking for at least one living creature and found none until, at the far end of the ruined village, Feslan Oakbeam had sung out, shouting "Got some!"

He'd found a clutch of children shivering in the cellar of one of the houses at the outskirts. They were weeping among the roots and the preserves and the pickle barrels.

Wind-stung and shivering, Lindenlea watched as Feslan hustled a survivor along the village street. Feslan was a warrior bold, not unaccustomed to the sights that lay all around him—the hacked corpses, the feeding ravens. But he was a father when he wasn't that, and so it was a father's hand that turned the boy away from sights, a father's hand that kept him walking straight on the road, past ruin. When Feslan stopped him before his commander, the boy's eyes were wide in his white face. Perhaps he'd never seen an elf before now, or anyone not of his mean little village.

"My lady," Feslan said in Common, his hand on the boy's shoulder. "This one will talk."

Lindenlea looked down at the boy, looked him right in the eye. She didn't waste time on false sympathy or pretend to empathy. This was a human after all. What could either of them know about the other?

"Tell me, boy," she said, a warrior tall and stern. She gestured, sweeping the village around, causing the boy to look where Feslan had not let him. "Who did this demon work?"

Lips trembling with shivering or fear, the boy started to speak. He managed a squeak, then had to swallow.

Lindenlea snapped, "Choke it out, boy."

He had long red hair, shaggy and unkempt. His face was filthy, and the soot that smeared his cheeks was only the newest layer of dirt. Urchins in the root cellar, they had likely been urchins in the muddy streets long before then. He lifted his chin, and a little his eyes narrowed.

"Ain't chokin' for you, elf," the boy sneered. "Ain't chokin' nothin' for the like of you."

Feslan's hand tightened on the boy's shoulder. He jerked him a little, but not hard. "That's a lady of the House Royal you're talking to, boy. Be mindful."

The boy snorted and twisted a grin that might never have known humor. "Aye, and so what does it matter to me? Reckon her sword'll kill me just as fast be she lady or goblin or bandit." He looked around again at the smoking houses and the broken well not five yards away. He looked at the ravens picking over the dead, at the smoke curling up from the last burning embers of what used to be his home. Then, right into Linden-lea's eyes he looked, his own blue eyes piercing as daggers.

"So, do it, royal elf. Kill me and get done. I ain't got much here to lose, eh?"

Lindenlea raised an eyebrow. The boy spoke like a bitter warrior, one who had seen too many battles and lost most of them. His face was all bones and hollows, his hands raw with cold, his lips cracked and bleeding. She didn't doubt that under that rag of a shirt, the boy had ribs like ladders. By the look of him, he couldn't count twelve years for himself.

Pawing the barren earth, scenting death and hearing ravens, Lindenlea's horse pawed the ground, restless. Bridle bits jingled and saddlebags bounced.

"Listen," Lea said. "You may have nothing to lose, but what about those who are hiding with you? Are you ready to let them suffer, too?"

Again the boy snorted. "What? Gonna kill us all 'cause I won't tell you what you want?"

She appeared to consider this, scratching her chin and looking at Feslan over the boy's head. Then, when enough time had passed, she said, "No. I'm not going to kill them. I was thinking," she said, gesturing with her head to the horse beside them, "I was thinking you might be hungry, and your friends, too."

Ah, there was the key. The boy's face set in stub-born lines, but those melted fast as he contemplated food. He swallowed, then again. He looked away, then back.

"Them was goblins done it," he said, his voice low and flat and dead. "Them was goblins, and one of 'em—" He looked up, his eyes narrowing, his chin jutting as though he didn't think he'd be believed. "One of 'em, it were the biggest goblin I ever seen, green-skinned and pig-eyed. But that ain't the whole of it. I'll tell you that ain't the whole. It had—"

He stopped, shaking his head. Away in the village, among the rubble, Lindenlea heard the voices of her warriors calling one to another or speaking together. She heard the horses and the wind as the boy's silence held.

"It had a fire-staff," she offered.

The boy's eyes went wide. "Aye, it did, and when it pointed it at things, they exploded. But it didn't stay. It didn't—" The boy shook his head, not having the words. "It didn't stay while its army did the killing. It set things on fire and left. It were goin'—" he turned around and pointed out over the stone-lands. "It said it were goin' away, back to the Fortress of Ghosts."

Lindenlea glanced at Feslan, who shrugged.

"Where?" she asked.

"The Fortress of Ghosts. Away out in the south, down in the stonelands." As though they were dim-witted, he said very slowly, "The Fortress of Ghosts. In the mountains."

Cold crawled up Lindenlea's spine. "Pax Tharkas?"

"Aye," said the boy. "There. The Fortress of Ghosts."

Eyes on the saddle bags slung across the back of the elf's horse, the boy licked his lips, dried and split by cold. "You really got food in there?"

Lindenlea nodded to Feslan, who untied the saddle bag and tossed the boy a cold half of the hare that was last night's supper. The boy caught it and darted away. Lindenlea hardly saw him go. She looked away south and east to where sunlight glinted, perhaps off the snowy heights of the mountains, perhaps from the very towers of Pax Tharkas itself.

Pax Tharkas was an ancient city, and long dead. Who knew what might be lying in some forgotten forge or storeroom? More weapons like the fire-staff, more and worse. Lindenlea knew the legends, knew her history. She knew that when dwarves and elves had lived in Pax Tharkas, ancient friends in peace, they had stored many weapons there—swords and axes and spears, bows of finest make, arrows with shafts as straight as truth. And there had been weapons of another make, not forge-made or fletched. There had been magic weapons.

Without doubt, the hobgoblin had found his fire-staff there, or thereabouts. And when Lindenlea looked over her shoulder, west to Qualinesti, it seemed there wasn't as much distance between that old fortress and the elven forest.

"My lady," said Feslan. "What are you going to do?"

"I'm going to think a moment, and this is what I'm thinking about: " 'Back to the Fortress of Ghosts,' the boy said. Back, as though Gnash had been there before."

Long deserted, the fortress could not have been swept clean of all that had once been there. Perhaps the hob had come upon some ancient mage's secret hoard. If that were the case, it would be best if the hobgoblin never returned there.

Lindenlea looked south to the gleaming peaks of the Kharolis Mountains. A softer breeze blew here than must be breathing there. There, so high up, it would still be winter. And there, or close to there, Prince Kethrenan hunted, questing to find his wife.

Lindenlea looked east to the stonelands where the hobgoblin and his army might even now be stopping to burn and loot before pushing on to Pax Tharkas. Last she looked to home, to the forest her prince had put into her care, her beloved kingdom.

Chapter 13

"I'm following gods."

The voice came out of darkness, and it sounded both near and far away. Elansa walked stunned, all her senses reduced. It was hard to see in the barely lit tunnel. She should have been able to discern the red outlines of her companions, the edging glow of their lifeforces. She could not. Only strangely—near and far, then near again and far again—she did hear the voice of the one who claimed to follow gods, the voices of those who scoffed or groaned in pain or exhaustion. A metallic taste filled her mouth, slick and coppery, and she knew that was blood. She had bitten her tongue, her lips to bleeding when she'd engaged the magic of the sapphire phoenix. Someone held her in his arm as she walked. She wanted to pull away, to cry out for the pain that caused. The ogre who'd gripped her had left a mass of bruises.

"Ah," said the one who held her, "nothing's broke, girl. Keep walking."

Brand. His impulse, his arm, his own strides moved her, not her own will. Left to herself, she would have crumpled to the ground.

She said so, once. "Let me go. Let me fall." In her heart she'd cried, *Leave me behind!*

All her bones screamed, as though they had been separated from their joints, wrenched from their sockets. She hadn't worked healing magic with the talisman. She had called upon the god to let her speak with the earth, the rock of the world, and that had been granted.

She had not asked for healing. She had asked for breaking. As her body had known how to gather the illness of trees and then feel the healing of the sapphire phoenix, now her body felt the breaking, the tumbling of stone, the cracking of rock. She had rent a piece of the earth and felt all the tearing pain in her body.

"Na," said Brand, "na, now, girl. You go on. You can."

Ah, she must have whispered that plea she'd thought had been a silent scream in her heart. She went on. She had no choice. He would not let her stop.

"I am following gods."

Char said that, and recognizing his voice felt like a triumph. Elansa looked up, looked around, and saw the dwarf standing head-cocked and looking up at Brand.

"I'm following gods, and if y' had but the one eye I do, you'd know it."

No one had the one eye Char had. No one had the ability to see in almost complete darkness as even a one-eyed dwarf could. Faint beams of light shivered down from the ceiling of the close tunnel; there were cracks above. This light, barely discernable to humans or elves, was enough for Char to find his way, enough, it seemed, for him to find something to follow.

"So y' just trust me," the dwarf said, his jaw jutting, his dark beard bristling. "I'm what y' got in here, Brand, so just trust me."

Brand held her, but absently, keeping her on her feet by holding her against him. It was the way you'd hold a sack. But leaning against him, she felt the breath he took, the considering breath. She felt his answer in the relaxing of his muscles.

"I trust you," he said, very quietly. "But all this talk of gods—" He tilted his head toward Elansa. "They liked the killing of the ogres, Char. They didn't like the way it was done, the magic and the crying out to a god."

Char made a sound far back in his throat. He sounded like his hound. "Then they're idiots. The rock fell, the stone cracked, a god lifted his hand. Blind fools."

Brand shifted his grip, his arm slid lower, circling Elansa's waist. She breathed a little easier for the lessening of pain.

"Might be," Brand said, his voice chill. "Doesn't matter. You spook them any more, and things aren't going to be easier."

"Ain't so easy now," the dwarf muttered. "Ain't been gettin' easier for a while."

He didn't say it hard. He didn't accuse. He spoke, and the tone of his voice touched Elansa like sadness. There had been a plan, a grand scheme between these two, to stand against their old enemies, to settle the feud with the goblins forever. He'd bargained in good faith with Kethrenan, or he had intended to. She believed, standing there, that if Keth had kept to the letter of the bargain, Brand would not have done less. He had no feud with elves, for all he thought of them as heartless neighbors. Maybe his plan would have worked, but Keth hadn't been minded to hand over a trove of weapons. Then goblins had come roaring onto the false field of exchange. . . .

Elansa's knees wobbled, and she began to sag in Brand's arm. Ah, gods, if only she could lie down, or even sit.

Brand shook his head, not conceding. "Listen to me, Char. There's enemies all around. Ogres in the caves and elves outside, and someone stole our weapons and sealed all our bolt-holes. Tell me later if you think our plan has turned in my hand. Now, get us to Pax Tharkas."

The dwarf turned. A thin drift of light showed his face, worn and weary, eyes sunken, skin gray. It was how he looked when he knew there was no drink to be had. His last lay in the ruined cavern among the corpses of two friends, ogres, and hounds.

"Come on then," he said, not to Brand, but to all those dark shapes gathered, breathing and muttering, and some groaning with hurt and weariness. "Come on. Let's walk."

Brand shifted his grip again. Elansa winced, but she made no cry. They followed Char, the line of them winding through the darkness. When pale glimmers of light sifted down from the ceiling, they saw the tunnel changing, the walls growing wider apart. Their own weary legs told them the way was rising now.

"We're getting close to the surface," someone said, whispering and hopeful. It sounded like Nigh-toothless Kerin. And Ley—she knew his voice, for it spoke in the accents of home—said he thought that was the case.

They stopped twice for water, to cup their hands under little rills running down the walls. It tasted sharply of minerals, but no one complained. Each filled up his or her hands with it and drank gratefully. Only Char didn't, wanting something else, and he kept his distance from his fellows, a surly space. He didn't stop talking about his godly guides though, and he took a sour satisfaction to see how that worked on his companions. Most, he seemed to take grim satisfaction in Arawn's sneering.

"He's mad. The damn dwarf's gone mad, and that's what they said happened the first time—"

Not more than that did Arawn say, though, for Char had stopped and turned. He didn't drop his hand to the throwing axe at his belt or make any other threatening gestures. He lifted only his head.

"Come along, Arawn," Char said, his voice a low mockery of coaxing. "Come along if y' have the guts, and see where gods are leading me." He laughed, but it sounded hollow. "Might be our raggedy little princess knows. Might be she could tell you what waits."

Whispers rustled in the passage, like the shuffling of bats' wings. Arawn said nothing. He was not one to bluster, but Bruin muttered, and Pragol hissed. Brand told them all to shut up, he said he'd bind the next one who wasted his breath on threat or challenge and leave him in the dark. Satisfied, Char turned and walked ahead, up the rising way and into the dim light that did not increase and did not fail.

As the outlaws marched on, it could be seen that Char did indeed follow gods. Here and there, barely seen, felt by hands reaching to steady a walker, hands reaching to find a place to stop and rest, were images chipped into the stony walls—a dwarf with a warhammer, a dwarven smith at an anvil, more like those. These were not the works of an artist with time to make them perfect. They were the offhand works one sees when men are idle and their hands resent the stillness. Dwarves had been here, thinking of Reorx, thinking of the god and the images they most liked to create.

The rough god, peering out from shadows under her hand, comforted Elansa. Here had been folk who knew the right of the world, who knew that gods lived. In the long ago days of this rough craft, the gods had walked with their children. They had visited Krynn in guises fair or dark. The great families of deities had been deeply involved with Krynn. Now, they were not. They were gone, but these little images, the faith in the hearts of those few races who remembered, argued that gods did exist, even if they were long gone from this realm.

The sapphire phoenix hung round Brand's neck caught a gleam of gray light and shot it back to her eye. He saw it too, and he slid the talisman back into his shirt.

Following gods, they walked, and as the ceiling of the tunnel dropped low, tall humans bent to make their way. After a time Nigh-toothless Kerin said, "Why, them's tools!' and the voices of others echoed to agree. Here and there, in corners, up against the narrow walls, lay the heads of hammers, rusted chisels, picks whose wooden handles had long rotted in the damp air under the ground.

Brand slipped his arm beneath Elansa's and helped her to stoop. "Bend low, girl. Head down. I don't think it's far now," he said, his lips right beside her ear. "See, there's light ahead. The way is climbing. Hang on."

Like a voice out of far memory, Char's drifted back, crying, "Ho! Come on! Come ahead!"

She stumbled, and Brand lifted her up. He moved her to the side, pressed her back to the wall while the rest filed by. They passed, and in each she felt the urgency of their need to be out of the cramping tunnel, to see what Char had found. Her legs sagging, Brand let her sit. As the last of them passed, he crouched next to her.

"Can y'walk?"

"In a moment."

He grunted, then sat beside her. He lifted her blouse and winced to see what the ogre had done. "Damn me if you aren't all luck, girl. Your ribs should be broken."

He eyed her keenly. "But that ain't the worst, is it?"

Elansa leaned her head against the stone, and a thin trickle of water crept down her neck. "No, the magic hurt the worst. It's better now. I'm tired."

He looked like he wanted to ask about that, but all he said was, "Only a little way now. Come on, get up." He took her hands and pulled her up. She stood, and he held her against him again, but not as strongly now. He helped her through the low passages, and when they came out he stopped.

"Ah, gods," he breathed, who didn't believe in gods. "Look at that, will you?"

Men had spoken that way as they entered the stony forest where the battle with the ogres had taken place. Their voices hushed with wonder, they had stared around them at that deep place sculpted by time and rivers and the hands of dwarves. The hardest among them had admitted they'd seen little to match the beauty. There was not that much of beauty here, but there was more of wonder, for all that lay before them was created by mortal craft. Ley walked the perimeter, looking up, looking out. He was of Qualinesti, and Elansa didn't know what his station had been—tradesman, craftsman, servant. His eyes met hers, and she saw it: He knew the lore, knew he stood on the doorstep of a wondrous place.

It was, indeed, a doorstep, and not a lovely one. They stood in a smelting cave, high-sided and long deserted. At one end rose a shaft, and from this light poured down as once, a long time ago, ore had, shoved from the open pits above. Great iron vats, gone to rust and ruin now, lined the sides. A pungent odor clung to the stone walls, strong enough to make

Elansa's eyes water. Far across the cavern a tall, broad opening gaped, like a mouth opened to scream. From there cold air drifted, carrying a fresher scent, the perfume of air that had never lived below ground, that only knew sunlight and starlight and the sweet breath of the seasons.

Elansa looked behind her, back the way they'd come. All those tunnels, all those dark ways, had been known to the dwarves who'd made Pax Tharkas and delved the open pits of the Tharkadan Iron Mines, that army of stonemasons and sculptors and smiths who had made real what kings had dreamed. Some of the tunnels they must have discovered and used, perhaps they even dwelt there for a time, for the making of Pax Tharkas had not been accomplished quickly. Perhaps they had delved some of those tunnels, though Elansa doubted they would have wasted much time at that. Through these tunnels the dwarves had traveled, roads beneath the surface of Krynn, unknown to any but them. One of those dwarves, she knew, had gone back and forth to Qualinost, perhaps by those underground ways for as far as they would take him, then overland. He'd seen the marks of the Lily of the Night, a king's lovely mistress. Perhaps the dwarf had crafted those lilies himself, small works of beauty to relieve an artistic hand that spent most of its time hacking a martial fastness out of the mountains.

Elansa's skin prickled with chill, and her breath caught in her throat. She stood in the least lovely part of the great fastness whose name meant Peace of Friendship, yet she could not help but feel awed. She had heard many tales of Pax Tharkas, and she had never thought to see the place.

She took a long breath. It hurt to do that, and yet the breath strengthened her. She breathed in a place known to her oldest kin, and it seemed to her that some of their strength yet lingered here for their distant daughter to borrow. She moved away from Brand, standing on her own. He let her go, and the look he bent on her was that same complicated look he'd given her on the night he'd shown her the sapphire phoenix.

Now, as then, she couldn't interpret it.

Turning, he shouted, "Hey! Char, where'd you bring us?"

He asked, knowing the answer. He asked so others could hear the dwarf's reply and acknowledge the feat he had performed.

"We are in a fastness of kings," Char said, his voice gone formal. The heavy gray sullenness fell from him, and his face lighted as Elansa had never seen it, graced by wonder and pride.

"What fastness is that?" Arawn asked, his voice thin with disbelief. "Ain't no king in the mountain, Char. Ain't no dwarf king. Ain't no elf king." Some of the others muttered agreement, Bruin and Loris. Ballu shifted a glance at Pragol, then away. Arawn's lips twisted in a sneer as he glanced at Brand. "Ain't no king at all."

Ley stopped pacing. His hand rested on the grip of his sheathed sword, then he looked at Brand and let his hand fall.

As though Arawn hadn't spoken, Char swept his arm wide, taking in all around. "We're in the ancient smelting cavern of Pax Tharkas." He pointed to the shaft rising high at the far end. "There is where the ore from the famous Tharkadan Mines was dumped into here. See the vats—" He sniffed deeply. "You can still smell the ore melting."

Char grinned, and he walked across the stony floor, not looking at his companions as they stepped aside for him, never looking at Arawn who stood in sulking silence apart from the others. The dwarf stood before Brand, his friend, and he winked his one good eye. Then he slid a glance at Elansa and nodded.

"There's a prettier place to rest than here, though, ain't there, missy?"

She stood there, a moment silent, and Char nodded, just once to say he didn't mock.

"Yes," she said. "There is a better place to rest than smelting caves." She lifted her head and stood as tall as aching bones and groaning muscles would allow. It had been a long time, a long time since she'd stood in elven precincts, a long and sorry season. "Make ready to enter Pax Tharkas," she said, as though granting permission.

Brand quirked a smile, but Char didn't. The dwarf nodded again, for he knew that none here had a better right to grant that permission than a princess of the Qualinesti House Royal, she whose ancient kinsman-by-marriage had caused this place to be built, Kith-Kanan who slept the long sleep in one of the deepest chambers of Pax Tharkas.

* * * * *

In a dark chamber of Pax Tharkas, a high hall and many-columned, in a place now long unlit and home to creatures no dwarf or elf or human who lived in the time of the Peace of Friendship had ever dreamed existed, two things stirred.

One was a gully dwarf, one of that lice ridden, flea-infested tribe of dwarves known as the Aghar. People down the ages knew about these pests, beings regarded by most of Krynn as no more than vermin, held in contempt by all clans of dwarves as disgusting two-legged rats.

This gully dwarf's name was Ygtha, and she was part of the plague of gully dwarves—"colony" she might have said had she known the word—who inhabited the ancient fortress. She'd been separated from her fellows, and in the space of moments utterly forgotten that she had, in fact, had companions at all. She'd come into this dark hall through a crack in the walls, momentarily thought she'd stumbled into a forest of stone whose trees either grew up from the floor or down from the roof. Then she saw the columns made a long aisle from one end of the vaulted hall to the other. A mile of an aisle, she thought, though she had no way of measuring that. The words just sounded good, and in her head they ran more like "aisle-mile," the rhyme jogging in and out of her mind.

Then she forgot the rhyme or the distance, for she became aware of high, wide doors on either side of the aisle. She pattered through the dust on the floor, and then forgot the doors, for the dust bore the marks of small creatures—the little dark piles of rat dung and the tracks of the rats themselves. Ygtha decided she'd come into a treasure hall, for what greater treasure could there be than food, and she saw sign of that—fat delicious rat!—all around her. Alas, she saw only sign, no matter how hard she looked, and a few little skeletons from which the flesh had long ago fallen.

She picked up a thigh bone and sat down on the floor, soothing her disappointment by sucking the brittle bones for marrow. Though she sat in near darkness, she wasn't unhappy about that or disturbed. Ygtha had learned that sooner or later light comes back again, either because it comes to you, or you wander out to it. One or the other thing would surely happen again, the coming or the wandering, and so she settled into the darkness of the mile of aisle, with all the doors around her, and sucked on rat bones.

When she heard the second thing stirring, she didn't give it consideration. She was eating, and if Aghar society had any commandment—that is, of course, assuming such a thing as Aghar society could exist at all—it would be that no one stops eating, no matter what.

And so the second thing that stirred, one of the doors along the far wall creaking, inching open, didn't trouble the gully dwarf's feast. She didn't hear the click or scrape of brittle feet on the marble floor. She didn't hear the tall thing sigh through very lean jaws, or notice its breath, cold though that was and filling the hall with winter's breath.

She sucked on bones, humming happily to herself, and she didn't know herself caught until she felt a cage of bones close around her.

The skeletal hand grasped. Flesh hung in shreds from long-lifeless fingers. The gully dwarf squealed, looking right into eyes that flamed with fire the same color as lightning. Unfleshed jaws gaped wide, and yellow teeth snapped. In an eerie voice, like that of stormwind, the undead creature lifted the gully dwarf and listened to her screech and scream for a while, then ripped off her head and flung the corpse against the wall.

It did this not because it disliked gully dwarves. It did this because if it and the others of its fellows who

slumbered behind the many closed doors of this hall
had a commandment, it would have been to kill as often
as it could.

When it was finished with the gully dwarf, the
undead thing, clothed in the last rags of its own
flesh, hung in the rotting silk and leather of a warrior's funeral gear, looked around for more to kill.
Finding none, it went back to where it had been
sleeping. It entered the crypt behind the opened
door, lay down upon its bier, and fell into a dark well
of dreamlessness. All around it, in other crypts,
behind other doors, more of its kind lay undreaming,
unaware. Some had been elves in life. Some had been
human. Some had been dwarves, and they all lay in
stillness until something living, smelling of blood
and flesh, came into the chamber. Then one or another of the creatures would sense the presence of something that needed killing. The urge that guided it, the
killing urge, would rise up to wake the sleeper, to
send it looking for the living thing that must not be
allowed to live.

They had been the honor guard of a king, a long
time ago when Pax Tharkas was new and Kith-Kanan
came often to stay there. Upon his death, he was
buried here, and each of his beloved guard was award-
ed a crypt outside the great king's burial chamber, one
and another to take up their charge in death as they
had in life: to guard the king. Their place had been
only ceremonial, an honored burial for those who had
served faithfully. But in these after days, when gods
had turned their faces from the world, when the races
of Krynn had turned their faces from each other, dark
magics crept and crawled, and the corpses of elves

and dwarves and humans, who had lived by shining codes of honor and faith, became corrupted into beings made to kill.

* * * * *

In the shadow of the rising hill they rested. Beneath a broad shoulder of the Kharolis Mountains, Kethrenan stopped and gave thanks to gods for the water they found there. A shallow stream darkened the stone, barely managing to pass the rocks. It ran from nowhere. Rather it sprang. Even as he thought so, Kethrenan decided that was too strong a word for it. The water seeped, oozing up from the earth. The weary horses dipped their muzzles into the thin stream, and the gulping sounds of their drinking echoed against the rocks. Bridles and bits jingled, and Demlin's mount shook its head and drank again.

Demlin took the water bottles, his and Kethrenan's, and filled them. It was a slow process, the trickle of water seeping in. One filled, he stopped it with great care and handed it to the prince. Patient, he began the next. They'd found little water in these days past. Kethrenan looked at the dark horizon, the pall of smoke hanging in the west. He shaded his eyes against the glaring of noon's sun.

"My lord prince, there's a great burning out there. How close to our forest, I wonder?"

How close? Kethrenan couldn't guess. The wind spread the smoke all over the sky, saving the darkest pall for the distance. There, he saw the work of the hobgoblin Gnash. In the night they'd seen the ruddy glow of fire on the sky, and Ithk said he reckoned Gnash was marching up and down the borderland. "Making goblin towns. He does that best."

Making goblin towns and manning them with his army. Kethrenan didn't bother to ask if the army increased in proportion to the goblin towns. He knew it did. He'd been fighting goblins off his border for many long years. They liked fighting, and they would be drawn to a powerful leader like Gnash as steel is to a lodestone.

His eyes on the pall hanging over the west, Kethrenan knew it wouldn't be long before that army would turn upon itself . . . unless it had a purpose. Lindenlea would keep them off Qualinesti's borders, and they would flow south, or north into Abanasinia to rampage among the humans.

Kethrenan shrugged. That wasn't his problem.

Wind moaned across the stonelands, raising grit and biting cold. Even so, it had the smell of spring on its chill breath. Somewhere in the forest surely the first blush of a kinder season quickened, the stirring of buds still furled, not green yet, no—red, and only faintly so. There in the forest, Kethrenan thought, the air must smell like hope, and the birds must be more active. There, it had snowed well in winter, and the grasses in the meadows would soon begin to thicken. Here, in the borderland, they had not felt rain in all the while they'd been riding south. Ithk looked withered, puckered, and weary. Demlin was like skin stretched over bones, and it seemed they spent most of their searching looking for water. Kethrenan, though, was a knife, gleaming and sharp, and he would not rest until he had spilled the outlaws' blood.

Kethrenan's horse snorted, dancing a little, restless. The best of Qualinost's stables, this one did not weary though they had been long days quartering the rocky land, searching for sign of the outlaws. The prince took up the reins and looked at the goblin, still on his knees drinking.

"You," he said. Ithk looked up, wiping his mouth with the back of his hand. They hadn't kept him tethered in days. He never showed sign of wanting to leave them. "How far to the last cache?"

"Not far." Ithk pointed east, and high up the slope. "In there. Do we go?"

Kethrenan said they would, and they tethered the horses and climbed. Wind dragged at them, and their fingers grew numb on the cold stone. The cave's entrance hid beneath an overhang of stone, a small slit in the mountain no one could see from below. They had to turn sideways to thread it, even the goblin. The elves had to duck, going bent into a small passage. When they could stand again, Demlin lit a torch, using flint and steel to ignite rags soaked in fat. It wasn't a good torch. It sputtered and stank, but it gave light. The cache lay far back, not in the first cave but in a smaller one beyond. Weapons, the keg of dwarf spirits, all were covered in oily rags.

Demlin's lip curled in disgust, and he toed the rags from the pile of swords and axes. This was a smaller cache, the last of what had been dragged here. By the sputtering light, Kethrenan took the count of what Brand had stolen.

"Do we destroy them?" Demlin asked.

The prince considered it. The weapons were of finest elven make, the steel more treasured than gold or jewels in these hard days. In the weeks past, he'd caused so many of their like to be broken, the blades made useless, the arrows shattered and axe heads broken. And this hoard, this last one, lay untouched. Brand had not been here.

Neither had he shown himself in the world outside the mountain. The elves had quartered the ground between the caches, like hounds searching after game. They'd seen no sign, not even a cast-off boot or the dark mark of a campfire. He'd kept within the mountain. Yet how had he hunted? How had he fared? He had a dozen men at last count. How did he feed them?

"Where is he going?" Demlin asked. He looked around at the slick cave walls, the dust on the floor. Tracks marked the dust—booted feet had passed here but not lately, not in a very long time. "He has to know all his other caches are broken, but he hasn't come here."

Kethrenan nodded, and he thought of the map he'd had Ithk make. The point of the triangle had looked south, right to Pax Tharkas. Could he get there? Kethrenan didn't know. Would he try? And why?

In the flickering light, the eyes of his servant and the shifting glance of a goblin on him, Kethrenan closed his eyes, considering his questions and receiving his answer.

Brand would try for Pax Tharkas. Kethrenan knew it, because he knew that if he were in the same position, beset by enemies, he would try for a place like Pax Tharkas. He would run there because there was no way to keep alive in the caverns, even if he knew all the ins and the outs. Sooner or later, he'd have to hunt, and the risk of that was too great. Brand wouldn't know who'd destroyed his weapons, goblins or elves. Outside, he was a hunted man. Wherever he turned, he was beset and outnumbered.

Kethrenan smiled. This one, this outlaw, knew the outnumbered man on the high ground still had a chance.

"Demlin, douse the torch and follow me."

They went out into the cold and stood on the highest part of the slope, a flat place above the mouth of the cave. Wind whipped their hair, and the goblin clutched his bearskin tight as the elves looked south across the stoneland, shading their eyes. The arms of the Kharolis Mountains reached out into the plain, dark and long. Because he knew his history, Kethrenan knew the fortress of Pax Tharkas spanned the gap between those reaching arms.

"Tell me," the elf prince said to the goblin. "Tell me all the ways you know to Pax Tharkas."

But Ithk shook his head, seemingly puzzled. "None, none. Go south, I only know that. Ain't never been to the Fortress of Ghosts. Don't go there. No one does."

The goblin wore the deepest look of sincerity, yet Kethrenan believed him not at all. Ithk knew ways— maybe secret roads through the borderland, maybe dark paths through the heart of the mountain itself. He could be forced, Kethrenan knew. He began to consider ways of doing that, of bending the goblin to his will, when Demlin's cry rang out.

"Prince!" He pointed north and a little west. Something bright ran along the stony earth, a swift horse on a stretch of an old road long forgotten. Sunlight leaped from a shining helm and a bright shield. "A rider. It's one of ours, my prince!"

The rider ran against the wind, bright against a pall of dark smoke. Kethrenan nodded to his servant, and

Demlin went bounding down the hillside, nimble as a mountain goat, leaping from stone to stone until he reached the low ground and the horses.

On the high place, the goblin shifted from foot to foot, and the elf prince watched his servant ride to meet the warrior. He heard him call out in their native language, shouting, "Friend!" He saw them meet, and he saw them confer. Demlin pointed upward and back to the prince where he stood overlooking the borderland. They turned their horses and rode to the little stream.

Kethrenan felt something on the air. He felt something like a shift in the wind, a change in fortune. He was not superstitious. He was not so devoted to the tending of gods as his lost wife was. Still, he felt something moving, luck or fate.

He went down the hill and kept the goblin at his side. When the messenger said he had word from Lindenlea, Kethrenan tethered Ithk and moved out of earshot. This he did because Demlin reminded him to.

"You think he's one of us, like us in his need for vengeance. He isn't, my lord prince. He's a goblin. I know what your cousin said about how the Stone in the temple showed him to be a liar about something. Don't mistake him, he isn't serving you."

Kethrenan didn't mistake the goblin. He tethered him and went aside to hear the warrior's message. It was from Lindenlea.

"Have a care, cousin. The hob Gnash is taking his army to Pax Tharkas, all of them burning along the way. If you go much farther south, you'll be caught between the fortress and him."

Kethrenan heard, and he looked once at Demlin, maimed Demlin who had ridden this quest beside him since the first snow broke the grip of the killing cold. "I know," said the servant to his master. "We must go back to the army."

They had to, for they must stop the hobgoblin before he reached Pax Tharkas.

Chapter 14

~

Ithk's every thought and plan was inspired by one passion: vengeance.

They didn't think so, the elves. The bastard elves thought he was driven by some kind of treachery, some kind of Gnash-inspired betrayal. He wasn't. Vengeance inspired him, the only true passion he knew. The elves didn't think goblins had hearts. Some few said they had lean hearts. Well, maybe there they were right. Lean hearts, hard hearts, the kind of hearts that liked to kill and take and grab. But their passion, that was vengeance, and they considered it a noble passion.

That was Gnash's shame and weakness, that he'd put aside the long feud with Brand for ambition. Now ambition was good, and greed was better, but vengeance—well, if goblins had poets, they'd be singing of revenges taken. Gnash would get no song of a goblin poet. Gnash thought of his own glory and let feuds fall. Ithk knew this wasn't the case with feuds. A feud, once lifted, must never be put down unless upon the corpse of the enemy.

And so he'd hunted in the stonelands all through the winter, hunted for Brand when no one else dared the cold or the wind. He'd sheltered in caves, he'd sneaked and he'd skulked, and he'd seen the outlaws at their work of hiding stolen weapons. One goblin against all of them was no chance Ithk would take, and so he'd made a plan. He went to the elves, who had good reason to hate Brand, and promised to lead them to him, the only fee required was that he alone be allowed to kill the outlaw. Kethrenan had agreed. Maybe it had sounded like a good bargain to him, and would have been if Ithk had been minded to keep it. Ithk had other ideas, and he didn't intend that Kethrenan should come back from this venture alive or with his woman. The elf would do the hard work for him, stripping Brand of all his weapons, closing up his hiding holes, then Ithk would be rid of Kethrenan and his servant at the gates of Pax Tharkas. He'd have help at that. He'd thought it might be a good idea to have a way back to Gnash. He hadn't liked what had happened to poor Golch the Beheaded, but the idea of imitating the deed and returning to Gnash with an elf prince's head in a sack seemed like a good one to keep in reserve.

But the damn elf broke the bargain before Ithk could, riding off to his army to stop Gnash from reaching Pax Tharkas. Damn Gnash.

But he had a single mind, did Ithk. He cursed, and he reworked his plan. It was, for him, all about vengeance. Jogging along beside the maimed elf, tethered again, he regretted the lost chance of killing them. He hated the smell of them, the forest-stink clinging to their clothing, their hair, their gear. They reeked of temple incense and scented candles, and they reeked of—Ithk almost gagged—perfumes, soap, and other vile scents. But as he ran along beside the tall horse, he knew that killing would have been pleasure-killing, after all. What he really wanted was to kill for revenge. More than anything he wanted to kill Brand.

Brand had done great slaughter of goblins in his time, and he'd made no secret that he'd liked that killing. He'd killed Ithk's brother, his father, and his . . .

well, they were probably his cousins, those orange-skinned idiots who'd got in Brand's way up around the Notch last year. Cousins, or close enough, and Brand had killed them. He hadn't hacked off their heads like Golch the Beheaded, but he'd killed them just the same. Wasn't anyone, Ithk thought, in all of Golch's army—or, Gnash's now—who couldn't say the same thing about Brand. And he laughed, doing it, the killing.

Ithk hated him, and he'd been happy to trot along after the bastard elves as long as he thought that would get him to Brand and the slaking of his vengeance. Now it looked like that wasn't going to happen. Now it looked like they had other things to do, or other ways to get the woman back. Ithk didn't know. He wasn't privy to their talk, tethered and running and keeping his eye out for stones and gullies and ruts for fear of falling and being dragged.

Something about Gnash, something about armies, something about Pax Tharkas, but they weren't talking about getting in there the quick way. They were talking about throwing themselves against the walls in crashing battle waves.

Idiots. Like his cousins, idiots.

Ithk ran. Sometimes he had to hold onto the tether to keep from falling, but he ran. When they stopped at night, still far short of their goal, the elves untied him and let him collapse where he stood. They made camp around him. The maimed elf, the prince, and the warrior set their fires, tended their horses, and talked about great armies in the south. Ithk listened, pretending to sleep, and he heard what he needed to know.

In the darkest hour of night, when the two scythe-thin moons had set and a scud of clouds obscured the stars, he rose. Two of the elves slept, the fire between them, wrapped in their cloaks. The other, the prince, stood looking south. Ithk glanced his way and saw past him to where a thin glittering line of campfires gleamed. One army or another.

A shadow, he slipped away, but not before he took the little knife from his belt that he used for eating and skinning. He slid it between the ribs of one of the elves with such deft swiftness that the sleeper made no sound as he died between one breath and the next.

A horse snorted, another stamped. Not one of the elves who lived so much as looked around as Ithk slid away into the night, a dark ghost savoring the smell of blood as he wiped his blade clean on his thigh and ran away south to find his way around two armies.

He knew ways into the Fortress of Ghosts. He had been long around these mountains. He knew the way in, and it didn't involve running into walls. He had friends waiting, and maybe he would be a little late, but he didn't doubt they'd wait.

* * * * *

O blessed light!

It rained down into the spacious bed chamber off the Hall of Thanes like gold pouring in, leaping through tall windows whose iron shutters were thrown wide. The sunbeams danced with glittering dust motes.

O blessed air, unfettered by tunnels of stone!

Elansa breathed it as though it were blown down to her from alpine meadows. To her, it smelled not of a musty closed room, not of the woven wall hangings falling to rot beneath a burden of mildew, nor did it smell of gully dwarf, that rank odor of filth and sweat that would have warned of the presence of the vermin if little footprints on the dusty floors had not. Others swore the place smelled of this, but Elansa smelled only air, free and clear and moving.

They had left the smelting caverns and walked out into a purple twilight, the first star pricking the sky, the moons but little crescents above the two tall towers of Pax Tharkas. Ley stopped to stare, his face turned up to marvel at the towers. In the courtyard stretching between, they were a dozen, and they felt small as sparrows before the great wall spanning the towers.

"I've never seen anything like it," Tianna whispered. She was a child of the stoneland and the mountains but had not dreamed that such a wonder as this could exist.

"It's called the Tharkadan," her father said, "and it's seen better days."

It was so. Even as she marveled, Elansa admitted that. Time had not dealt kindly with the fortress. The courtyard stone was cracked and heaved, the towers themselves had felt the digging fingers of frost. The broad high gate in the wall had slipped on its great hinges.

"We'll get in through there," Brand had said, nodding to the gap between gate and wall.

After the low cramped tunnels, after caves whose ceilings were not always high, whose way in and out were seldom broad, the space between the unhinged gate and the stone wall seemed broad as the door to a king's feast hall. They went in single file from habit, but they need not have. Once inside they found that the state of the inner court was the same as the outer—heaved stone, cracked stone, broken stone.

In good time Char found a way into the eastern tower, out of the wind and cold, but not out of the light. Once inside he did not hesitate, nor did Elansa question him. From legend, the elf woman and the dwarf had learned much about this place. They knew, the two of them, where they'd find the best place to keep from the night and the cold. Outlaws and their prisoner, wind-whipped and filthy, ragged in broken boots, they went to the Hall of Thanes and felt they had made a good choice.

"Used to be someone's bedroom," Dell said, turning from the window.

Elansa nodded. "A king's—elf or dwarf or one of the human kings from Ergoth. Now and then, even the Ergothian emperor. In the old times one or another of them came here often."

Arawn stood alone at a far window, his eyes on the sky or the tower across the courtyard. He had his back to the room, his back to his friends. Outside, far below, Brand and Char were scouting the broad courtyard. Within this chamber, this place where dwarven thanes had entertained kings, the rest of the outlaws had staked out their places, much as if they were setting camp in a cold cave.

They have drawn a line, Elansa thought, seeing what Brand had hoped to prevent. In the far part of the chamber, away from the dais where a bed had once stood, Arawn looked out. Bruin, Loris, Ballu, and Pragol had spread out their sleeping furs close by. The clack of the bones, shaken in Pragol's hand, sounded familiar to her now, as familiar as their rough voices, their conversations couched in cursing and hard laughter.

Near the window, the one with the shutters flung wide, Dell stood. Nigh-toothless Kerin crouched nearby, his back to the stone and his head on his chest, asleep. Ley stood not far from him, draped in the long shadows, and sighted down the length of an arrow's shaft. He turned it this way and that, judging whether it was straight and true or if it must be abandoned. Tianna lay wrapped in her cloak, the ragged hem of it muddy and so discolored that the original hue could not be guessed. She had her back to the wall, and Elansa didn't think she was sleeping.

"They sleep, but they must be hungry," she said to Dell.

Dell nodded. "I think there must be hares in the hills. Failing that, we could scare up some rats. I'll take a few men and see what we can find." She looked around at her companions, head cocked as she listened to their voices. "Char says this fortress was always manned. That means there must be armories in one of these towers."

Elansa nodded. "But nothing you find will be in very good condition."

"Don't doubt that. Still, I'd like to see. I can't get into much trouble. It's just us and the gully dwarves, after all."

At the door leading out from this ruined chamber that once hosted kings, Char's voice and Brand's mingled in echo, low and earnest. They came into the chamber with two helms filled with water, talking about a well in the courtyard with a spring still bubbling up pure and cold.

"Got to use old helmets for buckets," Char said, "but that's not too hard. The water's high enough for reaching down."

Nancy Varian Berberick

He said more, but Elansa didn't hear. She closed her eyes and sank down to the floor. She was thirsty, but she knew better than to look for a drink before anyone else. In the dark silence, she nodded, almost sleeping. A hand touched her arm, she jerked, startled, and Brand stood with an old helm in his two hands. He took a long drink, and offered the rest to her.

"Go on," he said. "You did good, girl. You did all right against the ogres. You held up on the way." He moved closer. In the dimming light, she saw the silver links of the chain around his neck. The sapphire phoenix slid against his chest.

She reached to touch it. He let her, and the pulse of power against her fingertips beat as the pulse of blood beneath her own skin. "I . . . I was going to Bianost with that phoenix. I was going to heal . . ."

Brand shrugged, and he repeated his offer. "Have a drink."

He didn't smile. He never did, but he looked at her with a kind of earnestness that made her throat close up with tears.

* * * * *

Lines of smoke wavered in the icy air, dark scars across the face of the sky. Flights of ravens marred the blue, sailing toward the smoke as though toward home. Beneath them on the stony ground, wolves loped down from the hills in the stonelands. Outriders of death, they ran and they soared. In the days when gods had walked on Krynn, when people had believed because they had felt the nearness of deity, those who had worshiped dark gods knew these creatures as the minions of those gods who most loved destruction. They used to say, those who believed in the times when it was easy to believe, "You can hear Takhisis in the raven's cry. You can smell Morgion on the wolf's breath and see Chemosh in the beast's cold eyes."

Those beasts of battle fed full in the border between the kingdom of the elves and the kingdom of the dwarves. They gorged on goblin flesh, and they feasted on the marrow cracked from the bones of elves. They followed in the wake of a war where the burning of villages had ceased, where the making of goblin towns was no longer on the mind of the hobgoblin Gnash. What was on his mind now, each time he stopped letting the elves chase him and turned to fight, was how much he hated those pale-eyed wretches out of Qualinesti. He fought with fire, wielding his staff, the weapon that looked like an old bent stick. He flung fire, and he went with the stink of burning flesh clinging to him like a cloak.

He fought at night, whenever he could, sweeping down from the hills. He had known how to make fists of his fire when first he began to use his staff. He had known how to reach out and grab his enemies in a flaming grip, sizzling their flesh and blackening their bones while their blood boiled. In the time since then, harried by the elf prince across the lands no king owned and no one ruled, Gnash had learned more and better skills.

One night, when the two moons hung like sickles over the reaching arms of the Kharolis Mountains, he'd not set an army of goblins down on the elves. He'd sent an army of fire, creatures man-tall and made of flame. He had seen the brave soldiers of Qualinesti break and run, in shame take to their heels.

Turning from that battleground, he had gone south again, and he didn't think any could stop him from reaching his goal now. He dreamed of Pax Tharkas, that Fortress of Ghosts, and he dreamed it was filled with weapons and magic to make his fire-staff seem like a child's toy.

* * * * *

Each history of Pax Tharkas, written in Qualinost or composed in Thorbardin, sung in the cities of humans, studied in the libraries of Palanthas or Tarsis, will tell that the mighty fortress withstood the incursions of goblins, ogres, and even, for a time, the vast army of the evil mage Fistandantilus. For centuries the mighty fastness rang with the voices of dwarves and elves and humans. It hosted kings and, now and then, an emperor. Armies manned the battlements, dwarven warriors and soldiers out of Qualinesti. The great elf king Kith-Kanan slept the long sleep in a crypt below the fortress, and a royal guard attended him in the long sleep, his loyal warriors in a crypt of their own.

Yet storms will blow and wars will rage. The treaties made on one day are burned to ash on another. Great Pax Tharkas, the monument to friendship between the races, fell from its fabled glory after the Cataclysm and the bloody Dwarfgate War. Abandoned by those who'd made it, Pax Tharkas, the Peace of Friendship, was taken by time, by wind and storm, by summer's heat and, finally, by gully dwarves.

"It's like they own the place," Nigh-toothless Kerin growled, his nose wrinkling as the breeze blew into the bedchamber of kings from the corridor outside where he'd been setting watches. "You never see the things, you just hear 'em squalling in the shadows"—he grimaced—"doing gods know what. There are so damned many of them. And you smell 'em."

Elansa covered her own nose, agreeing. She'd seen one or two of the gully dwarves—small creatures scurrying in and out of shadows. They stood no higher than her own knee. Known as Aghar and disowned by all tribes of dwarves, they didn't bear much more resemblance to dwarves than they did to humans or elves. Two arms, two legs, two hands, two feet, a head, and probably a heart, she thought as she closed the door to the corridor. As Nigh-toothless Kerin had suggested, the vast numbers of them proclaimed that they had their reproductive parts in good working order.

The hallway didn't always reek of gully dwarf, of creatures long unwashed and garbed in rags and cast-offs that hadn't seen soap since the wash day before the gully dwarf wearing them got hold of them. Some days the air smelled of the breezes coming cold off the mountains, fresh as the sky and only a little of whatever mustiness drifted out of chambers too long closed up and only lately thrown open. Other days it smelled of smoke, and on those days the outlaws who walked on the Tharkadan—as much to keep watch as to stretch their legs and see a wide sky—reported seeing the signs of battle and burning out in the stonelands. This day, however, only the faintest wind blew, the sky was still, and so the reek of every one of the innumerable vermin lurking in the cellars and dungeons seeped into the chambers of the ancient fortress.

Watchers on the Tharkadan . . . Elansa shook her head and crossed to the unshuttered window. She looked out, watching the guards walk. Dell and Pragol and Bruin and Tianna, they kept no orderly march. Used to seeing warriors on the silvery spans around Qualinost, Elansa hardly recognized these as watchers at all. They lounged at the parapet talking or sharpening steel arrowheads against the stone. They looked out, but not with any kind of keen glance. They seemed bored and restless.

With these, she thought, Brand thinks to hold a fortress.

She turned from the window and watched Brand sitting with his back to the warm western wall of the chamber. Sunlight sent blue gleams darting from the sapphire phoenix in his hand as he turned it this way and that as though it were a box whose key he'd lost. She knew his thought by looking at his face: How does it work?

How does it work, wondered the man who now claimed possession of Pax Tharkas and thought he actually held it because he had a handful of ragged outlaws, a few swords, some arrows, and a throwing axe in the possession of a dwarf whose hand wasn't so steady now as it was when he was drinking. Brand looked up, twirling the phoenix on the chain round his finger.

"Come here, girl."

Girl he named her. It used to be she had no name at all, only "you," in the days when the dogs ate before she did. She crossed the chamber, walking as though across the stony floor of one of the caves, stepping round little fires. Because they must have heated with braziers here—braziers long gone—by necessity the beautiful mosaic floor of this once-royal chamber now bore the dark scars of cooking fires. For fuel they had the arms and legs and backs of ancient oaken chairs, the planks of the broad tables found in the mess and barracks of the opposite tower. What time hadn't broken in Pax Tharkas, these outlaws had shattered.

Elansa stepped around sleepers, for those who didn't hunt or walk on the wall slept. Little changed in their lives. They moved in the rounds of need. Only Char didn't sleep. He sat alone in a far corner, away from the door, away from the windows, wrapped in shadow. If he missed his hound Fang, he'd said nothing to anyone about it, but no one doubted that he missed his drink; his hands were unsteady, and his mood was not good.

"Sit," Brand said, and though he looked where she did, he didn't mention the dwarf. He twirled the phoenix again, watching it catch the light.

She sat, but gingerly. She was a mass of aching muscles and bruised flesh. She slid down the wall, bracing against the floor with her hands to lower herself carefully. He watched her, the phoenix still flying round his finger.

"I've heard it said that warriors in mail shirts who get whacked in battle have to peel the links out of their skin after. Good thing you had only your little rag of silk when the ogre hugged you, eh?"

"The good thing would have been to go unhugged in the first place."

He tilted his head back to look at her. He wasn't going to smile, but he nodded. "That would have been the good thing."

They sat a while silent. How much time, she wondered, would have to pass before she didn't feel every muscle and bone's grief? She looked around at sleepers and the thin sunlight coming in the window. It lay, a golden shaft across the floor, picking out a bright pattern in the mosaic where footprints had disturbed the dust of ages. She followed the path of the light, the brightest thing in the room. It stopped an arm's length from the corner where Char sat.

"Brand," she said, the words coming before she could stop them. "Why is it Char grieves?"

Brand settled his shoulders more comfortably against the wall. He didn't touch her with purpose. He never did but when the sleeping furs wrapped them. Still, his arm was close to hers, the warmth of him familiar. The phoenix flew round his finger and round again, the light glancing from it in beams like blue needles.

"What makes you think he grieves?"

"I hear him dream. He told me once that Ley still grieves the death of his . . ." What to say, wife or woman or lover?

"Alissa was her name," Brand said, watching the phoenix fly. "Yes, he still grieves her. Char—I don't know that he grieves, but maybe. Everyone's lost something, eh? You don't keep much from the cradle to the grave, do you? Char, he did a killing that got him kicked out of Thorbardin."

"And he regrets it?"

"He does."

She thought about that for a while, and she thought about a thing she'd noticed in the days after Brand had given her the choice of him or the rest. Char had changed toward her. He'd grown cold and had hardly spoken to her since. She didn't imagine he'd cared about her or whether Brand took her to his hard bed or didn't. She thought, though, that it had reminded him of something.

Elansa put her head against the wall and turned her cheek a little to feel the gathering warmth of the late sun. "It had to do with a woman."

The phoenix flew, blue and shining, Brand seemed to be able to keep it whirling with little effort and no attention. "It did, but it wasn't a woman he killed. Ask me, he should have, but he didn't. He killed his brother. Loved him right well, or so I gather; two brothers were never fonder. Didn't love him enough to share his wife with him though. Should have killed the woman. Might be he'd sleep better if he had." He snorted, still flying the phoenix. "Might be there'd be a barrel or two more of dwarf spirits in the world, too, if he had."

He looked away from Char.

"Ah, girl, you think that's a hard story? You think so? We ain't your pretty courtiers here, little princess. We ain't no merry band gone to be robbers and highwaymen for the fun. Half of us don't like the rest, and for a while we manage because it's a hard old world. Char, I guess he knows that just like the rest of us. He'll come around, later before sooner without the drink. But he'll come back. He usually does when I need him to."

"And you?"

"Me? Ah, me, I'm just like the rest. Got lost things and I try not to get lost with 'em."

Something about his expression moved her. The

stirring felt like pain, she had allowed no such feeling in all the months since she'd been his prisoner. And yet here, now, with the late light on his craggy face, his eyes a little narrowed as though he were looking into some far distance, she wanted to ask him what it was he had lost. She wanted to know whether he'd lost kin or friend, a home . . . How had he become lost?

Brand's mood shifted suddenly. He snatched the whirling sapphire in mid-round and held it tight in his fist. "What is it, girl? What is this pretty bird of yours?"

As his mood shifted, so did hers. She wanted to say, *It is a godstone. It is magic. It is more powerful than you can imagine!* But she said none of those things. She doubted he could imagine the power contained in the stone, the power a god granted, her beloved Blue Phoenix. She didn't want him to know; she didn't want him to understand. This was hers, though it lay in his hard grasp. This phoenix, the sapphire found whole in the very bones of the world, unshaped by an artist's hand, made by magic, this was hers.

She said, "It is my inheritance."

He laughed then, a hard bark. "Only this?" He tossed the stone high and caught it. "Just this little thing? Did your kin spend all their riches on the dowry, girl? Left you only this?"

"It was enough when I needed it."

Again, he tilted back his head, looking at her. "I suppose it was. But what do you mean, inheritance? A gift from your father?"

Elansa put out her hand.

"Ah, no you don't. You don't get it back that easily." Brand tossed the stone and caught it again, closing his fingers around it. "Might be you don't get it back at all.

I don't know about magic, or not much, but I do know it doesn't take a mage to make a thing like this work. Tell me, how did you do it?"

Elansa closed her eyes, unwilling to watch him play with the power he didn't understand. "I pray. When I take it out to heal, I pray. When I broke the stone, I prayed."

He didn't believe her. His eyes went cold and hard. "Power like that can't be had for a prayer, and I'll tell you this, girl: You better start thinking of telling me how you used it or—"

"Or what?" she said, her eyes still closed. "You won't let me eat? You won't let me drink? You won't let me have a night's peace?" She opened her eyes and met his without flinching. "I eat at your pleasure as it is. I drink when you tell me to. If you want me, I have no choice. You can kill me whenever you like, and I don't think you have any plan to take me home to Qualinesti. So . . . what? What will you do to me if I don't tell you?'

He rose, stood tall above her, and she thought he would strike her. She didn't brace, didn't flinch, for she couldn't imagine a blow would hurt her worse than she hurt now. He opened his fist, a little. The silver links slid from his fingers, and the phoenix dropped the length of the chain.

"It's a prayer," she said. "It's a prayer to a god, and I'll tell you this: You don't know what you have to pay for that prayer, Brand. You don't know what it feels like to speak to the elements as though they were kin, to feel what they feel, to feel what it is you do when they lend you their strength." She shuddered. "I don't use that power without paying a price."

Brand touched her then, a swift light brush of his fingers against her cheek, and said, "I know the fee, girl. I saw you pay it." He put the talisman back into his pouch. "Go to sleep," he said. "I'll let you have some peace."

Chapter 15

～

In the camp of the elves little fires gleamed. Smoke like gray ghosts drifted low. The warriors had no tents. They carried no such luxury as that, not even the prince. They slept rough on hard stone, they ate what they could catch or hunt, and they drank water that tasted of stone and dirt. The horses, picketed this night near a small stony pool bubbling up from the ground, stamped and snorted, nickering in the night. Bits slipped from their mouths, ringing only a little as they stirred or dipped their heads to drink.

Generous as this spring was, none such had the army seen for several nights before, and it was the water the warriors thought about most. They didn't wish for joints of stag or fine fat grouse. They didn't much miss the sweet canopy beginning to go faintly green. They missed the running brooks and the flashing streams. For its lack they despised the stonelands most, and when Kethrenan heard his warriors talk among themselves he heard them talk about water.

Not tonight, though. Tonight was a grace, and he wished his cousin would accept it in stillness. She did not. Lindenlea paced the ten feet before her prince's campfire as though it were a matter of life and death to measure the space precisely and often. She paced head down, chin on chest, her hands clasped tightly behind her back. Kethrenan knew that she was not happy. Cousins, they had known each other for a very long time. They were battle-friends, warriors who had often stood back to back, so close that not even the narrowest blade could pass between. He knew her, and though others might imagine Lindenlea was angry with the enemy, with goblins who had rampaged through the stonelands and had sent the pride of Qualinesti soldiery scattering in panic before fire-wights, striding flames with eyes like blackest coals and jaws that slavered acid, Kethrenan knew better. He knew his cousin, his trusted second, was angry with him.

The prince lifted his lance and watched the green rag tied to the shaft as it fluttered in a vagrant breeze. He wore this rag from his wife's cloak for his token, as jousters on the tourney fields wore a lady's favor. The pennon was soaked now in more blood than that which had stained it when she had used it for a bandage.

Who'd worn that bandage? Had she? Was the first layer of crimson Elansa's dear blood on the rag? Or had it been torn from her to bind another's wound? Was it, then, an outlaw's blood?

Well, if it was an outlaw's blood, more would spill. Like rivers it would run.

"Do you think she's alive, Keth?"

The prince looked up, startled. No one asked that question, not ever. Captains, commanders, simple warriors, no one wondered—or not aloud—whether after all these months the princess yet lived. Not even Lindenlea had wondered aloud until now.

"It's been a long time, Keth. Do you think—?"

"She is alive," he said, as he always did, with iron conviction.

Elansa was alive. Stolen from her home, his gentle woodshaper wife was alive. He knew things about her that others did not. Others saw her and thought she was a girl sweet and fair, a creature of gilded courts and shimmering woodland glades, a gentle healer whose sighs were like the breath of wind through the trees. Kethrenan knew her, and he knew the strength of her.

On the day she had left Qualinost, she was going to lift an illness from the elms of Bianost, take it into herself, and banish it so that the trees might return to health. Elansa Sungold knew how to wield a god's talisman. She knew how to speak to the elements of the world.

"She's alive, Lea."

She is alive, he thought, if she is not murdered. And if she has been murdered the stones of Pax Tharkas will run red with blood.

"She's alive."

Lindenlea went back to her pacing, to her anger. Lindenlea rode with his army, ever strong at his side, her sword like lightning, her war cry pealing across the stony plain like battle horns as they harried the goblins, trying to catch them before they gained the mountains and Pax Tharkas. At that, they had no success. Gnash held them off with warriors he didn't mind losing and with fire. He built walls of fire and fists of flame to reach out and snatch an elf from his horse's back and burn him to death. On the battlegrounds, goblins howled for victory against their enemies, and they named their hobgoblin Master Shaman. In the midst of the battle, Gnash cloaked himself in fire, and no arrow could reach him.

A burning madman, Keth thought when he recalled the hob. An insane creature maddened by pursuit, wild for only one thing: to reach Pax Tharkas. But something had changed. Today something had been different in the fighting.

Nancy Varian Berberick

Little flames crackled in the campfire, Lindenlea paced, and the prince closed his eyes, remembering.

They had engaged Gnash and his army twice since the prince had returned. Once had been a rout, the elves scattered by fire. It had been a shameful running for which he could blame none of his warriors. No soldier could be ordered into fire. But they had come back, his army, they had come back, and their hearts could not be said to be afire with rage. No, fire was Gnash's. The elves' hearts had changed to steel, and Kethrenan had taken them and pursued the hob again, running across the barren land with the mountains always in sight, their peaks gleaming with snow. The plain stretched out flat and far, Gnash and his army like a dark blight upon the earth. Kethrenan wouldn't come in running. He had divided his army and sent them up into the hills, half and half. In that way they'd surprised the hob, falling on him from the high ground and tearing through the sleeping goblin army in bloody slaughter.

The elves had not prevailed. Gnash had come and lifted up his fire-staff to end the matter. But they had hurt him. They'd reduced his army by a third, and they had seen—Lea herself had been the first to discern—that Gnash's love affair with the flame was not doing well for him.

Kethrenan listened to his cousin pace. He listened to the little settling sounds his own small campfire made, the sigh of wood consumed and collapsing. He opened his eyes and looked at the wood, ashy scales and a beating heart of ember. Gnash had looked like that, consumed from within.

Kethrenan thought of Elansa again, of her blue sapphire, her phoenix. It charged a toll, the magic of the phoenix stone. All magic did. It wanted your strength, your heart. It wanted your soul sometimes. Magic always wanted something. He was no mage, but he knew that much. It might be that the fire-staff Gnash wielded could burn forever. Gnash himself could not.

Kethrenan, the warden of Qualinost, had commanded a king's army for many long years. He knew how to recognize a chink in a foeman's armor, and he was not one to need a second look. He took his plan and made a few changes.

He imagined this was the source of Lindenlea's anger. She did not like his new plan, and she could not convince him of her thinking. Nevertheless, this night, half of Kethrenan's warriors would go from him. By the light of the red moon and the silver and all the stars they would ride hard in the night, wide around the goblin encampment, and head for Pax Tharkas. Let the goblins run to the old fortress. Kethrenan and the forces remaining would escort them right into the arms of the elven warriors who would be waiting outside the gates of Pax Tharkas.

Between them, the two forces of elves would smash the enemy as though they were sea and cliff and the goblins hopeless shipwrecks. Then Kethrenan would lead his army into the fortress and take back his wife. This was a fine plan, and one Lindenlea didn't like, for she didn't like to split the army.

"Lea," said the prince when he'd grown weary of her walking. "Lea, do you want to have the discussion again?"

She stopped, but she was a moment before looking up. "About the division of the army? No. We've had that discussion."

"Then what, cousin? Tell me."

"Keth," she said, and the softness of her voice startled him. "Keth, you believe Elansa is alive. Maybe it is the strength of your own will keeping her so." She twisted a grim smile. "We know about the strength of your will, cousin. Sometimes I think not even gods would dare it, if gods were here to dare. I doubt luck or fate would. But have you considered how you might find her, if you find her alive?"

He'd asked himself this question, in dark hours when he took his turn at watch. He answered the question the same way each time: If Elansa were still alive and in the hands of the outlaws, she remained unharmed, untouched. She would have killed herself before letting one of the humans violate her. She would have taken up a knife and killed herself. She was an elf. She was a princess. She was, after all, his wife.

"What if you're wrong?" Lindenlea asked, seeing the answer in his eyes. "Keth, what if she is alive, and she begs the gods every night for mercy, and begs them every morning that this be the day we come to take her home?"

But he wasn't wrong, this he knew. Elansa Sungold was Qualinesti, and she was a princess. She was a woodshaper, and hers was sacred blood, rarely shared with princes and never shared with those not of elvenkind. He said this to his cousin, and he added, "You know that if she is alive, she is well. You know, Lea, that you'd never let one of those human scum touch you, that if you couldn't kill him, you'd kill yourself."

It was a man's answer, a prince's reply. Lindenlea stood a long moment looking at him, and in the end she didn't say anything. She bade him goodnight, and he wished her good luck on her ride across the stony plain.

"I'll see you at the gates of Pax Tharkas," he said, "and all the gods go with you till then."

With her warriors, Lindenlea rode away in the night, the whole strength of her troops shining silver and red under the light of the moons. She drove her warriors hard, demanding of them the kind of speed that would take them the rest of the way to Pax Tharkas and put them outside the gates before dawn. Theirs was a grueling ride, a mad dash, and all her soldiers sped like quicksilver. She could not imagine that they had any wit for hard thinking on that ride. She could not imagine they had wit to do more than concentrate on getting the best from their mounts.

She, however, did more thinking than she would have liked, and all her thought was for the secret blasphemy she held in her heart, perhaps the one every elf woman held but dared not acknowledge. Lindenlea would not choose death over life, no matter if she must make herself an outlaw's whore to see another day.

She did not doubt that Elansa Sungold felt the same way, and she wondered how it was that a man could share a woman's bed for as many years as Keth had shared Elansa's and not know that.

* * * * *

Ithk thought he was the most wronged of all goblins who lived. His good plan had gone awry in three directions at once. The scurvy miserable excuses for goblins who were supposed to meet him on the high road behind the Fortress of Ghosts had all deserted but one.

That one was Velg, and he was not the sort Ithk would have chosen to find waiting for him. Velg was not known for keenness of wit, and his whining could get on even a goblin's nerves.

"Gone to Gnash," Velg whined when Ithk demanded to know where the others had vanished to. "Saw him out on the plains and figgered it would be better to be with him killing elves than here." Velg ducked a blow and claimed he didn't understand it himself. "But I'm here, and we can still get in easier than you thought."

Ithk stopped him.

"How easy?"

Velg shrugged, and he cringed when Ithk aimed another blow. "Come with me," the goblin whined. "I'll show you."

Ithk followed. He was in no mood to have anyone at his back. They went carefully, silent on the road. Shadows gathered at the end of day, and they kept to these. Long deserted, years in the unkind hands of the weather, the road was cracked and the stone heaved in places. It was not, however, unpassable and a better road than Ithk had traveled in all the winter. The road turned round a tall peak, winding in broad easy curves right down to a vast courtyard bounded on all sides by mountain stone. Velg took him round the peak and warned him to keep to the shadows. There before them, the Fortress of Ghosts brooded in the dying light.

"Look," Velg whispered, pointing.

Lights gleamed in the East Tower, a golden glow of torches. The West Tower stood dark, like a blind eye. Between ran a great span of wall. Ithk's breath hissed in, sudden and sharp. Upon the wall three figures walked, passing before the flames of ensconced torches. They looked at the valley beyond, down toward the great stoneland.

"Brand," said Velg. "There he is."

Was it Brand? Ithk couldn't tell. The watchers on the wall were too far away.

"Is he in there?" Ithk asked. "You saw him?"

Velg nodded. "Saw him. Saw the others." He grinned, a toothy leer. "Saw that elf girl, too. They still got her. Better than that, Ithk. *I saw a way in.*"

Ithk looked down the road, the winding stretch. "What way? They'd see us and fill us full of arrows before we got halfway down the road."

Idiot.

Velg shook his head. "Wait. Wait till dark. You'll see."

Shivering in the cold, eye on the light and what he imagined must indeed be warmer quarters, Ithk decided he had little choice. He hunkered down, back to the stone until night came to cover. In time, he did see, for night came down upon the mountain like a shroud. The moons were slim, the stars shone, but their light didn't reach. On the wall, the watch changed, and if they turned to look into the courtyard they wouldn't have seen even a horde of goblins, let alone two.

Still, Ithk and Velg were careful when they left the road. The goblins drifted like shadows along the dark edge of the flanks of the mountain. They made no more noise than wind slipping over the stone of the courtyard. They kept to the shadow of the Tharkadan and the mountain itself until they came to the great wall. There they flattened themselves against the rising face of granite and edged along the perimeter. Above, outlaws walked on the heights, watching over the plains. None looked down. None thought to consider that enemies lurked so near as to be but a few paces from entering the Fortress of Ghosts through the gap in the sprung gates.

Through the opening they went, and it was their luck that the watchers on the wall didn't look down into the interior of the fortress. Why do that? They believed all their enemies were without, trying to get in. First Ithk, then Velg slipped inside, keeping to shadows and seeking the darkest places. Because they were goblins, they found at once the way to the lowest levels, the places humans and elves would not naturally seek. All up in the air, those outlaws.

No matter, no matter. Let goblins take the lowest levels, in safety to plot and plan, perhaps to see what weapons remained in this pile of dwarf-built stone. Then they would sneak up on the outlaws when the time seemed best. They picked up two stout branches on the way, blown in by storm. Wood for fire, for light and warmth.

Maybe, Ithk thought, he'd go back to Gnash with Brand's head in a sack and fling it at his feet. Or maybe he wouldn't. Maybe he'd just carry it around for a while till he got tired of smelling it and then boil it long to get rid of the hair and flesh, scoop it clean, and use it for an ale mug to drink to a good end to a long feud. He enjoyed this picture very much, and he fell asleep embellishing the grinning skull with chasing of silver, perhaps a polished bronze stand on which to set it.

* * * * *

In the chamber the outlaws had taken for their own, out of the wind and the cold, Elansa walked carefully around sleepers, disturbing only one: Arawn, who leaned up on his elbow to watch her pass, following after with his narrow glance. She heard his breathing among all those sleeping, the rasp in his throat like hunger. Careful not to look at him, she crossed the floor, noiseless in broken boots. She'd felt Brand leave her a while ago and knew he'd gone to take his turn on the wall. Restless, she'd been unable to sleep. Thinking of the air outside, imagining it crisp and clean and cold, she'd wrapped herself in her ragged cloak and risen. She longed to see the outside of the tower, to feel the cleaner air. On silent feet, she slipped out the door and into the stairwell leading up to the wall. Maybe he would send her back, bully her away and into the darkness of the tower again. Maybe he wouldn't, and it seemed to her that the risk was worth the chance.

Light drifted down from above. A door stood open, and torches flared and hissed. Elansa climbed up, taking the unfamiliar stairs slowly, eyes on the golden glow. At the top, she stopped and sighed as the first breeze touched her cheek. Brand stood at the far end of the Tharkadan, head low and talking to Char. They leaned against the wall, Brand with his elbow on the parapet, Char with his back to it. It was the dwarf who heard her first. He looked up, his face pale in the light of his torch, rough and white with his thirst, unable to ease it. He jerked his head in her direction, Brand turned to look, then looked away.

They left her alone, kept the distance of the wall between while she stood at the parapet, looking out over the valley. She tasted the breeze and listened to the profound silence of the heights. Dawn had broken perhaps an hour before, and new light spilled down the valley. Elansa filled herself up with it, and in that silence she prayed. She did not pray for rescue. It startled her to realize she'd stopped doing that—she couldn't remember when she had. She prayed only to be seen, to be known to gods who were so very far away.

See me, she whispered, soft in her heart, praying to the god she had always served. Wherever you are, O my Blue Phoenix, wherever you have gone, see me, for I am here.

Just that prayer she made, and then she left the wall, for the night was cold and her cloak was thin. Footfalls sounded behind her, echoing against the parapet. She knew the step, the measure of the tread. Brand followed, and he carried a torch to light their way.

"Peace," he said, low behind her. "Go back to sleep."

Elansa nodded, but she didn't turn to look at him.

* * * * *

In the dark cellars below the east tower, Velg had not been able to sleep. He took flint and steel from his pouch and broke the branches into pieces, kindling sized and larger. He made a fire because he didn't like the dark.

In a chamber not far from where he and Ithk rested, something woke, something thin and rattling and dressed in rusted chain mail and a helm that fit better when it was fleshed. Light didn't wake it, but the smell of flesh did, of pumping hearts and blood running in veins. Behind a closed door, it sat up on its bier, aware of a great hunger.

It cried, *"Brothers!"* in a voice like wind, and when it moved it sounded like naked branches rattling in storm.

Others awoke, not all, but the most hungry of them.

They opened the doors of their crypts. Darkness was nothing to them, these creatures who had no eyes but only gaping holes where eyes once had been. They left their cold beds, ancient warriors uncorrupted in life but corrupted in death. They woke from the dreamless sleep, and the waking was like a cold birth. Out from their crypts, they shambled across the great hall, wandering through the spaces between the pillars. Corpses of gully dwarves lay in the corners, headless, armless, crawling with maggots. The sickening odor of decay filled the cellar. The creatures hardly noticed. They smelled living things.

They had no voices, not anymore, though in centuries past their voices had lifted in praise to a king, in oaths sworn upon valiant hearts. Elves and dwarves and humans, they had made the Royal Guard of the elf king Kith-Kanan. They had loved him in life. Every one had guarded him, each willing to trade his own life for that of the great king. They had no voice now, though, nor heart or soul to remember the glory of kings or the legend of their own devotion. Wretched, corrupted, they made no sound at all. None, until one shoved its shoulder against the stout oaken door, trying to get past it, out of the hall to where it smelled warm flesh and blood. Others joined the first, flinging against the door, mindless and driven.

The thunder of their need boomed through the corridors and up into the towers of the fortress itself.

Chapter 16

Brand heard the drumming first. As he walked down the tower steps he felt it reverberating in the cold air.

Boom! Boom! Boom!

Behind the thunder came voices, and though the drumming was distant and the voices closer, those voices sounded far and frail, the startled sounds of men and women wakened from sleep.

"In the name of gods," Elansa whispered.

Up the stairs, four flights and distant, Char's voice called, "Brand! You down there?"

"Here! Down here, Char! What's—?"

"Trouble up here!"

"The banging, I know. I hear it."

Silence, a breath held, then the booming started again. Hinges squealed as though Char yanked the door wide. His voice echoed down the stairwell. "Don't know about banging. It ain't coming from here. Up here, we got real trouble, an army's worth of it and riding hard!"

For just that moment all the world stood still to Elansa, frozen in the bright glare of Brand's torch. Even the shadows held. She heard the voices beyond the door, she heard the banging, but she didn't move. And then she turned and said to Brand, "Go! Go up and see what's coming." *Boom! Boom-boom! Boom!* "I'll go see what's here."

If she startled him, suddenly commanding, he didn't show it. He was gone, leaping up the stairs after his shadow. Only once did he turn, and when he did, she saw his eyes bright and keen in the mage-light.

"Go!" she cried, "go!"

He went, and Elansa turned from the sight of him leaving, for she had the feeling that something had changed, like a wheel turning. The turning filled her with strength, as though gods had looked at her from far, far away.

* * * * *

"Oh, damn," Brand whispered.

Dawn's quickening wind caught his hair, blowing it back. It combed his beard and stung his face, for up here the wind never blew warm. He squinted against the blowing cold to see a bright line running across the stonelands. The army ran swift upon one of the old roads that stretched a good distance before failing. Gray as pearl, the sky breathed with the first light of the new day. Stars were fading, the moons had gone west beyond the Qualinesti Forest, and the bright line ran on, catching the predawn light and taking the frail glow for itself. At the wall Char turned, and the white look on him said he wished he'd had a fine fat skin of dwarf spirits.

"I reckon," he said, "there's got to be about a hundred of 'em, and those ain't goblins, Brand."

Brand leaned over the parapet, peering into the ghostly gray. "Too bright for goblins, that's for sure. And look at the dust; it's hanging high. Mounted men." He squinted at the twin lines of horsemen and the plumes of dust rising up in the cold air. "Elves."

"Elves, all shining in armor and bristling with swords and arrows and lances." Char spat over the wall. "And I'll wager I know what they're looking for."

Brand shook his head and squinted out over the plain again. "I don't think they're coming for her, or not just now." He slapped Char's shoulder and pointed west. "There!"

There went unmounted men, enough to be marked by their dust, only this cloud rode lower, from this distance like a smudge right above the ground. These did not ride but went on foot.

"Ah, now. Those are goblins." Char leaned his back against the parapet and looked up at Brand. "You reckon they're running for here?"

"I do."

"You suppose the elves are after the goblins?"

Brand nodded, and wind moaned around the towers.

"And we'd be idiots to think we're not going to get squeezed in the middle."

Brand agreed that they would be idiots to think so.

Char looked at the mountains and the towers and all the ancient fortress, the stone scarred by time, steadfast and standing. "Ah, well. It was a nice high fastness for as long as we had it." He heaved a gusty sigh. "Wish I had a drink."

Brand nodded, still looking at the dawning day. "I wish you did, too. But you don't, and we're here."

Brand leaned over the parapet, watching the cloud from the west and the riders from the south, listening to the wind. After a time, he looked at Char and said, "I'm thinking we're already squeezed." He pointed to the stone beneath their feet. "Something's going on in the cellar."

"So I hear." Char sucked his teeth. "What do you want to do?"

Brand turned away from the sight of advancing elves and running goblins. He put a hand on Char's shoulder and turned him toward the stairs. "Fight the fight we can win, old friend, and worry about the other when we have to."

The sound of the dwarf's laughter sailed out with the wind, harsh as a crow's call. He loosed the hard-edged throwing axe from his belt.

* * * * *

Elansa stood in the darkened stairwell, just at the top of the first of four flights leading down to the cellars. On the landing below hers, Dell and Tianna and Ley stood listening. They heard nothing more than Elansa did. The booming had stopped only moments before, the last of it seemed still to be ringing in her ears.

A quiet footstep sounded behind her, and she turned to see Brand dark in the doorway.

"What?" he whispered.

Elansa shook her head.

He looked beyond her, down into darkness where torches stood in iron brackets on the walls. The light flared, and the shadows ran tangling up the walls. As though she felt his presence, Dell looked up. Her face was a pale oval, her eyes like dark pits. She shrugged, Brand gestured, and she turned away. A moment later Elansa heard her footfalls, the sound climbing the steps.

"Don't know what happened," Dell said. Her dark hair hung over her shoulder in a thick braid. She tossed her head to fling it back. "It got quiet, real sudden. You have any idea—?"

He glanced at Elansa, his eyes dark. "What ways are there into the cellars?"

Chilled, shivering in the darkness, Elansa shrugged. "In the days of the king, the entrances from the courtyard, and two from the Hall of Columns." The name of the place meant nothing to him, and she didn't try to explain. "One of those ways is trapped, the other isn't. Anything—anyone could have gotten in from the caves. There are tunnels all through there. Maybe they were strong and unbreached once. Now, I don't know what time has done to the tunnel walls."

Brand grunted, considering this. "There are goblins outside, and elves. Could they have gotten in?"

"I suppose, but would they—either of them—make all that noise?"

He didn't think so, and neither of them could think what would. "All right," he said, nodding to Dell. "Whatever it is, we make 'em come up after us. We're holding the high ground."

Eyes glittering with sudden excitement and battle-lust, Dell turned and bounded down the stairs. Moments later, those outlaws who had been watching in the stairwell came leaping up the stairs. Brand sent them all into the tower with orders to arm themselves and prepare to hold the door.

"Tianna, go up to the wall and bring back—"

The scream cut through the darkness below, high and terrified. It shouted in goblin-speech, gabbling curses and pleas. Came another, and both screams turned to shrieking, then to sudden silence.

Tianna said, "Brand, if goblins got into the cellar, something worse is in there with them."

She shot a glance over his shoulder, and her long elven eyes met Elansa's. Nothing passed between the two women but that look, and each understood what the silence between them meant. As though Tianna had spoken aloud, Elansa knew her thought: *I am sorry, princess. Neither of us is getting out of here now.*

* * * * *

Another scream wound up the stairs, then silence, cold and empty. Inside the tower, the outlaws spoke in low, tense voices as they took up positions to guard the door. Quietly, with Tianna still on the stair, Elansa said, "Brand, you told me there are armies outside. If they are elves and goblins, as you say, I don't think we need worry about them battering down the doors here."

"They're after each other."

"And now what's in the cellar is after us. I don't know what it is, but I do know this: Whatever it is, I can meet it as I met ogres. In magic."

He stared, almost ready to laugh as she drew herself up as tall and straight as aching muscles would let her. She lifted her head, met his eyes, and held them. He did laugh then, the sound cold as ice cracking.

"Will you bring down the tower on whatever it is, girl?"

Tianna shifted her weight from one foot to the other, her glance darting from Brand to Elansa. Softly, she said, "Give her a chance, Brand. Listen."

Brand never turned to the half-elf. He kept his eyes on Elansa. Eyes narrowed, he said, "You trying to strike a bargain with me, girl?"

Elansa nodded. "I am telling you the terms. I will deal with what's below. When I have, I will walk out of here."

"And go where? They'll be fighting out there, your folk and the goblins."

Elansa shivered, but she did not break gaze. "They will be. I am their princess, Brand. I would rather go die with my people than stay here a moment longer than I must."

In the cold stairway he looked at her long, her face a pale shining oval in the dimness, her long eyes bright with the kind of light he'd seen on men right before a battle.

"So, I am supposed to give you the phoenix and trust you?"

In the depths of the fortress the booming had fallen silent, and yet all the air around them pressed close and cold with dread, a fear crawling up the stairwell, like a dark miasma. From within the chamber that once housed thanes and kings, the voices of the outlaws called, one to another, and fear edged every one.

"That's our choice, Brand," Elansa said. "I will do what I must to stop whatever is down there and trust you not to kill me with an arrow in the back right after I've done that. You can count on whatever it is down there coming to kill you, or you can trust me."

He clapped his hands hard, the crack like thunder in the narrow stairwell. He did laugh then, and the bright and brittle sound of it startled her more than the thunderclap. "Well said!" With one quick motion, he slipped the silver chain and the phoenix over his head and dropped it into her hand. "You kill what's down there, you can walk out the front gate, my girl, if that's what you want."

Heart beating swiftly, Elansa's fingers closed round the phoenix, the ancient inheritance of her family. The sapphire slipped along her skin, warm from his own skin. The magic wakened, roused to feel the beat of woodshaper blood beneath her skin, the rhythm of a heart attuned to its magic beneath her breast.

With more certainty than she had felt in many a long week, Elansa looked up at Brand and said, "There is a thing you have to do, Brand, to make this work."

He stood still, listening.

"Drive whatever is down there out into the sunlight."

Brand's was a long holding look, as though he had her by the shoulders. Right into her he looked, and she knew he wasn't gauging her trustworthiness. For good or ill, he'd made that reckoning. She felt herself seen, as she had prayed that gods would see her. She felt herself known and found worthy. Madness! She blushed, her pale cheek turning rosy.

"Go on, then," he said, and there was no way to know if he saw her color. "Do what you must, and I'll see that whatever is down there ends up in the court between the first wall and the second."

* * * * *

Elansa wanted to stand upon a height, but she didn't run to the Tharkadan where Brand had posted all his watches. She'd not be but a small figure, unheard and unrecognized at that height. And she wanted to be heard, she wanted to be recognized. An army of elves was coming, and she wanted to be seen by them. She had a warning to give, a command that no one interfere with what she would do, for her sake and theirs, for she feared that if she didn't defeat what haunted this place it would rampage out of Pax Tharkas and ravage the armies without. For goblins, she did not care. For elves—she was their princess. She could not let that happen.

Cold wind caught her breath as Elansa ran onto the second wall. Char, still on the heights of the Tharkadan, saw her and called out. She didn't hear what he said. Neither did she stop to look at him. Out on the plains she saw what Brand had described: two armies running fast. Even at this distance, she saw each was making a run for Pax Tharkas. Without doubt, the elves would reach the fortress in good time to hold the ground before the first wall.

Char called again, and again Elansa didn't look around. Looking for a way down to the first wall, she realized there was only one. Once, a long time age, there had been two, each tower having access to the wall from the lower regions. She could not go down into the deeps of the East Tower, but she could try the western tower.

The cold winter wind at her back, singing in her ears, Elansa ran along the second wall until she found the door into the West Tower and the long stairway down. She pulled on the door, and almost yanked it from its ancient hinges. Pale light ghosted in behind her as she ran down the stairs, making her best guess about how far she must go before she found the way out to the first wall.

She didn't hear Char's warning cry, and she didn't know that a shadow slipped along the second wall and into the stairwell behind her.

* * * * * *

In the gray light and shadows, Elansa ran, not bothering to count the flights down. The door she wanted was the last she would find, for none other would lead out. There were no levels beneath the first wall.

Her breathing sounded loud in her ears, and in her heart she wove a prayer to Habbakuk, her Blue Phoenix. The sapphire talisman grew warm on her skin, pulling to the beat of the blood in her veins. The beloved rhythm carried her, and she ran to the beat of her heart and a god's magic. In her mind she saw not the damp, glistening walls of an ancient tower. She saw a phoenix with wings wide spread, head proudly lifted. She heard not the echo of wind in the closeness but the triumphant cry of the phoenix, the god rising from the ashes of its own pyre. Life from death, spring from winter, fire from ash and ever the world turns from darkness into light, from despair into hope again.

It was a time before Elansa realized that the breathing she heard echoing in the tower, the panting from running, was not only hers.

Elansa stopped, heart pounding. She listened, her own breath held, and heard it. The understanding struck her like a blow. Someone had followed her.

A rough curse grated in the silence. She knew the word. Whoever was following her spoke in Common. Her heart pounding against the cage of her ribs, she recognized the voice. Arawn had followed her. Elansa pressed herself against the stone wall. Cold moisture soaked her shirt, the stone-sweat chilling her.

She listened to him breathing. She knew he was still, and then she knew he moved again. She didn't hear his footfalls. He was too quiet, but she heard his breathing coming closer, step by step. Down and down, nearer, and the closer he came, the harsher his breaths sounded. She smelled him now, the rank sweat, and when she looked up, she saw him as a darker form in the blackness of the stairwell, outlined in the red glow of his life force.

Elansa bolted. She clattered down the stairs, not caring if she made a racket. She wanted speed. Discovered, Arawn had no more need for stealth and silence. He, too, wanted speed, and he had more than she. He caught her on the next landing and slammed her hard against the stony wall. Grunting, he pinned her arms against her side, kneed her in the belly, and laughed when the shock of the blow drove the air from her lungs.

It was the only sound he made but for the harsh rasp of his panting breaths.

The weight of him held her as he clawed at her shirt, tearing it at the neck. Her head hit the wall as he forced a kiss, his lips rough and cracked with cold. She tasted blood, then she drew blood. When she bit him, he growled and shoved her harder against the wall. Holding her pinned with his shoulder, he ripped her shirt wide.

Struggling, Elansa tried to knee him but could not move. Raging, she tried to scream, and could make no sound that wasn't lost in Arawn's own mouth. He shifted his pressure, shoving his shoulder against her neck, freeing a hand to loose his trousers. In that instant, light flooded the stairwell, cold and gray and damning.

"Bastard!" The cry echoed down the stairwell. "Whoreson bastard!"

Elansa heard the whistle of something heavy sailing through the air. Arawn jerked against her, and then he fell, sinking to his knees and toppling over. Booted feet thundered on the stairs. Her name echoed in the stairwell, from a voice so ragged with rage she would not have known who'd come to her aid if she hadn't seen what had killed Arawn. A throwing axe was sunk between his shoulder blades.

Shuddering, Elansa backed away from the wall, her shirt hanging in rags, icy wind running down the stairs to touch her with cold fingers. Suddenly unable to breathe, she stared at Arawn, then she stared at Char. The look on him frightened her as much as the body at her feet. He looked at her, and she didn't think he was seeing her. He looked at Arawn, dead, and she knew he was seeing someone else.

His brother, killed by his hand. And what had become of his wife, the woman who had betrayed him with his brother? She had not asked Brand. Remembering his grief, the remorse he tried to burn away with the fire of drink, Elansa was afraid to know the answer.

"Char." She crossed her arms over her breasts, with her two hands clutching her shoulders. "Char, I—"

I am not the woman who betrayed you with your brother. I am not she and have no part in your grief.

She said nothing like that. Simply, she said, "Char, I'm cold."

Startled, the dwarf looked up. He drew a long breath then snatched his cloak, the ragged wool, from his shoulders and held it out. Shaking, she took his cloak and covered herself as best she could.

"Girl," he said, his voice rough. "What are you doing here?"

Elansa looked past Arawn, down to the place where the door to the first wall showed dark in the wall. "I have . . . I have something to do." She began to shake

251

harder, and then she forced herself still. "Char, I have to go out to the wall."

The dwarf put his foot in the small of Arawn's back and yanked out his axe. He wiped it clean of blood on the corpse, and then looked up at Elansa. His one eye shone in the dim light. Like obsidian, she'd once thought, and bright.

She told him, as best she could and with spare words, why she'd come. "Whatever it is down there, it—they—whatever it is, Char, goblins are dead of it. We don't know if they came in from the hob's army, or if they are from somewhere else. They died cursing in their own tongue, though. They were goblins, no doubt. Whatever killed them isn't finished."

She lifted the phoenix, holding it in her hand. Cries drifted up from below, voices Char knew well. With battle cries, hazing shouts, and mockery, Brand's outlaws engaged an enemy.

"Brand is driving whatever it is out into the courtyard between the first wall and the second. I . . . I will use the magic, as I did in the caves."

He cocked his head to get a better look at her. She felt herself judged, weighed in his look.

"Brand and I have made promises. Believe me, Char. You must believe me."

Whatever Char saw, he trusted. "Come on then," he said, kicking Arawn's corpse over the side. He nodded in satisfaction when it hit the floor with a sickening thud. "Come on. We'll go to the wall."

He went before, she followed behind, and all the while she tried to find her way back to the magic. She could not even think of the words of a prayer. Something had fled or been driven from her, and all she could think of was the pressure of Arawn's shoulder against her throat, his hands on her right before they dropped to tug at his trousers. She heard her own breathing as rasping, and when Char stopped her, his hand on her arm, she pulled away from him.

"Don't," she grated, feeling Arawn's hand like a ghost behind Char's. "Don't touch me, don't."

But he didn't let go. He held her arm till he knew she wouldn't stop shaking. When he understood that, he took her hand instead, gently closing his fingers round hers. "Nah, now," he said, his voice gruff with trying to be tender. It was a long unpracticed emotion. "Nah, now, girl. Don't let that remembering poison your magic away."

She shivered, holding his cloak tight at her throat. It was not made for an elf, too short for her, but enough to cover her for modesty if not warmth.

"There," he said, "you're all right."

He said so, and she laughed, a brittle, breaking sound. She had not been all right in months. She had been prey in the eyes of outlaws, an unwilling bedmate to one, nearly raped by another. She was not all right. She turned from him and looked into the valley. In the rising light, the waking day, she saw her hope. An army came riding, so close now she imagined she saw the plumes on their helms and heard the ringing cries of their horses. Behind, and closing, she saw another, darker force afoot. There were the elves and the goblins, and it seemed to her that the goblins far outnumbered the elves.

Char didn't let go her hand. "Take hold of your god, girl. Let him hear you."

She let the weight of the talisman sit in her hand, the silver chain slipping over her fingers. "We know a thing about gods," she said, wonder filling her voice as the magic against her fingers throbbed like a heart beating.

"We do," the dwarf said. "In Qualinesti, in Thorbardin . . ." He looked away across all the distance of the two courtyards, past the Tharkadan and to the mountains rising between him and Thorbardin, the kingdom under the mountain, the fabled city where he could never again go. "They forget, or never knew, the humans out here. But we know, you and me. We know. Trust your god, Princess."

Princess, he said. She had not been named so in all the months since before the winter.

In the courtyard between the first wall and the second, a voice rose up from the shadows against the tower wall. Wailing, keening, it sounded a death knell.

"By Reorx!" Char went white.

Elansa's hand shook. She clenched it round the talisman, and magic pulsed, catching the beat of her blood again.

"Hush," she whispered, perhaps to herself, perhaps to Char.

In the silence, she heard two things: a brittle rattling as of bones being shaken, and the low thunder of horses running. Char's voice rose in a sharp curse. Elansa looked down at her hand. The sapphire glowed, the black shadows of her finger bones showed through her flesh. High above, in the bowl of the sky, the light of day quickened. Behind, the valley and the low thunder of horses running, the elven army bound for the gates of Pax Tharkas, headlong to some battle of their own and soon to find a princess. Below, the keening and the rattling of bones.

Brand's voice rose above all the sounds, the thunder and the bones. "Swipe the heads off 'em! Don't waste your strokes!"

She lifted her eyes and looked into the courtyard between the two walls. Not but shadow did she see, for the day had not yet broken the night below. And then, as the keening rose, the voices of things long dead, she saw the little pricking gleams of the first light on honed steel. One shadow moved from out of the darkness, only a shape, but she knew it: Brand, and he was looking up at her. She felt it.

"Char!" His voice boomed, echoing against the walls. "Char! Don't leave her!"

And the light broke, at last seeping into the dark place between the first wall and the second wall of ancient Pax Tharkas. Elansa saw then, what until now she had only heard.

They had been the valiant guard of a great king. They still wore the wretched rusted remains of their gear— helms, leather gauntlets, a scrap of silk waving from the thin bones of a neck, and tattered ring mail hung on skeletal shoulders. In their heads, they had no eyes, only dark holes. In their mouths were no tongues, yet the keening howls never ceased.

"Reorx preserve," Char groaned.

In the courtyard Tianna shouted warning, but too late. A man's voice rose in agony then choked as bony fingers clutched his throat, clenching. Ballu died and in the instant he fell, Ley swiped the head from the undead thing that had killed him.

These things Elansa saw and heard, but only as though there were distance between her heart, her mind, and the soul that now sought to engage a god's magic. That, the magic of the talisman, the power of the rising phoenix, began to touch her, first as a caress, almost tenderly.

Low and wondering, she said, "Char, move away now. Move away."

Her voice had a hollowness to it, the same sound it had taken in the caves before she'd called out to the god. The hair rose on the back of Char's neck. He knew about gods, but it had been a long time since he'd been comfortable with their doings. He moved away, but he did not leave her. He took up his post at the door, never taking his eyes from her as, to gods few believed in but they two, she lifted the wondrous sapphire to the breaking light and began her prayer to the Blue Phoenix.

* * * * *

Lindenlea's heart rose to see the ancient fortress. On wings it rose, and it sang old songs, remembered old tales. The Peace of Friendship, it had stood a long time in the gap between warring kindreds, a monument to their hopes for the end of fighting. It had been that, for a time. Seeing it now, bestriding the gap between two arms of the mountains, she saw it marred by the hard hand of time, the gates in the wall sprung, fallen from hinges, the old chains that had pulled them open or closed useless. Still, she thought it was a magnificent embodiment of what it is to love and defend.

"There!" she shouted to her weary troops. With her lance, she pointed. "There! We'll hold it and wait for the prince to drive the goblins to us."

One of the soldiers laughed and said he thought those goblins would shatter against the wall of elves before they ever hit the walls of Pax Tharkas, and Lindenlea laughed with him.

"That's the plan, my friend. Now, all of you, we'll make the ground before the first wall ours. Don't set camp, but rest the horses and yourselves. You've done well today, my warriors. Rest, eat, and make ready to rid the Outlands of these goblins for once and all."

A cheer went up, starting from the middle ranks and rippling forward. The sound of it lifted Lindenlea's heart, making all the long weary ride through the night worth the ache and effort. She laughed, and they cheered louder. In moments, though, the sound took on another tone, a wilder sound as a rider came galloping from the west.

"Goblins!" he shouted, brandishing his lance, his face alight. It was maimed Demlin, who had come to Pax Tharkas in hopes of finding his princess. "Goblins coming right to our doorstep!"

More and better news he had. Scrambling down from his frothing mount, the scout made his salute to Lindenlea and said he saw the sun on lances across the plains.

"And not too far away. The prince is coming, my lady, with all his army."

Lindenlea praised him and thanked him for his hard riding. She sent him to the others, to rest and await the battle to come. Alone, astride her mount and watching the great silent fortress where, it was feared, the hobgoblin had found a trove of magic, she thought long about the tactics that would be needed. She wondered whether she would lose many of her warriors.

"To you all," she said, and gestured as though she were raising a cup in salute. "To all who will fight. To those who will ride home and those who won't."

It was in that moment Lindenlea saw the two figures on the wall. Keen-eyed, she didn't have to squint to see that one was a dwarf and the other was a woman dressed in rags, her hair a-tangle, an elf perhaps, or a human. The woman lifted her hands, and from her fingers something dropped, blue and glinting in the new light.

"Hear me!" cried the woman. She flung her head back, the wind caught her hair from her face. "My Phoenix! Hear me!"

"Dear gods have mercy," Lindenlea whispered when the woman called out, her voice ringing against the stone of the mountain.

Beside her, Demlin shouted, "It's the princess!"

Lindenlea saw Elansa turn, obviously startled and shaken. She staggered against the wall, torn from the magic.

* * * * *

"I cannot believe what you say, cousin," Lindenlea called up to Elansa. "You are captive, you are—"

Elansa could not stand alone, ripped from her magic and shaking. She was forced to lean on the dwarf's shoulder. This Lindenlea saw, but she did not see that the dwarf had to hold her steady with a hand at her back.

"You think I am a staked goat, Lea? Put up here to lure you inside so a half dozen ragged men can fall upon you and kill you?"

Behind and below, the high keening of the rattling undead pierced the silence of the courtyard. Brand's voice lifted in a curse, then in sudden wild laughter. Elansa let go of Char's shoulder and put her hands on the parapet.

"I swear it," Elansa cried. "I stand here freely. And I swear—" Her voice turned to ice. "I swear that I and those with me stand with our backs to the wall." She leaned far over the parapet, and the wind caught her cloak, tearing it wide and showing her naked but for her trousers, the rags of her shirt, and her bruises.

Brand's voice mingled with others now—Dell's high battle cry, the shouts of Nigh-toothless Kerin, and Pragol. In Elvish, two voices cried encouragement, one to the other over the piercing wails colder than wind. Ley and his daughter did battle together.

"You hear them!" Elansa cried. "You hear them, Lea, and I tell you these things cannot be killed with weapons! They cannot, and if you don't let me do what I must, these things will kill those in the fortress, and they will kill me. Then they will come out and find your army, Lindenlea, and they won't care if you have grudges against goblins or if goblins have grudges against you. They simply kill."

Lindenlea did not believe what she heard. She could not see her princess torn and bruised and standing in rags and understand.

"You say there are a half dozen. You are not held. Fine. I'm coming in, Elansa."

Elansa looked across the plain. Dust rose in thick clouds. Almost she could feel the grit of it in her

Nancy Varian Berberick

teeth, the dry lifelessness of it on her tongue. All of Lindenlea's army, restless before the gates of Pax Tharkas, made not even a quarter of what came across the plain, elves and goblins. And in the midst of the thickest cloud, that coming from the west and low to the ground, strange flashes of orange light showed, illuminating the dust like a sputtering sun rolling along the ground.

"I don't think you should come in, Lindenlea."

Elansa pointed west, and she turned away.

Chapter 17

Elansa stood upon the battlements, her phoenix in her hand, on her lips a prayer to her god. The fury of the battle below, the fighting of outlaws and the undead filled her up, lifted her prayer to a god who knew the round of life and death and life. She sent her cry to the Blue Phoenix, the god as he was rising from the ashes of his own death, alive and triumphant.

"Habbakuk, rise! O, Blue Phoenix, lift your wings, and lift me up!"

She raised her arms, and upon her breast the sapphire glowed. In her eyes, the fire of the god kindled, his power rising. The wind, cold around the towers, heard a god's command. Running up from the south and down from the east on the currents of the world, sailing on the paths of Krynn's sky, the wind changed direction. It turned, like a wide-winged creature summoned.

The howling of the undead echoed between the walls of Pax Tharkas. The light of the new day leaped from the edges of Brand's blade and Dell's. No blood dulled the battle-light, for their enemies' blood had turned to dust and vanished long ago. They bared their teeth in the warrior's grin, the two outlaws back to back.

"Heads off!" Dell shouted, laughing. She ducked as Brand swung, then came up and swiped the skeleton of a dwarf off his clattering feet. The thing fell but did not die. She kicked off the creature's head, and it came up again. She felt Brand's laughter vibrating in her own body, so close did their backs press.

Looking down from the wall, out from her magic, Elansa saw that, by the head count, the outlaws had killed their own number in the clattering ancient Royal Guard. They had lost only Bruin.

Brand looked up, as though he felt her eyes on him. Dell swung away from him, trying to swipe the head from a creature upon whose bones rags of silk fluttered, upon whose head a tarnished helm of royal silver sat. The outlaw lord's eyes met hers, and she felt the shock of his lust for battle.

"Char!" Brand roared. "Don't leave her!"

Char never did. He stood close, his dark beard and shaggy hair blown in the wind of her magic.

The undead poured out from the cellar beneath the eastern tower—humans, elves, and dwarves in rusted and rotting accoutrements of their ancient glory. Clattering, howling, their eye-sockets black as the end of life, they scented living flesh and hot blood and swung at the living with rusted blades. The blades could hurt. They had the edges to maim. One had run right through Bruin's breast. The touch of the undead thing had killed him, though. It was death's touch, turning blood to ice and marrow to dust, stopping the heart.

Nigh-toothless Kerin swung at one, an elf by the look of his ruined armor. He missed the head, shattered a shoulder, and fell screaming to his knees when the thing grasped him by the throat with its remaining hand.

Around Elansa the winds gathered. Char shouted something to her, but she did not hear. She lifted her hands, her arm high, and gathered the airs of Krynn, the breath of the world.

Ley shouted like thunder to his daughter, "Behind! Tianna! Behind!"

The half-elf turned, swift as lightning, to lop the head from a clattering skeleton. Shrieking, something like mist, gray and bodiless, poured out of the hung jaw of the fallen head. For an instant, Elansa thought she saw a figure form, a spirit-mist, a soul long trapped and finally released.

On the battlement, she shouted. "Habbakuk! Take their souls and quench their pain!"

She thought of storm and sent the wind of the world running out from her hand. It caught that spirit-mist in whirling tempest, sweeping it into the heart of itself, a gale directed by Elansa's own hand. She felt the presence of a god, wings spread wide and sheltering. Into that shelter the lorn spirit fled, the soul of a brave warrior held prisoner by the corruption of a foul magic, a spell anciently cast by a mage whose name no one alive remembered.

Shrieking, another spirit flowed out from a fallen head, a gaping jaw. This, too, her storm gathered. This the god took.

In the courtyard only Brand, Dell, Ley, and Tianna stood among the living.

The moment she counted them, the count of them decreased. Tianna, the half-elven child of a dark elf, died in the white, brittle grasp of a tall skeleton. A moment too late, Ley battered the head and broke the skull of the thing that killed his daughter. His roar of rageful woe bellowed high to the battlements, mingling with the shrieks of the undead thing at last dying.

A voice, Elansa's, shouted out from the maelstrom of winds, crying, "Brand, give ground! Go inside!"

Never questioning, his face alight with battle-lust, his eyes—she saw them from the height!—shining on her, Brand shouted in a kind of mad-minded laughter, "In! In! Dell! Ley!"

They ran, hacking through the bone-white warriors, Brand himself like a scytheman with his sword. Shrieking rose to the heights, lost souls set loose. Bones rattled, clattering, falling, and Brand, at the doorway to safety, turned and looked up.

"Princess!" he shouted, shining.

Upon her breast the sapphire phoenix lay, blue against her white flesh. He felt it beating, for he knew how her heart felt. He knew the rhythm of it. He had learned it on long, cold nights, as it beat steadily against his own breast. With his sword Brand saluted her, laughing he raised the blade before he plunged into the tower, into darkness.

On his heels ran a wind the like of which the granite fortress had never felt. It ripped bone from bone, tearing ribs from spines, shattering bony necks, flinging skulls in the whirlwind Elansa guided with her own will and shaped with her hands. She scoured the courtyard, broke the bones to powder and sent the poor scraps of once-proud armor and ancient clothing sailing up to the dawn, soaring out over the wall and into the valley where armies of the living gathered.

"Princess!" cried a voice, familiar, urgent.

Shaking, she looked away from what she had made with her magic, and she saw Char. She had known his face white with the pain of wanting his beloved dwarf spirits. She had known him gray on the morning after nightmare. She had never seen his face so drained of blood—of all color—as she did now.

"Princess, look!"

Over the valley, shreds of ancient glory and bits of bone whirled in the wind from the wings of the Blue Phoenix. Below, armies ran headlong toward dying, elves and goblins tearing up the stony earth to join in battle, and in the midst of the goblin army there was fire.

* * * * *

The warden of Qualinesti ran ahead of his army. Beside him ran Demlin.

"My prince!" the elf had cried. "We have seen the princess! We have seen her on the walls of Pax Tharkas!"

He'd delivered his message from horseback as he tore into the camp. Around him elven warriors had gathered, a silver army swirling, shouts of joy rising.

"Elansa! Elansa!" Her name had rung on the air like the call of a war horn. "Elansa!"

So did the cry ring now, from the prince, from his warriors galloping across the stony plain. "Ride for Elansa!" Kethrenan shouted. "Ride for our princess!"

The point of a spear, the hard gleaming edge of a sword, he drove his mount forward, the shining towers of Pax Tharkas in view. The force of his stern will carried his army behind, his warriors beloved of their prince. Kethrenan's war cry rang out, a terrible roar to shiver his foes and lift his warriors. The dark army of goblins halted and turned. He felt it like a shock in his own heart, the surprise of his enemy when they saw the silver army pouring down behind. In a moment's time, their cries of fear turned to battle cries, and in the midst of them a great bolt of fire shot upward and out. Caught between their master and his weapon, goblins burned, screaming, and the stench of the cooking flesh polluted the air.

And the hob—riding, Keth shuddered in horror—the hob himself looked like one of his own victims. Skin black and peeling in bloody shreds from glistening bones, the thing that used to be Gnash came lurching, clinging to its fire-staff. It did not scream in helplessness. It went with direction into the teeth of the elven army. It wailed in agony, consumed by its magic and generating fire with each shriek. Great gouts of flame shot out from the staff. They hung above the ground, struggling to form in the shape of the fire-wights that had so terrified past battlegrounds, but they could not. Like their creator, they staggered and fell. Stone didn't feed them, and Gnash's magic could not.

Elven voices thundered to the sky as the Qualinesti scented victory.

"Take him!" the prince shouted, pointing to Gnash. "Kill him!"

Behind Gnash, his army roared. Caught between their master's magic and the rage of elves, the goblins broke ranks. Some turned to fight, others fled, and one small bold line of them dug in and put up a wall of spears between the elves and their master, ringing him round while gouts of fire soared over their heads, unshaped but still dangerous.

"Gnash!" the goblins howled. "For Gnash!"

The first wave of elves broke on that wall, horses thrust through the neck, the belly, elves speared and pitched from their mounts. As the warriors fell, the goblins cheered, and those who hadn't fled their foe or their master fell upon them, hacking with their saw-toothed blades or filling the wounded with arrows. In the screaming fray, Kethrenan shouted orders to his army, and he found himself looking south and gauging the distance to Pax Tharkas. The fortress stood bright in the cold light, gleaming. Before it, he knew, Lindenlea's army waited, and now it was time to change the tide of this battle.

Even as he prayed for those who would obey him, Kethrenan cried, "Take him and damn the cost!"

Screaming, the elven army threw itself upon the spear wall, shattering their first ranks. The second leaped over the corpses of horses and elves and goblins to get to Gnash. For one instant, Kethrenan saw his foe, the hobgoblin reduced to an animated corpse. Their eyes met, the spear wall broke, and the hob was swept away on the tide of his followers.

Down the plain to Pax Tharkas they ran, and Kethrenan called off pursuit, refusing to let his army follow.

"Not yet," he said, leaning forward to watch the goblins run. "Give them a chance to get right where we want them."

He looked around at the stony plain and the corpses of elves and goblins. The stench of burning flesh hung in the air, turning his belly sick. He listened to the wind and the sounds of the groaning wounded. In the sky ravens gathered, and somewhere in the hills wolves must surely be lifting their noses to the wind. Kethrenan moved his army away from the killing ground, took them to a quieter place, and let them rest. He did not go back for the wounded, and he didn't spare men to help them. His battle was joined but not yet won. Neither would it be won until he had the head of the outlaw Brand on his lance. To get that, he must break the goblin army and the gates of Pax Tharkas.

Kethrenan spared a prayer for the doomed and the dead. Among them, he saw Demlin, his erstwhile servant, killed in Elansa's cause.

"May the gods have mercy," he whispered as he turned his back. "May the gods have mercy."

* * * * *

Elansa stood shivering in her rags. Hollowed by her magic, she leaned against the wall, looking down into the empty courtyard. Char helped her to sit. He put her back to the parapet and the battle below.

"Princess," he said, standing close. "Is it always so hard?"

She hardly understood what he meant until she saw him looking into the court and the scattered bones. Elansa rested her head against the wall and closed her eyes. "Char, I hurt." Not in the bones of her, or the muscles. Not that way. She hurt in the soul of her, for she was a wood-shaper, and she was not made to break and rend. She was made to shape and nurture and heal. Her breath caught in a ragged sob.

"Aye, well. It's done now." He patted her shoulder awkwardly. "You did good."

Elansa looked up, and she looked past him. Brand stood at the door to the tower. He lifted a hand, beckoning. She tried to stand but couldn't. Char pulled her to her feet. She could not stand on her own. She had to lean against the wall, and even that was an effort.

Brand covered the distance between them with long sure strides. He gathered her in his arms, holding her carefully. She smelled blood on him—his own, for his enemies had not bled in centuries.

She tried to say something, to ask him where he was wounded, but she couldn't. The winds of magic had blown all the wit and will from her. She saw Char's face though, and she didn't see fear there. Brand bled, but he wouldn't die of it.

Outside the fortress, beyond the stone walls, the storm of battle grew closer. Screams of rage, howls of fury, and the agonized cries of the dying filled the air. Elansa smelled the stink of burning flesh.

"I know the bargain we made," Brand said, his voice soft, his lips against her ear. He spoke for only her to hear. "But you can't walk out of here now, princess. Come inside. What will happen out there, will happen."

"No," she said. "I have to see. They are my people. I have to see."

He kissed her. He had never done so till then; she had not wanted it, he had never forced it. He kissed her, and it was a very gentle thing. He put her foot to ground, but he held her with his arm around her waist.

* * * * *

Lindenlea stood high in her stirrups, looking out over the plain. A slow smile spread across her lips, a wolfish tugging.

"Ready," she said to the elf at her side. "Get ready."

He nodded briskly and sent the order along the line of mounted warriors stretched before the narrow road that would lead to the first gate of Pax Tharkas. They saw the dust cloud first, and they heard the armies next—thunder of hooves, shouting voices, goblin-speech and Elvish all mingling into a distant roar of battle-song. One elf looked up and back, seeing Elansa on the Tharkadan. He saw her held close between a dwarf and a tall, bearded human. In his eyes, she stood a captive, and the blood in him burned to see the hand of the human on the arm of his princess.

"For the princess!" he cried, and the shout went long the line, a new war cry.

Lindenlea looked up to the wall, to the captive princess. She changed the battle cry. "To free the princess!"

The thunder of war came closer, the dark horde of fleeing goblins and the bright mass of elves behind.

"Stand," Lindenlea said to her aid. "Stand, hold, and wait till they're where we need them."

Stand! Stand! Stand! The command went down the line. Horses snorted, bridles jingled, and soldiers held their position.

The goblins came on, running in no formation now, and it seemed they followed no one. Indeed, they were driven. In the rear a terrible creature ran, a thing with black flesh peeling from its bones, its eyes white and staring, its mouth a bloody gash from which curses and screams of agony poured. Fire ran on it, like a cloak blown back by wind; fire poured from its hands, burning all those who did not get out of its way.

"Hold," Lindenlea said, and the horses stamped restlessly, catching the scent of fear. "Hold."

The goblins saw the road and the waiting army in the same instant. They broke, screaming, then reformed, for there was no place to go but back. The hob drove them, and Kethrenan drove the hob.

"Go!" she cried, and her army thundered forward.

They crashed together, the elven army and the goblin army. Mounted elves trampled the goblins, and the goblins did not die easily. They thrust swords into the bellies of horses. They held ground and hacked at the legs of the riders. When horses went down, the goblins swarmed them, yanking elves from the saddles, cutting throats and turning the stones red with blood.

"Get the hob!"

The order roared out over the heads of the fighters, and Lindenlea's heart leaped to hear it. Across the battle she saw her prince, Kethrenan at the head of his warriors. Spurring her mount, Lindenlea sprang to obey. She slashed her way across the bloody ground, trampling goblins. Those of the elves who saw her coming cut a path for her, laughing and cheering her.

"Lindenlea! Lindenlea! Lindenlea!"

And someone shouted, "Free the princess!"

Lindenlea had her eye on Kethrenan when that cry went up. She saw him hear it, and his head snapped around. She saw him look upward. She saw his face when he saw his wife, his Elansa Sungold standing on the Tharkadan, hemmed by outlaws.

It was the seeing that killed her, her attention on her prince. Lindenlea didn't see the goblin's arrow winging from her left. And of course, she didn't feel it. She fell to the bloody ground, dead before her horse trampled her.

* * * * *

On the Tharkadan, Elansa saw the elves cut a path through the goblins. She saw two bright figures, elves in gleaming mail, spur their mounts for the place in the dark horde where the fire flashed. That light. She knew it. It was

271

magic's light, and she knew that it ravaged the hobgoblin.

Char sucked in a sudden breath.

"That's him," the dwarf said. "There's the hob." He laughed, and he nudged Brand with his elbow. "There, it looks like a couple elves have an eye for him."

Char leaned on the parapet, watching as one of the elves fell, like a star falling out of the sky, bright to the ground.

Elansa groaned. It was as though she had fallen. It was so far away she couldn't know who that was. She couldn't see the elf's face when the arrow plucked away life. She heard a cry, though, faint and far and carried on the cold wind.

"Lindenlea! Lea!"

So cried her husband, the warden of Qualinesti, in the moment he lopped the head from the hobgoblin. Then, his sword dark and running with the blood of all this killing, Prince Kethrenan looked up, and again he saw his wife on the battlements of Pax Tharkas. Who else of the elves saw her, saw a princess held captive, kept close between two outlaws, a dwarf and a rough human. Kethrenan saw another thing, and all the heat of battle drained out of him. His blood ran cold in his veins. Whoever else of the elves saw her then, saw her bow her head to weep. Kethrenan saw her rest her cheek upon the shoulder of the bearded human, of Brand the outlaw. He saw her turn in his embrace and hide her weeping against his chest.

* * * * *

While the lengthening shadows lay on the stone floor of the room that had, for days, been her home of sorts in Pax Tharkas, Elansa sat with her back against the wall. Brand's cloak covered, and his sleeping furs made her warm. The broken tiles of the mosaic floor shone where the shadows did not fall and the dust had been scuffed by foot traffic. A great silence sat upon the room, upon the fortress itself. For a time there had been a flurry of coming and going as Brand and his few had gone into the cellar to see that no threat remained. None did. They found the corpses of gully dwarves and two dead goblins, only lately gone cold. It had been Char who had found the Chamber of Columns and the opened crypts.

"Ain't but a few got opened," he said, "and nigh more than a dozen or two left closed." He shuddered. "You can feel them in there, behind their doors. You can feel them smelling the blood, the flesh on your bones."

Raised in Thorbardin and on all the proud stories of the dwarven past, Char knew his history. He knew as well as Elansa who those undead had been, a long time ago when honor had moved them and a dark magic had not yet touched them. At Char's insistence, they sealed the doors as best they could and left the corpses behind.

Through this, Elansa sat alone, waiting.

Outside the battle had ended. She heard the martial voices of elves, soldiers setting up camp, giving orders, accepting orders, now and then laughing in the flush of their victory. The cries of ravens haunted the sky when night came, and wolves padded down from the mountains. Most of the killed goblins burned upon a high pyre. This Kethrenan commanded not to do them honor but to clean the field before the gates. Over the elves, small cairns of stone were being laid. It was a small honor to keep the wolves away. No one expected the little piles to stand long.

Sometimes Elansa slept, close in Brand's arm. He held her against him, gently. In her sleep, she smelled the blood of his wound, the sword cut that had torn the flesh of his right arm below the shoulder. The wound was bound and no longer seeping. He never groaned over it or even looked at it after Dell cleaned and dressed it. He was used to these things, the pain and the healing. When she did not sleep, she simply sat waking, as now.

And so she saw the shadows of the day's ending on the floor as she listened to the elves outside the wall. She looked around and saw the outlaws, Dell and Char and grieving Ley, these few who remained to Brand. They looked like they always did, like foxes in the den. Wary, they watched the door, and they talked in low whispers. Brand himself said nothing. He simply sat with the princess in his arm.

"You will go when you wish," he said to her. "We made our bargain."

But Elansa was too weary to go. She had strength only for sitting, for leaning against Brand. This he let her do, hearkening to the ravens and the cries of elves on the battleground, listening to the opening of the gates of Pax Tharkas and the clatter of hooves in the courtyard. If he wondered what fate he would meet, he and his three friends, he didn't speculate aloud or burden her with his thoughts. He simply let her rest.

But Brand did rest with his sword across his knees.

In the room, the outlaws stirred. Near the door, Char stood straight. Mail sang in the corridor, jingling. Booted feet trod the stone, heavy. Only one came, an elf off the battleground. None need guess who he was. Char went to the door, opening it before Kethrenan could.

"Welcome to Pax Tharkas," said the dwarf to the elf prince. His voice held only a small note of irony. "We've been expecting you."

Kethrenan stood in his battle gear, mailed and helmed and weaponed. He stood covered in blood and dust, his face all keen edges, his eyes like swords. Elansa's breath caught in her throat, as it had so many times before when she'd seen him like this, the prince come home from battle. Then, in the halls of the Tower of the Sun, she had felt a thrill to watch him stride into the room, to smell the battle still on him. Now, she did not thrill to see him. Now he looked dangerous, and fear snaked cold in her belly, for the look he turned on her was one of disgust.

When she moved, Brand loosed his hold on her a little.

"Keth," she said.

Kethrenan ignored her. He glanced at Char only to see that he was no threat. He pushed past him, swept the room with a cold stare. One and another, the outlaws looked at him. None stood, and Dell, in the far corner, honed the blade of her dagger, making steel and stone sing. Kethrenan dismissed it. Last, he looked at Brand.

"You," he said. "Move away from my wife."

Brand kept his place. He did not move his arm. Elansa felt him quiver, as a hound does to a call. He lifted his head. The danger she sensed, he understood.

"Move," Kethrenan said.

Brand's lips moved in a long slow smile. His eyes

narrowed. Elansa's belly tightened. She tried to move, but he held her.

"My lord prince," Brand said, naming the elf courteously.

Dell rose from her place in the corner, and the singing of stone on steel ended. Near the window, Leyerlain Starwing had the dark look of one who stares at an end. Perhaps it wasn't Kethrenan in his thoughts, but it was the prince at whom he directed his glance. Behind the elf prince Char stood with his back to the door, his throwing axe to hand. No one offered harm, but no one stood down.

Brand rose, and he stood before Elansa. In his left hand, he held his sword. It was not his natural hand for holding a weapon. Still he gripped it strongly, neither raising it nor grounding it.

Kethrenan lifted his head. "Do you threaten me?"

Brand appeared to consider the question, then allowed as how he probably did, indeed, threaten. "But it doesn't have to come to that if you go gently with your wife."

The color drained from Kethrenan's cheeks. Beneath the grime of battle and burnish of the sun, his skin went ashen.

"Elansa," he said, his voice cold as the winter of her captivity. "Move away from that human scum so I may kill him."

She rose, and the doing was easier than she'd imagined. She'd found strength, but she knew not where. Head high, standing in her rags, she said, "You will not kill him, husband. I do not wish it."

Kethrenan's eyes widened for the briefest instant, then they narrowed.

"Husband, I am ready to leave here with you, but I

won't leave over the bodies of these people. Brand and I made a bargain between us. I upheld my part, and doing that I made certain you had only goblins to face, not worse." She put her hand upon the sapphire phoenix, the wide-winged bird upon her breast. Soft, Elansa said, "Now Brand is prepared to uphold his part of our agreement. Let it be, Keth."

She spoke, without considering her voice and what the softness of it might reveal. Elansa saw horror and disgust warring in her husband's eyes as he understood, as he gleaned the true meaning behind her words. She saw them overwhelm disbelief and change into anger.

"He . . . he has had you."

Had, he said. That word made her skin crawl.

"He has had you, and you stand here shameless without the decency to have killed yourself!"

In the silence between them, the cries of ravens sounded very close, the call of death.

Brand moved Elansa aside and named the elf prince a coward.

"Coward, aye, that's what you are. You'd rather she killed herself than lived? You'd rather find her corpse than find her alive? Elf, you have no idea what courage your wife has. You have never seen it in your fine and golden towers. I have seen it. I have tested it, and I have tasted it." Sneering, he said, "You don't deserve her."

White to the eyes, Kethrenan drew his sword. Steel sang from the scabbard, the blade flashed up, and someone cried out.

Kethrenan shouted in Elvish. *"Valth! Caslth! Valth!"*
Whore! Slut! Whore!

Two swords rose. Kethrenan's flashed first and fell

to kill the woman he named whore. Brand moved swiftly. He took the blow, the whole blade into his breast. Elansa screamed and fell, covered in blood as a dagger whistled past her ear. Again, blood, spurting, spraying, and she saw her husband fall, Leyerlain's dagger in his throat. The room erupted in cursing and cries of fear. Elansa wailed, for she knelt with her back to the corpse of her husband and Brand's body in her arms.

Brand looked at her, his eyes dim, blood bubbling at the corners of his mouth. Kethrenan's sword had cut so deeply into his lungs he would soon drown in his own blood. Still, he held her with his eyes and tried to speak.

What was to say? What words would serve? None.

"My girl," he whispered. Only that, for a long moment, while someone sobbed, and someone else cursed. Only that, and then, "I loved the courage of you. I love . . ." And then, the soft sigh, the last breath leaving.

Elansa felt him go. She felt him die. There in her arms, she felt it, and she saw the life go out of his eyes. She lifted up her head to keen.

"Wa-la! Wa-la! Wa-la!"

The terrible grief-cry silenced the room, and then Char took her and pulled her to her feet. Brand slid from her, fell away, and she tried to cry out, but she had no voice for anything but keening.

* * * * *

Elansa would not go with the elves. She said so with the last of her tears on her thin cheeks. She would not go with people whose prince would have killed her for choosing to live. The outlaws gathered around her when she stated her will, and Char shook his head.

Dell didn't understand.

"He's dead," she said, glancing scornfully at Kethrenan. "Who's to know what he said or didn't say, what he knew or didn't? Go home, princess. You can now."

Leyerlain understood well, though.

"Let her do what she wants," he said. He said so wiping his bloody dagger on the leg of his pants. Not once did he look at the prince he'd killed or the outlaw lord whose life he'd hoped to save. Ley knew about endings, it seemed, more than anything else. He didn't look at Elansa. "Let her do what she wills. I'm out of here. Kethrenan's warriors are going to come looking for him soon. I'm not going to be here when they show up."

So saying, he turned and walked away. He didn't go alone. Wordless, Dell followed. They would find their way together, or they would part. This was the pattern of their lives, the way their fates were woven. Only Char remained, and of the last three outlaws, he grieved the dead man most.

"Princess," he said, his voice rough with emotion as he took Elansa's arm and helped her to stand. "We have to leave, if that's what you want to do."

She nodded. She wanted nothing else.

"Then we'll go through the tunnels again," he said. "Just you and me, we'll get back to Hammer Rock and see what we can think of after that."

Again, Elansa nodded. She heard his words, she understood, but she couldn't think about that now. Neither could she take her eyes from the dead, her husband and the man who had been her kidnapper, who had, by some mysterious alchemy of events and emotion, become, almost, her lover.

Slowly, with great care, she took the sapphire phoenix from her breast, slipping the chain over her head. Here was the inheritance of ages, a treasure she was obliged to pass from her own hand into that of her daughter. She did not think, kneeling beside the body of a man who had seen in her the kind of courage she herself had not known existed, she did not think of unborn daughters. She thought of him and how in the courtyard he had harried creatures of darkness into the light so that she might kill them. She remembered how he had looked at her upon the high wall, his eyes shining to see her. He had seen a thing about her that her own husband could not see, and he had valued it to the cost of his own life.

With great gentleness, she slipped the chain over Brand's head and settled the phoenix upon his bloody breast. She bent, kissed his cold lips, and felt all the coldness of winter and stone settle in her heart.

"Char," she said, "we cannot let him lie here like this."

Him, the outlaw. She didn't think about the prince.

But Char said there was no time. Out in the courtyard the voices of elves had taken on the tenor of those who are wondering: Where is the prince? Where is the princess?

"We have to leave him," the dwarf said. "Let him lie here in this his stone fastness." His mouth twisted in a bitter smile. "It's all the reason he took you, princess. Just to find a high place, a fortress in the mountains where he could harry goblins and fight feuds you in your golden city never knew existed. And here he died.

Leave him. Let it be his tomb till time makes his bones into dust and all the tale is forgotten. It's time to go now, if you mean to leave."

She went. Her hand in his because he would not let go, she followed Char out of the ancient chamber that had once hosted elf kings and dwarven thanes, the chamber that now hosted only the dead.

Chapter 18

Elansa looked down the road, the long road leading out of the stonelands and into the forest and all the way to Qualinesti. She had not seen the place through all the winter. It seemed as though years had passed. As she had left the city, so would she enter, on horseback. Char had bought a good mare for her in one of the hamlets between Pax Tharkas and the forest—a little roan with white spots on her shoulders like sun-dapple. On this mare she'd ridden the hard road, and though the dwarf never left her, he did not ride. He led her mare, walking. At first he did so because she was too bowed down with grief to guide the mare. The deaths, the run through the tunnels and back to Hammer Rock, these things were like measures of stone upon her heart. She did not rouse from that grief until the night she knew she was with child.

"How can you know?" Char had asked, for he thought that not enough time had passed for her to know in the usual way. "How can you be sure?"

She'd smiled, but sadly. "You are a man," she said. "You don't know what it is to feel your body talking to you. I am a woman. I know."

He took a long drink of dwarf spirits, for he had some again, a fine fat skin of it—bought, bartered, or stolen one day when he'd gone out of the tunnels to hunt. Drinking, he considered what she said. In the end, he simply shrugged, unable to argue.

"But what's to do?" he asked. "What will happen to an elven princess who comes home carrying a human's child?"

She would be cast out. She would become as Leyerlain Starwing had become. She would be named dark elf. No one would speak to her. Her name would be as a curse. This, not because she had lain with a human. It happened. It was tolerated, though barely. She would be cast out because she had betrayed a prince by failing to erase with her own blood the shame of having forsaken her lord husband to be with a human.

Char heard all this in sorrow, drinking. He thought about it long and hard. For days he said nothing as they went through the weary tunnels, and then in the cave below Hammer Rock, he told her he had an idea.

"Tell them you were raped," he said.

She looked at him long. "No. Brand never raped me," she said at last. "He gave me a choice between him and—"

"Between him and rape," Char said. "He did that for complicated reasons, but you're right. One was because he wouldn't see you raped. It's no matter now, though. That was then. Now you have to do for yourself, princess. Tell them in Qualinost that you were raped. Tell them that, and tell them your prince died bravely defending you against your rapist." He took another drink, enjoying the fire of it. "And tell them you've known for a time you got a child from Brand. That should take care of the matter of you not having the decency to kill yourself."

Elansa considered, but she said nothing.

"Tell them," he said, "for the sake of the child."

If she said she'd been raped, her child would have a home. It would be able to live among its mother's people, and that might not be a perfect life, but it would be better than the life of an exile. Whoever this child would be, maid or man, it would have the strength of its mother and its father. Whoever this child was, it would endure and thrive.

The sun lay on the road, lighting the way home. Elansa sighed and leaned down from the mare's back to touch Char's shoulder.

"Will you come with me?" she asked.

"All the way. Don't worry, princess. I'll tell them your tale and make it stick. You don't have to do more than nod to it."

Elansa pressed her hand to her heart, and then, shyly, to her belly. There lay her child. As greatly as she had grieved an unknown child lost, a long time ago in winter, that greatly did she love this known child now. These lives, she thought, the lost one and this one found, started with men, but they always came to her to keep or lose. She must keep this one safe. She must see this child to the light.

Char took the reins, leading the mare along the road into the forest. The chill shade closed around them after the hot sun of the stoneland; green embraced. They went in silence, and now and then, they stopped to look back out to the borderland between the kingdom of the elves and the far kingdom of dwarves.

The last time they stopped, they looked a long while. Hammer Rock was the tallest thing they could see. Then Char took the reins, and softly he said, "Come on, princess. Let me take you home."

DragonLance®

THE BARBARIANS • VOLUME TWO

BROTHER of the DRAGON

Paul B. Thompson

and

Tonya C. Cook

Available August 2001

Wizards
OF THE COAST®

Chapter 1

~

Flames roared into the chill blue sky. Jetting from every crack and fissure in the stone wall, they combined in the open air into a great eruption of fire. Loose rocks and a few unfortunate men were hurled skyward. A loud boom, flatter and deeper than thunder, reverberated off the walls of the valley. The fireball blossomed like a monstrous flower and quickly burned itself out. In its wake came a column of gray smoke, then nothing.

Amero opened his eyes. For a moment he was dazed, seeing blue sky above him instead of the foundry roof. His ears rang from the detonation. Lifting his head, he saw he lay on the ground, six paces from the foundry door. Inside the shattered building, all was smoke and flickering flames. His workmen staggered to and fro, stamping on smoldering embers.

"Arkuden, your arm!"

Dully Amero looked down and saw his left sleeve was on fire. The little flame was creeping up his arm.

Daran, the apprentice who'd warned him, slapped at the burning material, extinguishing the fire.

"Are you well, Arkuden?" The boy's eyes were ringed with heavy smudges of black soot. "Say something!"

The pain in his arm brought Amero to his senses. "I'm all right," he said hoarsely.

"What happened? I was carrying wood for the firebox, but before I could unload it—whuff! And I was out here!"

"Sounds like the journey I made. Go see if anyone else is hurt." The apprentice got up and headed to the workshop door. Amero pulled himself to his feet and called, "Count heads, Daran! I want to know if anyone's missing!"

"Aye, Arkuden!"

Dusting soot from his hide trews, Amero followed the boy inside.

The foundry was a shambles. Through the swirling smoke, Amero saw his new fire-feeder was wrecked. The wood-and-leather fan, powered by the legs of six sturdy apprentices, had been too successful. Too much air had been forced into the firebox, causing it to burst.

He found a man sprawled on the floor. It was Huru, his shopmaster. Hauling the unconscious man to his feet, Amero draped Huru's arm over his own shoulders. He was sliding toward the door when timbers in the roof gave way, sending a shower of burning splinters to the floor.

"Everyone out!" Amero shouted. "Get outside, now!"

The stony beach below the foundry quickly filled with coughing, bleeding, smoke-blackened men. The early morning air was cold, and they shivered in the short kilts that were the usual attire inside the sweltering workshop. A few sat on the damp, sandy ground, nursing burns or bruises received from flying debris.

Amero called for water. The first dipper he gave to Huru, and the cold liquid brought the shopmaster's dark eyes fluttering open.

"Arkuden . . . who threw the thunderbolt?" he grunted.

"I guess I did," Amero said ruefully. "The furnace blew back in our faces."

A head count showed everyone had made it out. One of the copper pourers, Unar by name, had the most severe injury. Hit in the eye by a flying stone chip, half his face was bloodied. Amero sent him to a healer with an apprentice to lead him by the hand. The rest of the workers were in reasonably good shape, though shaken by the blast.

Passersby stopped and stared at the sooty crew and the shattered remains of the foundry. The people of Yala-tene were accustomed to their chief's odd ways, but this was a novel sight.

Once he was sure his men were all right, Amero went inside. The foundry roof was completely wrecked. Sunlight pierced the drifting dust and smoke in a hundred narrow beams. Shards of gray roofing slate littered the floor. Charred wood, still smoking, lay everywhere.

He went to the crucible, a great stone pot cut from a single block of granite. Rough ingots of copper and tin were visible inside. Though the heat had fused them in numerous spots, they were not melted together. After all the fire and fury, his dream of making bronze was still unfulfilled.

"It's a wonder we weren't all killed." Amero turned to see Huru standing in the doorway. The shopmaster added, "What do we do now?"

Amero kicked a still-glowing ember with his bark sandals. "Start again," he said. "Bronze won't make itself. We'll have to fix the workshop first, then build another fire-feeder." He grimaced. "A smaller one, this time."

Back outside, they found the workmen being tended by a dozen young men and women dressed in white doeskin robes. The well-scrubbed youths moved among the sooty men, administering cool water and dabbing their cuts and burns with pads of soft, boiled moss. Amero frowned. He knew he ought to be grateful for the help, but he wasn't. This help came with an unpleasant price.

"Greetings, Arkuden," said Mara, one of the white-robed youths. "Praise the dragon you are well!"

"Why are you here?" he said. "I didn't ask for help."

"I sent them."

Standing on the gravel path to the village was Tiphan, son of Konza, leader of the *Sensarku*, the Servers of the Dragon. Not yet thirty, Tiphan was tall and sharp-faced, with shoulder-length blond hair and a beardless chin. Out of reflex, Amero clenched his hands into fists, then forced them to relax.

"Greetings, young Tiphan," he said, brushing stone chips from his short brown beard. "What brings you to my humble workshop?"

"I was on my way to the Offertory when I saw a column of fire in the sky," Tiphan said. Though young, he had a deep, resonant voice. "My first thought was that the Great Protector was paying us a visit—"

"Duranix isn't here," Amero said bluntly.

Tiphan looked over the chaotic scene and dusted his hands lightly together. "I see that now. The fire was your doing, Arkuden?"

"An accident."

"Still trying to make bronze?"

"Still trying. We have a lot of repairs to do, so if you would take your people away—"

"As you wish, Arkuden." Tiphan clapped his hands, and the Sensarku ceased their ministrations and fell into line behind their leader. Huru cajoled his men to their feet, and the foundry workers filed back to the ruined workshop.

"Your efforts to make bronze have not yielded much success," Tiphan said. "How long have you been trying, Arkuden? Ten years?"

"Twelve."

"Perhaps men weren't meant to make bronze. It is, after all, the hide of our Protector."

"The elves have been making bronze for generations," Amero observed.

"Elves are not men," Tiphan countered.

Amero bit back a sarcastic reply, saying instead, "You'll excuse me, Tiphan. I have much to do, and I don't want to keep you from your own work."

"The fields, Tosen . . ." said Mara, standing close behind Tiphan. *Tosen* was a term of respect meaning "First Servant."

The young Sensarku leader nodded. "My father and I are going to view the planting of new seedlings in the orchard. The dragon has given us word that winter is over."

Amero folded his scratched and bruised arms. "Planting, now? It's too early. The seedlings will perish in the cold."

"It is the Protector's word."

"Duranix is not a weather seer."

"What the Protector says must be so," said Mara. Tiphan nodded approvingly.

Amero looked at the proud, serene faces behind Tiphan. How firmly they believed their leader's words! He envied the haughty Sensarku chief. It must be pleasant to have such unshakable confidence, to inspire such unquestioning loyalty.

Four burly men in hide shirts and fur leggings arrived, bearing Tiphan's father, Konza, in a litter. Behind them came four more bearers with an empty chair for his son.

"Greetings, Amero!" said Konza with a wave. In his early life, he'd been a tanner, and his arms were stained red-brown up to the elbows from years of working hides. Now he was nearly sixty, and his gray hair hung in limp strands around his deeply lined face.

"Long life and health to you, Konza," Amero replied, and he meant every word. Konza, though a bit foolish, was a good-hearted friend. He was also a valuable check on his son's ambitions.

For twelve years, Tiphan and his father had taken over sole responsibility for feeding the dragon. In the old days, any hunter in the valley could offer up part of his catch to Duranix, in gratitude for his protection. Then Konza had started the practice of choosing only the finest beasts for the dragon's meal. It was only fitting the dragon should get the best, Konza said. It demonstrated how much he was revered by the people he guarded.

Tiphan refined the procedure further. Believing the dragon shouldn't have to snatch his meals off a pile of dirty stones, the young man began scrubbing the dragon's cairn himself. Other young men of the village sought to share the honor of serving the dragon, so he gradually gave over the onerous cleaning duties to them. Younger boys and girls learned to wash the sacrificial animals, and later, the enclosure around the cairn itself.

Father and son received no direct encouragement from Duranix for their efforts—the dragon seldom spoke to anyone but Amero—but where once he'd merely swooped down and carried off a raw carcass, he now perched atop the high wall surrounding the cairn and ate the cooked offering in full view of the reverent youths below. Everyone took this to mean the dragon was pleased by their labors, and over time the cult of the Sensarku grew in size and prestige.

The four bearers lowered their poles, bringing the empty chair to ground level. As Tiphan climbed in, Konza said to Amero, "We're off to the orchards."

"So your son said. Have a look at the bridge as you cross it, will you? The winter's been hard. I hope the supports aren't stretched or rotted." The vine-and-plank bridge across the river feeding into the lake was one of Amero's early projects. Anyone crossing the river had to use the bridge or pole over on a raft. The current was too swift to swim safely.

"Yes, the bridge," Tiphan said, signaling his bearers to go. "One of your *useful* creations."

Before Amero could retort, the bearers took the two men away, followed by smiling acolytes. More than a little angry, Amero left Huru to supervise the cleanup and stalked away.

He crossed the spray-drenched beach below the waterfall that dominated the valley and gave its name to the Lake of the Falls. The sheer cliff face had just one visible opening on the north side of the falls. A complicated tower of timber and vines rose from the ground to the hole. Amero went to the base of the log tower and pulled hard on a vine rope. The apparatus squeaked, and a large rattan basket sank slowly toward him. This hoist was another of his early inventions.

He climbed in and started the counterweight down. As he rose, the whole village of Yala-tene was visible, spread out beneath him.

The settlement had grown against the base of the cliffs like a cluster of toadstools on an oak stump. In the twenty-two years since its founding, it had changed from a random collection of tents and lean-tos to a permanent town of eleven hundred souls, the largest concentration of human beings in the known world. Narrow dirt streets snaked between the field-stone houses (some of which had as many as four floors), and smoke curled up from over six hundred chimneys.

Twenty-two years, Amero mused, a lifetime by nomad standards. Time enough to grow up, mate, and raise children. Instead of children, Amero had raised a village under the watchful eye of his friend, the bronze dragon Duranix. The dragon dwelt in a cave hollowed out of the cliff face behind the waterfall, and though he had little to do with the daily lives of the villagers, Duranix remained Amero's mentor. Amero's parents had perished long ago, before the founding of Yala-tene, and the boy had grown up with the dragon as his only family.

Though Duranix stood ready to defend the people of Yala-tene from dangers natural and unnatural, he often left the valley for days or weeks at a time, flying to all quarters of the sky, keeping a watchful eye on the land he claimed as his domain. His absence at the time of a nomad attack twelve years earlier had convinced Amero a more reliable defense for the village was needed. From this was born his notion of a protective wall.

Curving out from the mountain north and south of the village was the great stone wall. The wall didn't look imposing from this height, but at ground level it was a different story. Four-fifths of the wall around Yala-tene had been completed, and the last gap, a fifty-pace stretch facing the lake, would be finished after the next harvest.

Work on the stout barrier was done mainly in the winter, when fields were fallow and the herds were kept shut in their pens. Women, men, and children alike labored on it, and the work was hard. Loose stones littering the valley floor, tumbled round by the river, were not stable enough for the wall, so heavy blocks had to be cut from the living rock of the cliff behind Yala-tene. These were dragged on log sledges by gangs of villagers and piled up. Early sections had collapsed before attaining their full height, and the budding masons learned to make the wall wider at the bottom than the top. Then the structure stood solid and firm.

Two other structures stood out from Amero's vantage-point. One was the Offertory, where Konza and Tiphan served meat to the dragon. This was a square, roofless building, surrounded by a wall six paces high. Konza handpicked the whitest stone in the valley for it, and the Sensarku acolytes kept the place spotless inside and out. The courtyard inside was covered with washed white sand from the lake, regularly raked and cleaned by Tiphan's young adherents. In the center of the Offertory was the altar itself. Once a rude pile of stones, it was now made of dressed blocks laid in sloping courses.

The other major building in Yala-tene was Amero's workshop, lately the scene of the furnace explosion.

The basket bumped to a stop. Amero tied off the counterweight and climbed out.

He was immediately struck by the smell in the cave. For years he'd lived here with Duranix, becoming accustomed to the pervasive odor of the dragon. These days he spent most of his time in the village, and the sharp aroma—animal-like and oddly metallic—was very noticeable.

"As if humans don't stink," boomed a voice from the rear of the cave.

"You're hearing my thoughts again," Amero called back.

Duranix's broad brazen head rose from the stone platform on which he slept. "You think so loudly, I can't help it."

"Don't listen, then."

His sharp tone caught the dragon's attention. Duranix's huge green eyes, slit by vertical pupils as long as daggers, followed his human friend as Amero went to the cold firepit and sat down with his back to the dragon.

Duranix crawled off his bed with peculiar serpentine grace. With no more sound than the scrape of a few bronze scales on the rock floor, the huge creature drew up beside Amero.

"What vexes you? Speak," Duranix ordered, "or take your gloomy spirit to some other cave."

"I demolished the foundry this morning," Amero said, smiting his knee with one fist. "The fire-feeder I made forced too much air into the furnace, and it burst."

"I thought you smelled sootier than usual."

"I failed again. The foundry is a wreck."

Duranix shrugged, a gesture picked up from Amero. "Build another. Your devices have failed before."

"Yes, so Tiphan has reminded me!"

"Ah." Duranix coiled his tail around Amero, surrounding him with a wall of living bronze. "This is the true cause of your mood."

"Tiphan wants to be chief of Yala-tene." Now that the words were out at last, Amero was surprised by how angry they made him feel.

"There was a time when you didn't want to be chief. Now you fear Tiphan will take your place?"

"I only want to do what's best for the village. Tiphan wants what's best for Tiphan. And you help him!"

"I?"

"Yes! You eat your meat for all to see, encouraging them to think you honor the Sensarku with your presence. Why don't you eat in the cave, like you used to?"

"They amuse me. All that washing and cleaning! Tiphan's the funniest of all. His mind's so narrow I can hardly hear his thoughts, but he's so obvious in other ways, he makes me laugh."

Amero stood up and stepped over the dragon's tail. "Did you tell him that winter was over?"

Duranix blinked. The movement of his eyelids sounded like swords being drawn from scabbards. "The boy asked me if I thought it would snow again this season. I said I didn't look forward to any more snow."

Amero shook his head, seeing how Tiphan had misread the dragon's casual comment. "If he tells the planters to start now, we may lose the year's fruit crop!"

"I could pluck his dull-witted head from his shoulders," Duranix suggested. "That would put an end to your troubles."

"Oh, be serious! It's not worth Tiphan's life."

"Isn't it? You said the harvest might be ruined."

If the harvest is ruined, Tiphan will be too.

Amero's thought carried plainly to the dragon, and Duranix narrowed his eyes. "You'd let folk in the village go hungry to best Tiphan?" he asked, the barbels on his chin twitching in curiosity.

Amero flushed at having his selfishness discerned. "I'll not let anyone go hungry. Once the foundry is repaired, we'll have bronze to trade with the wanderers who come through the valley. We can barter metal for food."

"And if your metal-making fails? You're gambling with the empty bellies of a lot of people."

Amero lowered his head. "Maybe the weather will stay mild, and the seedlings thrive."

"And maybe I'll start eating roots and berries," said Duranix dryly.

* * * * *

A score of men and women, still clad in winter furs, hunched over their work. With hoes they grubbed small holes in the sandy soil, and into each hole went a tiny fruit tree. By the shore of the lake they planted apple trees, because these needed the most water. At the foot of the mountain slope the villagers placed walnut trees. Sturdy walnuts could stand the rockier soil and occasional slides of dirt and stones from the higher slopes. In between the apples and walnuts were planted the most valuable trees of all, the burltops. A single burltop tree could provide a family with bushels of brown fruit to be dried, eaten fresh, or pressed to extract the sweet oil inside. Windfall limbs made excellent handles for tools, and sloughed-off bark could be made into shingles, sandals, baskets, or buckets.

Everyone thought it was too early for planting. Snow still lay on the slopes above Yala-tene. A four-day thaw had broken winter's ponderous grip on the valley floor, but the boggy land held meltwater too well. Yet, as Tiphan had ordered, the planters had come to break ground on the west side of the lake for a new orchard. Seeds held back from last year's harvest had been planted in small pots and carefully tended all winter. Exactly when to transplant the green shoots into the ground was a critical decision.

A gentle chiming filled the air, a sound like the fall of icicles from the plateau above the town. One by one the diggers raised their heads, the distraction offering them an excuse to ease their aching backs. Morning sun glinted off burnished bronze, flashing in their eyes. The Servers of the Dragon were coming.

Two litters appeared, coming down the path from Amero's bridge. Eight sturdy bearers moved slowly, their feet gripped by the same gritty mud that hampered the planting. The men in the chairs were covered from neck to ankles in heavy robes made from hundreds of small bronze scales, sewn to an underlying doeskin shirt. The scales tinkled as the chairs swayed from side to side.

The planters leaned on their tools, waiting for their visitors. When the bearers arrived, they halted and lowered the litters to the ground. With a distasteful glance at the mud around him, the younger bronze-clad man remained seated, but the elder left his chair to join the workers in the mire.

Jenla, eldest of the planters, raised her hand in greeting. "Welcome, Konza. Welcome, Tiphan, son of Konza."

"Greetings to you all," Konza replied cheerfully. With every step his bark sandals sank into the sodden turf. The hem of his heavy metallic gown dipped into the mud.

"Father," said Tiphan. "You're in the dirt."

"These good people spend their days in the mud," his father replied. "Why shouldn't I dirty my feet to speak to them?"

"We are Sensarku," Tiphan said, his tone indicating the number of times he'd had to remind his heedless father of this fact. "To be worthy of the great dragon's favor, we must be pleasing to his eye. You won't be if you muddy his scales."

"I'll wash before I return to the Offertory. Don't be so proud, boy! We're all Servers of the Dragon." He gestured to the diggers, waiting patiently in the cold mud. "Aren't we?"

Tiphan sighed. "Yes, father."

Turning back to Jenla and the rest, Konza smiled. "I bring good tidings: We have the dragon's word no more snow is expected this season. You can plant your seedlings knowing the weather will only get warmer."

Jenla's square face brightened noticeably. "That's good, Konza. When I dug my first hole, I tell you I was thinking ill of our Protector. The soil is too wet, but so long as there's no snow, the land will dry and the trees will grow."

"You should always believe the words of our Protector," Tiphan said coldly.

"They believe," Konza said, grasping the old woman's hand fondly. "Jenla remembers how hard life was before Amero and the dragon taught us how to live."

Tiphan said loudly, "We must return and prepare the evening's offerings."

Konza smiled indulgently, his deep-set brown eyes gleaming with gentle tolerance. "My son was very young when we came to the valley," he explained. "He doesn't remember wandering the plains each day, searching for food and shelter. He's very proud of that."

The old man clasped hands with the diggers he could reach, wishing them all fair sun and dry skies. By the time he resumed his seat in the litter, not only were his feet and hem muddy, so were his hands and sleeves.

Eight pairs of brawny arms hoisted father and son off the ground. Hampered by the soggy earth, the bearers slowly worked their way around until they were facing Yala-tene.

The planters resumed work. Jenla stood idle a bit longer, scanning the sky. Most of it was a clear blue, but heavy gray clouds crowded around the western peaks, as if ready to slide down into the valley.

Jenla frowned. Like all the villagers, she believed in the power of the dragon, but she also knew snow clouds when she saw them.

* * * * *

Tiphan's bearers were younger and stronger than his father's, and they soon outdistanced their fellows. Even if they'd been close enough to converse, Tiphan would've remained silent. All the way back, across

Amero's bridge and up the eastern shore of the Lake of the Falls, the younger man fumed.

His father was hopeless. He had no sense of dignity, no feel for the importance of their positions as Sensarku. That he would descend to the ground and soil his robe was bad enough. That he would clasp hands and consort with ordinary diggers was worse. He would have to remind his father yet again of the proper way to comport himself. To be worthy Servers of the Dragon, they had to be more serious and more pure than ordinary folk. They were not common people any longer, but they had to be worthy of their place.

When Tiphan's litter reached the outskirts of the settlement, cattle herders tending their beasts greeted him. The older ones hailed him the traditional way, by raising both hands high—a plainsman's greeting meaning "I'm a friend. I'm unarmed." The rest, villagers of Tiphan's generation and younger, bowed their heads low as he passed. No one knew where this custom came from. Some said it was the way elves showed respect to their lords. Whatever the origin of the gesture, Tiphan liked it.

The stock pens were full of long-horned oxen, lean from subsisting on dry hay all winter. When the outer valleys thawed, the herds could be turned loose to graze on the fresh green grass growing there. Their flesh would sweeten and be all the more pleasing to the Great Protector.

Behind the pens were the long, narrow horse corrals. Some of the mares had foaled early and were trailed by leggy offspring. Tiphan frowned. He did not approve of horses. They reminded him of the savage nomads who had chosen not to live under the wings of the dragon.

The nomads roved the plains outside the valley, many on horseback. Filthy, lawless barbarians, they stole cattle, kidnapped women and children, and did not respect the Sensarku.

Tiphan forgot his dislike of horses and the people who rode them when the village wall came into view. Where finished it was eight paces high and three paces thick, and even the haughty Sensarku chief thought it a grand project, worthy of the dragon's people.

Under the wall were clustered an ever-changing forest of tents and ragged lean-tos. Wanderers of every stripe came to the valley to trade. Born in the open, some folk could not adapt to the close streets and roofed dwellings of the village. They pitched their tents and remained for one day or a hundred, trading game, labor, or objects for food and handicrafts.

Something in the muddle of scruffy tents caught Tiphan's eye. He leaned forward quickly, saying, "Leave me at the wall." The lead bearer grunted acknowledgment and steered his comrades to the open defile.

To prevent enemies from simply storming the necessary openings in the wall, Amero's builders created a low, extra wall in front of each opening. Those entering Yala-tene by these baffles had to zigzag around the short wall before they could enter. In times of trouble, heavy timbers or boulders could be set in the baffles to block them.

The bearers lowered Tiphan's chair to the ground. He rose with a musical clatter of bronze scales and stepped down. Moments later, his father's litter arrived.

"Why have you stopped, son?" Konza called.

"I want to check the progress of the wall. You go ahead. Preparation of the offering must commence by midday. Will you see to it?"

The old man blinked. "Gladly." He sat back, plainly puzzled. "But I thought you were in a hurry to get back."

"I was." To Konza's bearers, Tiphan said, "Take my father to the Offertory."

With a concerted shout, they set off, giving Konza no chance to countermand his son's command.

Tiphan sent his own bearers away as well. He strolled along the outside of the wall, admiring the evenness of the stonework, the precision of the seams between the blocks. Amero's masons had learned a great deal about laying stone in twelve years. This newest section of wall was their finest effort yet.

Turning away from the wall, Tiphan walked to the wanderers' camp. Eyes watched him from scores of open tents, yet for all the roughness of the encampment, he had nothing to fear. The inhabitants might call their town Yala-tene, meaning "Mountain Nest," but to outsiders such as these, it was known as Arku-peli, or "Place of the Dragon." No one dared interfere with Tiphan. His dragon scale robe made it plain he had access to the powerful Duranix.

He spied a tall, conical tent near the center of the camp. Bark walls meant the owner was too poor to have a tent made of deerskin. A flap of woven ivy hung over the entrance, reinforcing the image of poverty, yet on the leafy door flap hung a bronze disk two hand spans wide, embossed with an image of the sun. Bronze was rare and valuable, quite out of place on such a lowly shelter. It was this artifact that had caught Tiphan's eye.

The Sensarku swept back the flap with one hand. The interior was dark and smelled of sour mold and raw meat. He saw crossed feet, clad in bark sandals. They retreated from the shaft of light Tiphan let in.

"May I enter?"

"As you choose, but close the flap." The speaker—his name was Bek—had an edge in his voice, the sharpness of danger and guile.

Tiphan stepped in and let the mat of vines fall shut behind him. Sudden darkness closed around him. Tiny points of sunlight pierced the interior through chinks in the bark shell. By these Tiphan could see Bek sitting on the far side of the tent. A few rough stones piled in the center of the floor served as a firepit. The rest of the tent was crowded with rattan baskets and bags of moldering leather.

"What do you have for me this time?"

"What you asked for," Bek said.

Tiphan's eyes widened. "Show me."

"It wasn't easy to come by, and won't be cheap."

"Show me!"

The shadowy figure stood. Bek was little taller standing than sitting. As he slipped past, Tiphan caught only glimpses of his strange host: tattoos scrolling down his neck, a blue stone fixed in a pierced earlobe, a reddish pigtail hanging down his back. What was hanging from the back of his belt? A panther's tail?

Bek knelt by a tall basket and pushed off the lid. The rattan container was crowded with cylinders of stiff white parchment. The tattooed man drew out one scroll, checked the glyphs on the butt of the wooden rod it was wound around, and handed it to Tiphan.

"*Kinshesus Talikanathor* is its name, more or less. In the argot of Silvanesti priests it means 'The Way to Bind the Sun.'"

Tiphan parted the scroll. It was filled from side to side and top to bottom with Elvish script. Glosses on the black text were scribed in red. He was still learning the language, and the poor light did not make deciphering the ornate, feathery writing any easier.

Tiphan let go of one side, allowing the scroll to roll itself shut. "What do you want for it?"

For the first time the little man looked his customer in the face. Both his eyes glowed in the dark, and in different colors. His right eye was cool, greenish blue, like the belly of a carrion fly. The left eye was yellow, like the stars in the constellation of Matat, the dragon.

"Give me your robe," Bek said.

Tiphan laughed. "This robe is worth more than your life!"

"This book is worth more than both our lives." Bek removed the scroll from the Sensarku's hand and carefully returned it to the basket with the others. "You can't walk into a scribe's shop in Silvanost and ask for these tomes, you know. They're forbidden! I took many chances getting it." He drew a stubby finger across his throat. Tiphan ignored the ugly gesture. "This book has commentaries by Vedvedsica himself! Did you see the passages in red ink? His hand, his wisdom."

Tiphan knew the fame of the elf priest Vedvedsica. For many years he'd been the first sage of Silvanos's realm. Then, a few years ago, rumors had reached Yala-tene of his downfall. It was said the wily Vedvedsica had been exiled to an island far away in the southern sea.

"I'll give you four pounds of bronze," Tiphan told him, "or six pounds of copper. I also have some gemstones."

The bookseller shook his head. His eyelids closed for the space of two heartbeats and when they opened again, his irises had switched colors. Now the right one was yellow, and the left blue.

"I want the robe off your back, nothing less," Bek said, grinning. His teeth were uncommonly long and pointed.

"There's ten pounds of bronze in this robe!"

"With this book you can command the elements!" The little man held the lid poised over the basket. "Last chance. What say you?"

Tiphan's hands ached to hold the manuscript. Jaw clenched, he unclasped the buckle of his belt and let it fall to the dirt. Dropping his arms, he shrugged the heavy robe off. It piled around his feet like musical, golden snow.

The little man handed Tiphan the scroll. "Wise choice, my friend," he said. "Knowledge is much more valuable than bronze." To Tiphan's amazement, the panther tail attached to the back of the man's belt moved, lashing once from side to side.

"You seem to crave bronze well enough," Tiphan said, slipping the parchment roll inside his white doeskin shirt.

"A fella's got to eat. While you're here, can I interest you in another book? It's also from Silvanost, very rare, suppressed by five priesthoods." In answer to Tiphan's questioning look, Bek elaborated. *"Girthas Laka Morokiti*, 'Dialogue of the Courtesans.' It tells of the amorous doings of highborn Silvanesti ladies."

Tiphan sneered. "Keep it. I seek wisdom, not lechery." He picked up his belt, raised the door flap, and added, "But if you find more like this, contact me in the usual way."

"Good fortune to you, excellent Tiphan!" Bek called cheerfully. "Always a delight to serve you."

The Sensarku walked away. He glanced back once and regretted it. The bookseller stood partially concealed in the door of his tent. Where sunlight fell on him, the illusion of humanity failed utterly. One leg, one arm, and his shoulder were covered by charcoal fur. A single yellow fang protruded from his whiskered upper lip. The supposed panther's tail curled around Bek's ankle, twitching with feline amusement.

DRAGONLANCE

The War of Souls
THE NEW EPIC SAGA FROM
MARGARET WEIS & TRACY HICKMAN

**The New York Times bestseller
—now available in paperback!**

Dragons of a Fallen Sun
The War of Souls • Volume I

Out of the tumult of a destructive
magical storm appears a mysterious
young woman, proclaiming the
coming of the One True God.
Her words and deeds erupt into
a war that will transform
the fate of Krynn.

Dragons of a Lost Star
THE WAR OF SOULS • VOLUME II

The war rages on . . .
A triumphant army of evil Knights
sweeps across Krynn and marches
against Silvanesti. Against the dark
tide stands a strange group of heroes:
a tortured Knight, an agonized mage,
an aging woman, and a small,
lighthearted kender in whose hands
rests the fate of all the world.

April 2001

DRAGONLANCE is a registered trademark owned by Wizards of the Coast, Inc.
©2001 Wizards of the Coast, Inc.

CLASSICS SERIES

THE INHERITANCE
Nancy Varian Berberick

The companions of Tanis Half-Elven knew of their friend's tragic heritage—how
his mother was ravaged by a human bandit and died from grief.
But there was more to the story than anyone knew.

Here at last is the story of the half-elf's heritage: the tale of a captive elven princess,
a merciless human outlaw, a proud elven prince, the power of love, and how
tragedy can change a life forever.

May 2001

THE CITADEL
Richard A. Knaak

Against a darkened cloud it comes, soaring over the ravaged land: the flying citadel,
mightiest power in the arsenal of the dragon highlords. An evil wizard has
discovered a secret that may bring all of Ansalon under his control, and it's up
to a red-robed mage, a driven cleric, a kender, and a grizzled war veteran to
stop him before it's too late.

DALAMAR THE DARK
Nancy Varian Berberick

Magic runs like fire through the blood of Dalamar Argent, yet his heritage denies
him its use. But as war threatens his beloved Silvanesti, Dalamar will seize the
forbidden power and begin a quest that will lead him to a dark and uncertain future.

MURDER IN TARSIS
John Maddox Roberts

Who killed Ambassador Bloodarrow? In a city where everyone is a suspect, time
is running out for an unlikely trio of detectives. If they fail to solve the mystery,
their reward will be death.

DRAGONLANCE is a registered trademark owned by Wizards of the Coast, Inc.
©2001 Wizards of the Coast, Inc.

DRAGONLANCE

The tales that started it all...

New editions from DRAGONLANCE creators
Margaret Weis & Tracy Hickman

The great modern fantasy epic – now available in paperback!

THE ANNOTATED CHRONICLES

Margaret Weis & Tracy Hickman return to the Chronicles, adding notes and commentary in this annotated edition of the three books that began the epic saga.

SEPTEMBER 2001

THE LEGENDS TRILOGY

Now with stunning cover art by award-winning fantasy artist Matt Stawicki, these new versions of the beloved trilogy will be treasured for years to come.

Time of the Twins • War of the Twins • Test of the Twins

FEBRUARY 2001

DRAGONLANCE is a registered trademark owned by Wizards of the Coast, Inc.
©2001 Wizards of the Coast, Inc.

New characters, strange magic, wondrous creatures.

**ADVENTURE THROUGH THE HISTORY OF KRYNN
WITH THESE THREE NEW SERIES!**

THE BARBARIANS
PAUL THOMPSON & TONYA CARTER COOK
Follow a divided brother and sister as they lead rival tribes of
plainsmen amidst the wonders and dangers of ancient Krynn.

Volume One: *Children of the Plains*
Volume Two: *Brother of the Dragon*
August 2001

THE ICEWALL TRILOGY
DOUGLAS NILES
Journey with an exiled elf to the harsh, legendary land known as Icereach,
where human tribes battle for life and ogres search to reclaim lost glories.

Volume One: *The Messenger*
February 2001

THE KINGPRIEST TRILOGY
CHRIS PIERSON
Discover for the first time the dynastic history of the Kingpriest
and how his religious-political rule of Istar influenced the world
of DRAGONLANCE for generations to come.

Volume One: *Chosen of the Gods*
November 2001

DRAGONLANCE is a registered trademark owned by Wizards of the Coast, Inc.
©2001 Wizards of the Coast, Inc.

THE DHAMON SAGA
Jean Rabe

THE EXCITING BEGINNING TO THE DHAMON SAGA

— NOW AVAILABLE IN PAPERBACK!

Volume One: *Downfall*

HOW FAR CAN A HERO FALL?
FAR ENOUGH TO LOSE HIS SOUL?

Dhamon Grimwulf, once a Hero of the Heart, has sunk into a bitter life of crime and squalor. Now, as the great dragon overlords of the Fifth Age coldly plot to strengthen their rule and destroy their enemies, he must somehow find the will to redeem himself.

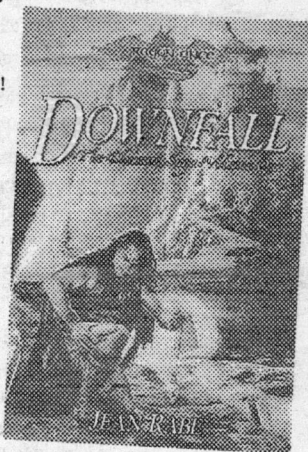

Volume Two: *Betrayal*

All Dhamon Grimwulf wants is a cure for the painful dragon scale embedded in his leg. To find a cure, he must venture into the treacherous realm of a great black dragon. Along the way, Dhamon discovers some horrible truths: betrayal is worse than death, and there is something more terrifying on Krynn than even a dragon overlord.

June 2001

DRAGONLANCE is a registered trademark owned by Wizards of the Coast, Inc.
©2001 Wizards of the Coast, Inc.

THE CROSSROADS SERIES

This thrilling new DRAGONLANCE series visits famous places in Krynn in the pivotal period of time after the Fifth Age and before the War of Souls. New heroes and heroines, related by blood and deed to the original Companions, struggle to live honorably in a world without gods or magic, dominated by dark and mysterious evildoers.

THE CLANDESTINE CIRCLE
MARY H. HERBERT
Rose Knight Linsha Majere takes on a dangerous undercover mission for the Solamnics' Clandestine Circle in the city of Sanction, run by the powerful Hogan Bight.

THE THIEVES' GUILD
JEFF CROOK
A rogue elf, who may or may not be who he claims, steals a legendary artifact, makes an enemy of the Dark Knights, and rises and falls inside the Thieves' Guild in Palanthas.

DRAGON'S BLUFF
MARY H. HERBERT
Ulin Majere and his companion Lucy travel to Flotsam, and battle against a dragon terrorizing the local populace.

July 2001

THE MIDDLE OF NOWHERE
KEVIN KAGE
Kevin Kage's debut DRAGONLANCE novel tells a tale of irrepressible kender, a forgotten town, and an act of pure bravado.

December 2001

DRAGONLANCE is a registered trademark owned by Wizards of the Coast, Inc.
©2001 Wizards of the Coast, Inc.